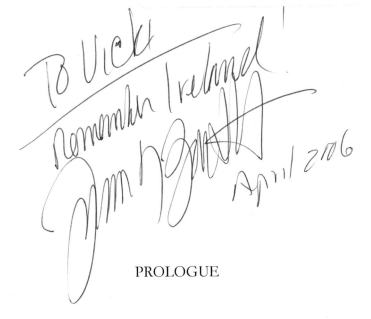

To Vicki
Remember Ireland
Jim Barrett
April 2006

PROLOGUE

T he kid driving the carts out of the barn almost ran
him down. He stopped the kid and read him the riot
act. *Can't let these little shits get too comfortable or
sooner or later they'll think they own the place and do whatever they want. Gotta maintain control.*

*When he was done with his lecture, delivered in a loud voice
and with finger waved in the kid's face, he walked into the darkness
of the cart barn, looking for his clubs. The pro said he had seen them
in back against the wall. He waited a moment or two until his eyes
began to adjust to the darkness. There. Still about a dozen carts
parked in neat rows, electric umbilicals reaching down from the ceil-
ing-mounted chargers. Motorized abominations! Where's the sport in
golf if one is sitting on one's ass all day, driving through the grass?
Sure, the revenue helped pay the bills. But still …*

The damn kid would probably take his time coming back to move these last few out into the morning sunshine, especially after the lecture he had just received. These kids today! Had no concept of what it took to succeed in this day and age. Hard work, playing the angles, getting the other guy before he got you. The world is made up of two groups: predator and prey. If you aren't the first, you will sure as hell soon become the second.

He strolled to the back of the barn and found his golf bag leaning against the wall. The thick yellow electrical cord connecting the last cart in the row had been pulled from its socket on the cart, and was dangling on the floor. Damn that kid! Should have been neater! The correct procedure is to coil the cords neatly and hang them from the hooks on the frame up above. Get them out of the way and eliminate the possibility of tripping or, worse, that some member's kid would wander in and stick his finger in the socket. That would be a 10,000-volt shocker! Must speak to McDaggert. Have the kid disciplined. Maybe fired. God knows there are enough kids out there who'd love to have this job.

He bent over to unzip one of the compartments in his large staff bag, and rummaged around for the new golf glove he had placed there yesterday.

A tap on his shoulder startled him. He hadn't heard anyone come into the barn. He straightened up and turned around. A sudden burst of pain exploded with Technicolor effect in his right eye. He staggered backwards and struck his head on the hard edge of the cart roof. The world went black.

He struggled out of the blackness. His eye throbbed. Something was wrapped tightly around his neck. He gasped for air. Bright lights in kaleidoscopic effect circled at the edge of his vision. He couldn't see. He couldn't breathe. His fingers clawed at his neck, trying to remove the constriction. Have … to … breathe!

Suddenly, he was swept off his feet, dangling in midair. He scrabbled for a foothold, something to relieve the pressure that was now crushing his windpipe. The pain, the panic. Have ... to ... breathe!

He heard a soft laugh, and then nothing. He hung there, fingers pulling at his neck. Couldn't get hold. The pressure. Have ... to ... breathe. His mouth was open in a futile attempt to get air through the passageway.

He kicked his legs, once, twice. Have ... to ...

The lights swirling around got faster and faster, blending into one bright halo, which got brighter and brighter and finally exploded and went out. He stopped struggling. One hand fell limply to his side, the other frozen at his neck, still trying to pull the thing away.

The body hung limply in the darkness of the cart barn; the only sound the low humming of the electrical chargers still running juice into the handful of carts. The door at the front of the barn swung shut. The air grew still.

ONE

It was rapidly turning into one of those days. I was back in the newsroom at the Boston Journal the day after Labor Day, feeling as I did every September that time and the summer had passed all too quickly. Once, I felt awful after Labor Day because it meant I had to go back to school. Now I felt awful because it seemed everyone else was going back to school and I wasn't.

A cold, early fall rain pelted against the ancient windows on the sixth floor just outside the city room. A summer's worth of grime and grit had built up on the glass and the rain split into rivulets as it ran down the windows. I stared out at the urban vista of wet brick, boarded-up windows and overall gloom while the rain came down hard and Boston's usually inspiring downtown skyscrapers drifted in and out of view in the wet white mist.

Part of my feelings of gloom could be laid to the fact that the golf season, for the most part, was over for the year. After the PGA Championship and one of the World Golf events, the golf season peters out. There were still tournaments scheduled every week until November, but they were not events worthy, in my editor's eyes at least, of justifying the expense of my leaving this depressingly damp city to go cover. It was not a Ryder Cup year, so I didn't have that biennial international madness on the schedule. In early November, the season-ending Tour Championship would dole out millions, but that was probably the only tournament left that I could get approval to attend. Mainly because my editor, the world's largest jackass, had always wondered what it would be like to try and make a five-foot putt for a half-million bucks. "Jeez," he'd say every year, "I'd never be able to pull the putter back for that kind of money." I always resisted, so far anyway, the urge to tell him that if he took his overweight, under-exercised flabby body out on the first tee of a PGA Tour event, the stress would kill him dead in seconds.

No, after Labor Day, golf recedes into the background of American sports. There are still a few story lines: The handful of players trying to make it into the top-30 money list to qualify for that Tour Championship. But even that field is pretty much set by the end of August. Or the rush of the Tour's wannabes and has-beens to make the top-120 money list for the year, so they can avoid going back to the Tour Qualifying School. That annual event is hardly a school, but a six-round do-or-die tournament that makes Chinese water torture seem like a refreshing soak in the hot tub. The truth is that the fans of the golfing world, so attuned to the exploits and achievements of Tiger Woods and the ten or so pros who try to keep up with him, could care less if Hobie

Millcot can somehow find the game to make a top-ten finish in the Texas Open and avoid going back to the Tour
School for the sixth time in seven years. Hobie probably
cares a lot, along with his wife, Mom and Dad and whoever
is putting up the cash to keep him on Tour, but the rest of
the world has trouble giving a rat's behind.

I sighed, took another sip of the acidic black coffee in
my Styrofoam cup and stared out the grimy window. My
nine-month season of golf writing was about over. From
now until Christmas, I would be doing fill-in duty. Sidebars
on Boston College's new ace quarterback, who couldn't
throw a neat spiral if they grafted Joe Montana's arm on
him. Personality features on the football coaches of the
Yankee Conference ("Northeastern's Hendrick 'Spuds'
Deirdorff raises dinner-plate dahlia's in the off season.")
Previews of hot new talent on the Bruins hockey squad.
("According to 18-year-old right winger Pierre LaChance,
that PlayStation computer hockey game is 'awesome, eh?'")

I was contemplating prying open the window, probably for the first time in that window's fifty years of exist-
ence, and dropping myself the six floors down to Dorchester
Avenue, when I heard my name being bellowed.

"Hacker! Get in here!" The dulcet bark came from the
office of my boss. I walked back down the hall towards the
city room, bright with its rows of neon lighting, alive with
the constant clang and clatter of telephones, reporters running back and forth, keyboards softly clicking as the staff
of the Boston Journal cranked out yet another edition of
the important news of the day to a waiting public of damp
and unhappy citizens who didn't, really, give a damn.

I turned into the last doorway on the left, home of
executive sports editor Frank Donatello. His office overlooked the city room through an impressively large plate
glass window, which helped block out most of the under-

current of noise that enlivened the place. Frank's office looked pretty much like every other newspaper editor's office I had ever seen: an unmitigated disaster zone. The only unoccupied space was a small wooden folding chair in front of Frank's desk. Every other usable square inch of space was covered with something: stacks of old newspapers, file folders spilling over with papers, printouts of stories ready for editing or ready to send back to the writer, pink telephone message slips, press kits, media books, dictionaries, telephone books, and Post-It notes. Growing out of this pile of stuff were Frank's computer screen, his keyboard, a green-shaded desk lamp and his telephone, on which he was talking loudly as I walked in.

Frank's appearance matched his office décor. He was fat and disheveled from his head to his feet. His face hung with thick jowls, which jiggled as he talked. His hair, thin, gray and greasy, was scattered atop his head in a style that was too chaotic to actually be termed a comb-over. His thick, bushy eyebrows fought for attention with his large ears, and the huge bulbous nose in the center of his face carried the evidence of many years of smoky, boozy late nights. He wore a short-sleeved blue dress shirt over a huge chest that expanded outwards as it disappeared below the desk line. Dark half moons of sweat had risen underneath his arms. He wore a loud necktie in a width that had been in style during the '70s, with the knot loosened and pulled down to the second button. The collar was open, but still seemed to cinch against his thick and burly neck.

There was a waxy bag from Dunkin' Donuts on top of the stack of papers on his desk, and an ashtray next to the telephone was filled with crushed butts, save for the one which sent a thin trickle of sickly gray smoke up into the air, in weak defiance of the Journal's prohibition on smoking in the building. Frank Donatello had apparently been grandfathered in for most of the company's new politically correct rules and regulations.

Frank ended his conversation and slapped the phone down. He took a final drag on his cigarette and tamped it out. With a smooth and practiced motion, he tapped out a new one from the crumpled pack on his desk and lit it.

"I believe the official smoking area is outside near the parking lot," I told him helpfully.

He wagged his bushy eyebrows at me. "In case you haven't noticed, it's raining," he growled at me. "Put that in your official pipe and smoke it." I just shrugged. I figured the more he smoked, the quicker he might die and get off my back.

"Hacker," he said. "You like kids." It wasn't a question. It was a statement. I said nothing. But I didn't like the sound of this. At all.

"We got a deal with the local J-schools," he went on, waving his cigarette in little circles over his head. "Every term, they send over a half dozen kids who wanna spend a few weeks watchin' what we do, working on small stuff ... you know ..."

"Interns," I said, glaring at him. I really didn't like where this conversation was headed.

"Whatever," he waved his smoke at me again. "So, Human Resources got this one kid wants to be in sports. God knows why. Need to set him up with someone who can show him the ropes, y'know?" He took a drag on his butt and chased it with a bite from a jelly donut and a swig of cold coffee.

"I want you to do it," he finally said.

"No."

"Won't be that bad...maybe a couple hours every other afternoon."

"No."

"Might get to like it, y'know? Like Big Brother or something. Bond with him."

"No."

"I ain't askin'. I'm tellin' ya."

So I did what any mature adult would have done in my situation. I stood up, called Frank a few unprintable names, and went back to my desk to sulk.

The gloom of the day had finally and officially hit home. Bad weather, end of the golf season and now I had some snot-nosed college kid to babysit. I thought about calling my friend at Sports Illustrated to see if they had any job openings, but, as was always the case when I contemplated bolting for the big city, I quickly came to my senses.

Just in case, I flipped open my PGA Tour media guide to see where the boys were playing this weekend. The B.C. Open. I sighed again. Of all the places in the world I didn't want to go — and with all that was coming down on me I would have gone anywhere — the B.C. Open in Endicott, New York was probably at the top of the list.

First of all, there is no there, there. Endicott is upstate and outstate New York, and about as far away as one can get without leaving the country. Between Owego and Johnson City and just down the road from East Boondocks, Endicott sits alongside the Susquehanna River, about eight million miles from anywhere.

Why the PGA Tour elects to hold a golf tournament there with all the Orlandos and Las Vegas's and Los Angeles's to choose from is one of life's eternal mysteries. The En-Joie Golf Club, where the tournament is held, is not listed among the top courses anywhere, for any reason. It was originally built for the workers of the Endicott Johnson Shoe

Company, the only horse in that one-horse town. When the shoe business went bad, the company sold the course to the town of Endicott. Money or some pretty detailed sexual photos of the commissioner of golf must have changed hands at some point along the line, is all I could ever figure, because the PGA Tour comes in every year. The tournament, now called the B.C. Open, is named after that prehistoric comic strip, yet another unusual distinguishing characteristic for a golf tournament on a Tour otherwise supported by multinational companies like Mercedes-Benz, Shell Oil, and American Express.

Most of my fellow golf writers, none of whom have ever covered the tournament on purpose more than once in their lives, agree that the tournament's sponsor is appropriate: the place is a joke. There's nothing to do out there in East Boondocks. Because of the lateness of the season, most of the marquee players have gone home to watch college football and practice a little for the Tour Championship. So the tournament frequently comes down to a close battle between the 68th and the 101st leading money winners, about whom nobody in the world of sports much cares. The only semi-interesting event of the entire week is the annual caddie tournament, when the loopers get to play and the players carry their bags. Fun, yes, but hardly the stuff of which daily newspapers are made.

In addition, there's just one hotel in town, and it's always booked solid with players and Tour officials. And it contains the only halfway decent restaurant within 30 miles. So everyone else scrambles for places to stay. The nice folks of Endicott try to help by offering spare bedrooms. But the one year I went, I ended up staying at the home of a single gentleman of late middle age who kept me up until two in the morning explaining to me in a cold dead monotone how it was that the U.S. Supreme Court had secretly converted all the Congress to Judaism and were awaiting just the right time to have the President and all the governors executed and bring in the Knesset. Or something like that. It was the most frightened I have ever been, and I have followed Boston PD SWAT teams into drug lords' rat-infested tenements. I nodded politely through the guy's monologue, finally interrupting him to tell him I had to get some sleep, and barricading myself in my tiny attic room for the rest of the night. I didn't sleep a wink, and bolted out of there at first light, never to return.

I was musing on these and other charms of Endicott, New York, when a shadow fell across my desk. I looked up.

The kid standing there was tall and thin, with stringy, slightly greasy black hair spilling down over his forehead. He wore rimless glasses, a good case of acne and an attitude of sheer fright. He was dressed in light khakis, a solid brown sport shirt and a necktie underneath a high school letter jacket. He was a bit damp from the rain, and was hopping from one foot to the other as if in imminent need of the men's room.

I stared at him wordlessly.

"Uh, they said you were Mr. Hacker?" the kid said, his voice thin and nervous.

I continued to stare.

The kid's face turned red. "Uh, well, my name's Zec? ... Tony Zec? ... And I go to Northeastern? And I'm supposed to, like, you know ... intern here?"

He kept putting question marks at the end of his sentences, waiting for me to gasp in recognition, jump joyfully to my feet and embrace him into the brotherhood of journalism. Which I didn't do. Hell, nobody embraced me into the brotherhood of journalism when I was a young punk.

I swiveled around in my chair to see Frank Donatello staring at me balefully through his plate glass window at the end of the room. Tony Zec started hopping from one foot to the other again.

"Sit down, kid," I growled at him, pointing to the chair next to my desk. He practically leapt into the chair in relief and looked at me with the air of an expectant puppy. His eyes were round and wide behind those round, rimless frames. I think if I had said "Go jump out the window over there" he would have obeyed, instantly, gratefully and completely.

But I didn't. "What kind of name is 'Zec?'" I asked him. I knew it was politically incorrect and probably illegal to inquire about the kid's ethnic background, but after all, this is Boston, where one's family and religion pretty much determine one's position in the pecking order. I wouldn't have asked if his name was O'Malley, Pagliacci or even Cabot Lodge. But I'd never met a Zec before and I was curious.

"Armenian," he said. "I think it was longer back in Yerevan. I live in Somerville." It was the town next to Cambridge where I knew there was something of an Armenian enclave. Armenian-American enclave, I mean.
"You ever written anything?" I asked.

"Oh, yessir," he barked happily, reaching into his backpack and pulling out a thin manila file folder, which he handed to me. My telephone rang as I opened the folder and extracted a thin stack of about ten clippings from the college newspaper. The first two were stuck together, with what substance I dared not imagine.

"Yo," I said into the phone.

"Hack-hack-hack-Man!" sang a cheerful and instantly recognizable voice into my ear. Unconsciously, I broke into a wide grin.

"Jack-Off," I replied. "What's goin' on?"

The caller was my longtime friend, former college golf teammate and occasional drinking buddy, Jack Connolly. "Got any extra tickets to the Red Sox tonight?" he asked.

"In case you hadn't noticed, it's raining cats and dogs," I reminded him. "Besides, don't you own a skybox at Fenway?"

"Oh, yeah," he laughed. "I guess I do."

That was Jack Connolly. One of the richest people I knew, Connolly was the publisher and sole owner of the Lowell *Citizen*, "The Oldest Newspaper in the Merrimack Valley," as the front-page logo proudly proclaimed. That was probably the only positive thing one could say about the paper. Let's just say the Lowell *Citizen* was not an odds-on favorite to win a Pulitzer Prize anytime soon. But it was also the only newspaper in a medium-sized town and, as such, a license to print money for its owner, Jack Connolly. After we had partied our way through college, I went out on Tour while Jack had gone home to Lowell where he found gainful employment at the publishing company long owned by his family, where they had to take him in. He had planned to work as little as humanly possible while drinking, screwing around and generally goofing off as much as possible until his father threw a monkey wrench into Jack's career plans by unceremoniously pitching over dead from a massive heart attack. It was quite a shock when the lawyers informed Jack that his father had left the whole shooting match to his one and only son. There had been an uncle with a minority interest, but Jack quickly bought him out and took full control of the company. His next move was to sell the newspaper's ancient downtown Lowell building and build a brand new and modern printing plant on the outskirts of town. Jack's new presses spent only a small time every night printing the *Citizen*. Otherwise, they were busy three shifts a day cranking out brochures, annual reports, fliers, magazines and anything else that needed ink applied to paper.

The newspaper bumped along at break-even, but Jack didn't care too much about its profit statements. The printing operation made millions. Jack used those profits to buy some radio stations, a couple cable-TV outlets, some small suburban weeklies and then, as the head of a mini-media empire in the Merrimack Valley, he returned to his original career plan. He turned all the operations over to loyal subordinates and began to travel around the world. I'd get postcards and post-midnight phone calls from the strangest places: British Guyana, the Canary Islands, North Efate. Jack loved the life of the international playboy, and I'd see his name in the paper now and then mentioning his exploits with some European countess or a Hollywood starlet. He did pretty much want he wanted to do, and didn't care a fig about money. Which is why he could forget he owned one of the most sought-after pieces of real estate in New England: an air conditioned, glassed-in, skybox suite at Fenway Park.

"Aren't you tired yet of being filthy rich?" I needled him. "Why not sell everything, donate it to the poor and come work with me?"

Connolly laughed. He loved to laugh. "Up yours, Hacker," he said. "Listen, I need your help."

"Sorry," I said. "I just loaned my last million to the Russians."

He laughed again. "No, really," he said. "This weekend is the member-guest at Shuttlecock and I need you to be my partner."

"Whatsamatter, Nicklaus couldn't make it?"

He chuckled. "No, don't be offended, but I first asked a buddy of mine from Tokyo to fly over. I thought I might be interesting to watch the dynamic between the bigoted Irish-Yankee establishment and the new economy from the Orient."

That was like Jack Connolly too. Although his own family had struggled its way up the social ladder and ended up quite wealthy and solidly ensconced in what passed for the establishment in the small pond of Lowell, he never failed to try and tweak the comfortable class. Perhaps his eccentricities and strange behavior were the way he dealt with the inner struggle he felt in being one of the upper crust he professed to despise.

"But Tagaki couldn't come – his bank's in the toilet. So I thought of you," Jack continued. "I figure, let's bring in a ringer like Hack-Man, keep an ample supply of booze at hand and just have a blast. Whaddya say?"

It sounded great to me. Spending time with Jack Connolly, even though it usually resulted in a nuclear hangover, had never failed to be anything less than a laff riot. Furthermore, the prospects of playing a few rounds of golf at the Shuttlecock Club whet my appetite. Shuttlecock is one of those hidden gems, a course not famous for anything nor the site of any history-rich tournament, but simply a good, honest test of golf. The course is not overly long, nor particularly difficult, but it's challenging in a great many subtle ways. Like many courses in and around Boston, it was the work of the peripatetic turn-of-the-century architect, Donald Ross, who never lets the golfer know he's getting into trouble until he's already there. Shuttlecock had all the elements of the master's work: long par 3s, short 4s that seemed easy until the tiny crowned greens rejected an approach; and at least one Redan hole, with bunkers marching diagonally across the fairway. I began to play the holes in my head until I remembered Tony Zec sitting next to me, waiting expectantly for something to do. Dammit.

"When do you need to know?" I asked Jack.

"Cripes, Hacker …yesterday!" he replied. "I had to slip the pro a coupla hundred just to let us in; they cut off registration weeks ago. So … are you in or are you in?"

I drummed my fingers on the desk, thinking hard. Glancing down, I saw the PGA Tour media guide, still open to the page on the B.C. Open.

"Hang on," I said to Jack.

"Zec!" I barked, making the kid jump. He sat bolt upright.

"Yess-sir?"

"You got a car that works?"

Yess-sir?"

"You know anything about golf?"

"Uh-a little, I think."

"Can you keep your mouth shut?"

"I-I think so."

"Jack?" I said into the phone. "I'm in."

"Far freakin' out, Hack-Man!" Jack yelled. "Meet me up at the club on Thursday for lunch and a practice round."

"Got it."

I put the phone down and turned to face Zec. "OK, we got work to do," I said, wagging a finger at him and enjoying the startled look on his face. "What you are about to hear and do is between you and me. You will not repeat any of this to anyone, or not only will I make sure you flunk out of Journalism 101, but I will arrange to have the interior line of the Patriots come beat the snot out of you. Is that clear?"

He couldn't talk. His throat had tightened up. All he could do was nod, once.

I got busy.

First I called Suzy Chapman, the PGA Tour's ever-efficient assistant press secretary, who was already in the newly set up press room at the En-Joie Country Club. I told Suzy I was sending a college intern up to do some golf pieces and interviews, and she promised to look out for him for me and try to find him a safe place to stay.

"Is he good looking for a college man?" Suzy asked, with a slight wistful tone in her voice that said she knew the pickings of non-scary men in Endicott, New York that weekend were going to be scarce.

I looked over at Tony Zec, whose greasy hair had fallen even further over his eyes, and whose acne-covered face had turned even redder since he first walked in.

"He's a dreamboat," I told Suzy and hung up.

Next, I called down to accounting and had them send up $250 from petty cash, which was the most I could get without Frank's approval. They sent the money up in an envelope with a runner. Is this a great country, or what?

I gave Zec the money. "This is for gasoline, food and incidentals," I told him. "Keep track of it and bring me back a receipt for everything including toilet paper. If you play your cards right, it won't cost you much to eat. The pressroom will have free breakfast and lunch every day, and you can usually find some party to go to at night with pretty good eats. At your age, we won't worry about cholesterol.

"Don't play cards with the caddies—they'll skin you alive. If you go out drinking, and you should, don't flash your wad at any bimbo dressed in a black mini with thigh-length leather boots. OK? I do not want to be driving to Endicott, New York this weekend to bail your ass out of jail."

His head was bouncing up and down rapidly.

I tossed him some reporters' notebooks, the tall skinny kind that fit perfectly into your hip pocket, and a handful of Flair pens that are newsroom standard issue. I fished around in my desk drawer to find the embossed press card I hadn't used in years, and handed it to him.

Then I told him what I wanted. Story a day. Tournament updates. Personality profiles on local players. Maybe a feature on the caddie tournament. Whatever. I wanted the kid out of my hair and busy for the entire weekend, so I loaded him up with assignments. I didn't have the heart to tell him that none would see the light of day in the newspaper, since the sports desk, if they found space for the B.C. Open anywhere in the section, would just grab a couple graphs from the AP wire. He didn't need to know this. He was just trying not to pee himself in excitement.

He wrote down his assignments, my cell phone number, and the telephone number for Suzy Chapman. I got him directions to the golf course, about a six-hour drive from Boston. Then I looked up the number for the clubhouse phone at the Shuttlecock Club and told him to call me there or on my cell phone every afternoon at 6 p.m. for an update.

"Go home, pack some clothes and get going," I finished. "You want to get there a day early and get the lay of the land. Just watch what the other guys do and sort of follow their lead. Find Suzy if you run into trouble. Got it?"

"Yes-SIR!" There was no question mark this time. I looked up in surprise and saw the excited spark in his eyes. His shoulders and spine had straightened up. The kid was into it.

"OK. And remember…this is between you and me. Nobody else. You pull this off and you get an A-plus from me," I told him.

We walked out of the newsroom together. As we passed in front of Frank Donatello's window, he looked up at us, frowning, with the phone screwed into his ear. I smiled and put my arm affectionately around Tony Zec's shoulders, and gave Frankie a little wave. His frown deepened.

TWO

By Thursday morning, the rain had moved off and the sky was so cloudless and blue that the sun hurt your eyes. It was a perfect New England fall day. The air was fresh and clean, carrying a tang of the sea, and the weatherman had predicted an afternoon high of at least 75 and more of the same for the weekend.

I stood on the balcony – really not more than a slightly overgrown window ledge– in my third-floor North End apartment and craned my neck out and down to the right where, on a nice clear morning like this, I could see a tiny sliver of water in Boston harbor. The street below was quiet and empty at this hour, except for Enrico sweeping the sidewalk in front of his little bodega.

The North End is Boston's Italian neighborhood and I was the only non-Italian I knew who lived there. As usual, there was a good story behind the explanation. It had been about four years ago, as I was working a late shift at the paper, when a call came in. It was a friend of a friend of the cousin of a nephew once removed of Carmine Spoleto, the *capo* of the North End mob. It was made known to me by the caller that a close relation of Carmine's, a young man named Cappaletti, had met an unfortunate end that morning. Something involving a business disagreement in a grimy apartment in Everett. Anyway, the unfortunate stiff now lying in the city morgue had a young wife and daughter, and Carmine didn't want them to read any scurrilous gossip in the man's obituary the next day.

"Why me?" had been my question. It turned out that the dead Cappaletti was a distant cousin of Gino, once a famous placekicker for the old Boston Patriots, and it was felt someone in sports could put the proper spin on the young man's obit. What the hell, I wasn't busy and it sounded fun, so I called the morgue, talked to the city desk and ended up writing a ten-grapher. I made much of the fact that the dead Cappaletti had played football a couple years at Boston English High School, and made him sound like he coulda been a Heisman contender if only he'd gone on to play college ball. Which, of course, he couldn't since he got busted for armed robbery in his senior year and got sent to Concord for three-to-five. I left that part out and waxed eloquently about how he was considered an up-and-comer as an executive in the family business.

It was a couple days later that I got another call from the friend-friend-cousin-nephew expressing Carmine's heart-felt appreciation for my work. It's always a plus to get good reviews from that quarter. I mentioned that I was looking for a new apartment, something in the $800 a month region, and within an hour an envelope arrived on my desk with a key and an address to the third-floor flat in the North End. I took it.

In one of the little ironies that make life so interesting, it turned out that my downstairs neighbor was the widow Cappaletti and her daughter Victoria, who was now six. I had never mentioned to her my role as her husband's obit writer, and she had only mentioned him to me once, when she told me he was dead. Mary Jane had quickly become a dear friend, who watched over my apartment when I was out of town, which was a lot, and invited me over for coffee and canolli when I was home. Victoria was a doll who never failed to brighten my day.

I had dropped in on them the night before, along with a hopelessly fat and lazy cat named Mister Shit who had adopted me, for some strange reason. I had been planning to take him on a one-way drive out to Milton or some other fancy suburb, but hadn't quite gotten around to it yet. Mary Jane said she and Victoria would love to cat-sit for the weekend.

"C'mon in, Hacker," she had said. "I'm making us a cappuccino. 'Toria! Mister Hacker is here with his kitty!"

Victoria's little feet had pounded down the hall and she burst around the corner, all dark curly hair and ribbons. She immediately took control. She took Mister Shit in her arms and cradled him like a baby, cooing and clucking at him. Mister Shit looked resigned to his fate.

"What's his name?" she asked.

"Mister Sh——." I caught myself just in time.

"That's a strange name for a kitty," Victoria said seriously. "I'm going to call him Ducky. C'mon Ducky, let me show you my room." She disappeared.

Mary Jane cocked an eyebrow at me and then grinned. She was in her early thirties, with a pretty face and fine black hair swept back in a ponytail tied with a red ribbon. She wore a man's white oxford shirt knotted in front at the waist and tight blue jeans that showed off a trim, athletic body. We took our coffee into the living room and caught up on the neighborhood gossip.

Mary Jane and I had always kept our relationship on the "just friends" level, by mutual consent. She had often told me of the attempts of various men to get her to go out, and while we laughed together at their feeble attempts, I always heard an undercurrent that said "hands off – not interested." And, I knew that she was connected, in whatever strange, labyrinthine way, to that other world that kept the streets of the North End safe from punks, but could in other circumstances be dangerous to one's health. So I always kept it nice and light.

I told her about my plans for the weekend. And about Jack Connolly.

"Rich, huh?" she took a thoughtful sip of coffee. "Think he'd want my number?"

"He's the last playboy of the western world," I said. "I'm not sure he'd appreciate what you have."

"Oh, thanks a bunch," she said, sticking her tongue out at me. "You mean, he wouldn't like a stay-at-home mom with a six-year-old and no life."

Just then, Victoria came around the corner pushing a baby carriage. Inside, Mister Shit, wearing a pink bonnet, was lying on his back and looking strangely content.

Mary Jane and I laughed aloud. A few minutes later, as I was leaving, I turned to her and said, "He wouldn't appreciate the love that keeps this place together."

She punched my arm, lightly. "Didn't think you'd noticed," she said. "But nice recovery, anyway." She was smiling as she closed the door.

THREE

I t was such a nice morning that I put the top down on my Ninety-something Mustang, a process which involved so much tugging and cursing that it usually wasn't worth the effort. My car has more than a few years and miles on it, and all the rusty corners and peeling paint show it. But in Boston, the auto-theft capital of the world, it pays to have an old, beat-up set of wheels. At least you can usually count on them being there when you're ready to roll. The thieves tend to concentrate on Jeeps and Porsches and Acuras and other vehicles that look like they have some residual value. My heap looks, and probably is, totally value-free.

Clubs, shoes, clothes and a supply of new balls stashed in the Mustang's trunk, I motored out of the Back Bay, up Storrow Drive past a Charles River that sparkled in the bright fall sunshine and reflected the whitewashed bell towers of the Harvard campus. *Ve-ri-tas* you mothers, I waved across the river, I'm going to play some golf.

I followed Route 2 north through Arlington and Belmont, cut eastwards a way on 128 and then swung north onto the ancient Route 3 highway signposted for Lowell and New Hampshire. This highway had been built roughly at the same time that cars had been invented and the bumpy, cracked pavement looked every bit its age.

Traffic was light at midmorning, so I had the luxury of being able to admire the trees and meadows as they flashed past. Outside of Boston proper, Massachusetts quickly becomes quite rural. The quality of light changes, I believe, at some point during Labor Day weekend, when the harsh, humid and hazy glare of summer changes over to a crisper, softer light slightly tinged with gold. The trees sharpen in definition as fall proceeds, and the leaves begin their annual turn from deep green to golds and russets and bright yellows. Sometime around Thanksgiving, the quality of light changes again, just as the leaves drop, and the icy blue tones of winter seep through the barren woods.

The low-lying wetlands along both sides of the highway were choked with waving masses of purple wort, a tall, spindly weed topped with masses of purple buds. The paper had carried a story a few weeks earlier about the environmental problem posed by the purple wort. Originally, I had read, the seeds for the plant had been imported accidentally from England, carried in the bales of sheep's wool shipped over to New England's finishing mills. Once it took root around the many ponds and streams of eastern New England, the purple wort took off, far from whatever natural predators controlled it back in the Olde Sod, and its fastgrowing root system was now threatening to choke out the ecosystems of most of Massachusetts' wetlands. Aghast, environmentalists were thinking of importing a special breed of English beetle to help keep the spread under control. And after the beetles are done munching on purple wort, they'll probably start in on the red maples, the wolf's bane pines or some other indigenous plant we don't want to lose. When will they learn to stop screwing around with Mother Nature?

The purple wort waved happily in the breeze as I rumbled over a bridge that spanned a dark, serpentine creek identified as the Concord River. I wondered if there had been any purple wort growing on the banks when ole Henry D. Thoreau paddled his canoe downriver from Concord to explore. If there had been, I'm sure he would have described it for us in exhausting detail. Since the son-of-a-bitch never worked a day in his life, he had plenty of time for providing rich detail.

Certainly, Thoreau wouldn't recognize today's Concord River, especially when he got to its confluence with the Merrimac River that poured out of New Hampshire on its way to the Atlantic. There, he would have happened upon the ugly brick-factory and old mill town of Lowell.

When Henry David had paddled through, Lowell was just beginning its run as the cradle of the industrial revolution in America. In the early years of the 19th century, a group of Boston capitalists had gone looking for some good manufacturing sites. Because the technology of the day was powered by water, they came to a place along the Merrimac River where it descended, in a series of rapids and waterfalls, several hundred feet in less than a mile. The capitalists' engineers built an elaborate series of canals and waterways designed to harness the power of that falling water and transfer it to the huge turbines that were built to power the looms of the mills that sprang up overnight along the river's banks. Thus was Lowell born.

Lowell's main product was textiles. The Boston capitalists had been to the great English mill cities of Birmingham, Manchester and Stoke-on-Trent and had come home absolutely appalled at the squalor, the slave-like conditions of the workers and the widespread use of child labor. American industry, they declared, was going to be different and better.

But as the rows of mills were built, the capitalists needed warm bodies to run the looms. And in the New England of the 1830's, there was really only one readily available source of labor: farm girls. Huge families were the rule in the rural communities of New England, in part because life expectancy was so limited, and in part because farms needed lots of willing young hands to operate. But girls were less advantageous than a family of strong boys. Girls could keep house, but not work in the fields. Keeping them fed and clothed added to the farm's bottom-line expense.

So the mill owners proposed a deal to New England's farmer fathers. Send us your daughters to work in the mills of Lowell, they said, and we'll pay them a good salary (about five cents a week), house them in dormitories, make sure they eat well, and are protected from moral decay. The farm girls, it was promised, would also be taught to read and write, and the mills will bring in lecturers and musical concerts and plays to further the culture and discernment of the young ladies. In two year's time, they will return to the farm wiser, more educated, more cultured and with some pocket money … all of which might help them land a good husband.

To both farmer and daughter, this all sounded too good to pass up. So thousands of farm girls from Maine, New Hampshire and Vermont made their way to the big cities, especially Lowell, to seek their fortunes in the mills. Of course, the mill owners had conveniently skipped over the part about the workday lasting from 6 in the morning until 8 at night, with but a brief stop for lunch. Or the part about the incessant, eardrum-bursting noise of a thousand looms working at once. Or the part about the excellent chance of losing fingers, or a hand, or an entire arm in the never-stopping gears and flywheels. Or the part about the deductions from that nickel a week for room and board and "extras." By the time the farm girls had settled in, the contracts had been signed and they were forced to live out the two or three-year term.

It was called the Lowell Experiment and it was celebrated around the world as the model of enlightened industrialism. Charles Dickens, no stranger to the horrors of the Industrial Age, dropped by to see for himself and deliver a lecture to an audience of exhausted farm girls. The mill owners, of course, made a killing, and it was their greed that eventually undermined the entire system.

For after some time, the educated farm girls realized they were being exploited, and asked for more than that nickel a week. Horrified, the mill owners fired the farm girls en masse and shipped them back to their rural lives. The new labor force consisted of immigrants — new arrivals from Ireland and Italy, from French Canada and Greece — who were more than willing to do the endless, back-breaking work in the mills for the very same nickel a week. A few generations later, those immigrants began to organize unions to ask for a bit more, and the mill owners closed down the plants in Lowell and took them South, to the hills and hollers of Carolina and Georgia and West Virginia where there were plenty of people willing to work for a nickel a week. And in recent decades, the process has continued as the mill owners close down their Southern plants and take them to Indonesia and Honduras and China where, once again, there is an unending supply of people desperate for that nickel-a-week bonanza.

It was not a pretty history, I mused as I motored past the city and headed north towards New Hampshire. But at least the lucre of the mills had created a wealthy group of families in Lowell who in turn had founded the Shuttlecock Club. Out of all those decades of human misery, a great golf course had been born. Not exactly a balancing out on the scales of Justice, considering all the lives, from farm girls to Indonesians, that had endured a sweaty misery. But for a weekend of fun, I decided I was grateful.

The Shuttlecock Club, located on a small island in the broad reaches of the Merrimac River north of Lowell, had originally been a true "country club" for the wealthy elite of the city. It had been a place to escape for a weekend or a week or two in the summer, where members could pitch tents in the woods, swim in the river, hike through the hills, canoe or row, and just kick back away from the noisy and grimy city. Rowing had been a popular early pastime, followed by biking, until, around 1909, the members had constructed the first rudimentary holes of a golf course. Those first few holes were kept on Shuttlecock's small island, across a narrow creek from the mainland. But a few years later, as the game of golf became popular among the wealthy class in America, the members had called in Donald Ross, the premiere architect of his era, to construct a full-length course. The club purchased a hundred acres of farmland on the mainland, across that narrow creek, and Ross was turned loose. His routing started and ended on the island, crossing the creek twice and running through the hilly terrain before returning to a beautiful final green positioned in the shadow of a gorgeous, cedar-shingled, three-story clubhouse perched on a bluff at the north end of the island.

Shuttlecock was Ross at his finest. He was a master of subtlety who could make what looked to be easy incredibly hard. Many of his holes left the golfer with an out, a place to miss or to lay up. But then he demanded the most precise of recovery shots to challenging targets. Shuttlecock was favored with Ross' favorite defence, the crowned green. Shaped like an inverted saucer, the greens on many holes looked big and inviting, but because they fell off sharply at the edges, the acceptable target for getting and keeping a ball on the putting surface was actually quite small. Shuttlecock also had typical Rossian short holes that looked wide and inviting, but with a combination of overhanging trees, deep bunkers or fingers of gnarled rough, actually demanded precise play. There were short par-fives that invited a golfer to go for the green in two, but contained all kinds of evil places lying in wait for a ball that was not quite perfectly struck.

The one thing I remembered most about Shuttlecock from the handful of times I had played the course with Jack Connolly was the greens. Jack had explained that some years before the club's greens superintendent, a rather feisty Portuguese immigrant, had developed his own strain of northern bentgrass. Through careful propagation, this new variety, called Shuttlecock Velvet, had eventually been installed on all the greens, and exported to other clubs in the region. The result was a putting surface unlike any other I had ever seen, including those at the famed Augusta National. Shuttlecock Velvet, especially after years of careful cultivation, grew unusually thick and rich, so that even a high-flying sand wedge from 70 yards would make hardly a dent in the surface. Yet the grass provided an incredibly smooth and fast surface, making Shuttlecock's greens lightening quick and treacherously sloped. I knew that in preparation for the weekend's Member-Guest, the greens superintendent would shave those greens down to make them even quicker. He'd want to show off his course to the guests of his members by making it as tough and therefore as memorable as possible.

My stomach lurched in anticipation. There is nothing more fun than playing a wonderful old course in good weather, with good friends, in a spirited competition. The weekend promised to have everything I treasure: camaraderie, laughter, fun, good golf and a competition designed to test both mind and skill.

I exited Route 3 just before it crossed the line into New Hampshire, motored through the tiny, whitewashed village of Tyngsboro, and crossed over the Merrimac on a rusting, green-girder suspension bridge. Turning right, I headed downstream. The river ran broad and deep beside the road. The Merrimac started as a pristine stream deep in the rocky foothills of the White Mountain chain in New Hampshire. For generations now, it had been anything but pristine. Starting in Concord, the river flowed through a succession of ugly, brick-lined mill towns that all had roughly the same history as Lowell. Over the generations, each of these cities – Concord, Manchester, Nashua, Lowell, Lawrence, Haverhill – had used the river for its free-flowing power, and, as a way of thanks, had dumped sewage and wastes and toxic nasties into the water's downstream flow. By the time the river reached the Atlantic at Newburyport, it had been turned into a disgusting mess. In the 1960s, the river had been considered one of the most polluted waterways in the entire nation. Then, thanks to governmental action and a better awareness of ecological system management, they started to clean up the river. All the cities along the route installed waste treatment plants, and with most of the textile mills moving South, there wasn't as much toxic crap being dumped into the river. I had read that some Atlantic salmon had been caught recently, well upstream from the river's mouth. Perhaps there is some hope for us, after all.

The river disappeared from view as I rounded a bend, and then I caught sight of the Shuttlecock Club's imposing clubhouse on its bluff at the end of its island. The thin stream that separated the island from the mainland was no more than 100 feet across, but I could imagine that it must have seemed miles wide to the factory workers and immigrants who gazed across at the verdant green fairways, the shingled clubhouse and the beautifully dressed set that partied gaily on the other side.

I drove across the rumbling boards on the old bridge that spanned the stream and glided to a stop on the other side. The entry road cut directly across the first fairway, a short par-four, and I remembered to stop and look for golfers who might be teeing off to the right. I didn't really care about getting another dent in the body work, but I did have the top down and I wasn't anxious to field a Titleist to the noggin.

Coast clear, I guided my heap down the curving driveway and under a canopy of broad oaks and tall pines. The roadway swept past the 18th hole on the left, and then forked. Straight ahead was the clubhouse, rising majestically in the bright autumn sun. I took the road to the right and found a place to park near the old, ivy-covered golf house. The squat little brick-and-clapboard building sat apologetically behind the first tee. Where the imposing main clubhouse bespoke generations of wealth and power, with its broad lawn, flower beds in a riot of late-season color, and a towering flagpole which carried a huge Old Glory and a somewhat smaller state flag – the golf house was something of an afterthought. It was obviously designed merely as a place to change one's shoes, buy some golf balls and perhaps have a drink. There was a newer, tacked-on section that held a windowed grille room, and a narrow porch overlooking the first tee. Still the place had a lot of charm, in a weathered, old-golf-club kind of way. I'd seen a lot worse.

I unloaded my golf bag, handed it to a kid dressed in a Shuttlecock Club golf shirt and went inside to find Jack Connolly.

FOUR

I climbed the wooden stairs onto the front porch and walked through the old screen door into the pro shop. Standing behind the counter at the end of the room, frowning at a thick sheaf of papers, was Shuttlecock's head pro, Ted McDaggert.

"Hey, Teddy," I called out.

He looked up from his work, recognized me, and his face broke out in a wide smile.

"Hacker!" he exclaimed, coming around the counter to shake my hand. "How the hell are ya? Jackie told me you were coming up to play with him this weekend."

McDaggert was about six feet tall and thick around the torso. His ruddy Irish face was topped with a mop of unruly orange hair – I'd heard it called an "Irish 'fro." His face was freckled, slightly jowly, and, I noted, unusually pale for someone who nominally spends a good part of his time out in the sunshine playing and teaching golf. But I also knew that few people who actually work in the golf business get to play the game, especially club pros. He was wearing the "uniform:" Kelly-green polyester Sansabelt slacks, a white pique knit polo with a green and purple geometric design, and black-and-white oxford teaching shoes.

As we made small talk about the events in the world of golf during the summer, I glanced around Teddy's pro shop. The room was small, maybe twenty feet by forty, and dark, with just one side window and the screen door permitting some filtered natural light to penetrate. The golf merchandise was crammed into every nook and cranny. Four wooden shelves took up most of the center of the room, and were filled with stacks of golf shirts, shorts and sweaters. More clothes hung on racks against two of the walls. Boxes of iron sets and long rows of drivers and putters competed for attention with a glass-fronted counter filled with boxes of balls. It was claustrophobic.

I have been in pro shops around the country that rival the selling floor at Bloomingdale's for retail presentation, with soft, indirect lighting, piped-in Muzak, stylish mannequins modeling the latest chic couture, and thick plush carpeting. Teddy McDaggert's pro shop was the antithesis of that kind of retail elegance. His carpets were worn in wellused traffic patterns in and out the doors, his fixtures were old and scratched, and he seemed to be presenting the theme of golf as chaos. But I imagined it worked for Teddy, who, after all, had something of a captive audience in the members of the Shuttlecock Club. He probably knew exactly where everything was, too.

"Have you seen Jackie this morning?" I asked.

"I think he's upstairs playing cards," Ted said, smiling at me. "Hope you can keep him sober enough to play some golf this weekend."

"Good luck to me and the Red Sox," I said, smiling and shaking my head. We both knew that Jack Connolly pretty much did whatever Jack Connolly felt like doing, and never worried much about the consequences. And if he decided he wanted to get, and stay, tanked for most of the weekend, golf tournament or no, that's what he would do.

I waved Ted back to his paperwork and pushed through the swinging door that led into the main grillroom. There were about a dozen men having an early lunch, drinking beer or staring at some sporting event blaring out from the huge television screen that hung from a corner of the ceiling. Big windows along the front of the room looked out on the first tee, where a foursome was getting ready to set off. I wandered to the back of the grill, past the long mahogany bar, pushed through another door and ran up the stairs.

The top floor of the golf house at Shuttlecock was the sanctum sanctorum for the male members of the club. While political correctness had invaded even the hallowed fairways here, where women had equal membership rights and could get prime weekend morning tee times, there was still once place in the club where men could act like men, and that was the upstairs locker room. It was mostly one big, open room, with the ceiling following the lines of the hip roof and gables. Rows of old metal lockers ran off a wide center aisle, and in the middle of the space, there was a row of brown-tiled showers. On the opposite side, a bathroom area held stalls and urinals, and a row of sinks outfitted with combs, brushes, throwaway razors and even a couple hair dryers.

The front of the room, with a row of large windows overlooking the first hole, was the game room. There was a big billiards table on one side, its brilliant green baize gleaming in the light of a Tiffany swag. On the wall, a wooden rack held a half-dozen cue sticks, and a dusty blackboard showed the score of a recent game. Three hexagonal card tables were grouped opposite the table, also covered in baize, with wooden shelves along the edges to hold drinks and stacks of chips. Two big ceiling fans whirred slowly overhead in a useless attempt to move the thick, steamy, cigar-scented air around.

Only one of the card tables was in use, but the six men sitting there were fully engaged in their game. The colorful chips were tossed into the pile in the center, the ashtrays were overflowing with crushed butts, and the drinks glasses of the players were beaded with moisture in the fetid air.

Jack Connolly sat on the left side of the table, his face a profiled study in concentration. He didn't see me right away, and I let him play his hand while I watched quietly from the side of the room. Jack was a handsome man. In college, he had been absolutely irresistible to women. His hair was still a tawny shade of gold, cut short, with small curls around the edges. He had a high brow, deep blue eyes, a patrician's hooked nose and a wry, off-center way of grinning. The fingers that held his cards were long and elegant and I noticed his well-trimmed, manicured nails. He wore a thin gold chain around one wrist, but was otherwise without watch or jewelry of any kind. He wore casual golf shorts and a shirt that was neatly pressed, but not expensive looking. Jackie was never flashy or loud. But he did have a nice-looking cashmere sweater casually draped around his shoulders and knotted at the front.

The poker hand was nearing its denouement. The pot was being fought between Jack and a fat guy sitting across the table from him. I watched as Jack coolly raised his eyes from his cards to stare at the man.

"Fifty," he said quietly, throwing a handful of chips into the center of the table.

The other man stared back at Jack for a long count, then blinked and folded his cards in resignation. Jack just smiled quietly to himself as he raked in the chips.

"Roland!" he called out. A pudgy young fellow dressed in medical white from head to toe materialized from out of nowhere at the call. "Drinks all around," Jack ordered, motioning at the table. "They need it. Hell, I need it."

Roland vanished as quietly as he had appeared. Jack finally looked up and saw me standing there.

"Hack man!" he said with genuine pleasure, and stood up to shake my hand. "Gentlemen," he announced to his pals at the table, "This is Hacker, my able-bodied, poor son-of-a-bitch partner for the weekend. He will accept your pity, but would appreciate your dollars instead."

Jack introduced me around the table, and I shook hands while giving up trying to remember all the names. The fat guy who had lost the last pot to Jack held my hand for an instant longer than normal, and peered at me through his thick round glasses.

"Hacker, eh?" he said softly. "I've heard about you. Didn't you used to play on the goddam Tour?"

"Only a couple years," Jackie said, a huge grin breaking across his face. "And before that we were college teammates at Wake. Hacker made it to the finals in the Amateur before he turned pro. He's since regained his amateur status, so he's legit."

"Legit my ass," the fat guy said. "What's his handicap, plus four?"

"I'm a certified three," I said, smiling. "Don't get to play as much as I used to."

"He's too busy raking muck for that despicable fishwrapper in Boston," Jackie said, laughing.

"Three? That's awful strong for a former Tour player," said the fat guy. "I don't think that's fair …"

"Oh, Charlie, quit your whining," Jackie snapped at the guy, although he was still smiling. "You'll be getting, what? Ten shots from him? Besides, he's gotta carry my sorry ass around all weekend, and that'll put anybody off their game."

There were nods of assent all around, and the table began a spirited discussion of handicap strokes and the general inequities of golf in loud and happy voices. Roland came bustling out of wherever he hid with a tray full of freshly made cocktails. Jackie grabbed his, pushed back from the table and motioned at me to follow. He led me back to his locker in the last row at the rear of the building. An ivy-covered window overlooked the parking lot down below.

"You can change and stuff here," he said, pulling his locker open with a loud clang. "Now, for tomorrow, when the tournament starts, I want you to wear this."

He reached into his locker and pulled out a hanger with slacks, a golf shirt and a belt. The slacks were a strange blue color the clothing catalogs like to call teal. The shirt had a white background, with a scattered design in greens and blues that looked like someone on crack cocaine had gone wild with a brush. Embroidered over the heart on the front of the shirt were the words "THE BROTHERS."

"If we're gonna play team golf, we're gonna dress like a team," Jackie said happily, pulling out the exact same outfit for himself. "You know, it's a gang thing, like the Crips and the Bloods. We'll strike fear into the hearts of our opponents. I got different outfits for each day. Wait'll you see Sunday! That is your size, isn't it?"

I was just staring at the clothes and shaking my head. "'The Brothers?' Jack, you just invited me to play in this thing a couple of days ago. When did you have time to custom order matching outfits?"

"Hell's bells," he said. "You gotta look stylish if you're gonna kick some Shuttlecock butt. Now look, here's the piece de résistance!"

He reached up on a shelf inside his locker and came out with two huge, wide-brimmed white Panama hats, trimmed in a wide band swimming in colors of red, yellow, pink and green.

"We're each going to go outside wearing one of those?" I asked, unable to mask the incredulity in my voice.

He nodded.

"In the daytime?"

He grinned his wry, one-sided grin at me.

"On purpose?"

"I thought the Greg Norman straw hat look would complete the look, even if he was one of the biggest choking dogs who ever lived. Did I ever tell you how much money I lost on his sorry ass in the Masters of '90?"

"You are certifiably insane," I said. "What have you got for Sunday?"

Jack Connolly laughed. "I knew you'd like it," he said. "You'll just have to wait and see."

FIVE

Jack wanted to get back to his card game since he was on something of a roll. I wanted to go hit some balls, since it had been at least three weeks since I last touched a   club.

"Okay," he said, edging back towards the card room. "Check back with me in about 45 minutes. We'll play a practice round at around one o'clock. You need anything to eat or drink, just tell 'em to put it on my tab. I don't want you to spend a dime this weekend, buddy. Just play good and make lotsa birdies."

I waved him away as I started to change into my golf shoes.

"Who we playing with this afternoon?" I asked.

"I dunno, we'll pick up a game with someone."

When I looked up, he was gone. I laughed quietly to myself. I had long ago learned not to try and keep up with Jack Connolly. In our college days, his staying power at parties was legendary. When we had traveled away from campus for a golf tournament, he had always figured out a way to defeat the usual bed checks and snuck out to sample the nightlife of wherever we were. Rarely did he get back to bed before dawn, or get much in the way of sleep, but he never missed a tee time and he was always a solid golfer. How he did it, I never was able to determine.

So I left him to his card game and drinking. I walked outside, picked up a bucket of practice balls and shouldered my clubs for the short walk up a hill next to the 18th green to the practice range.

The sun was shining brightly in a cloudless sky. Huge beds of summer annuals waved in a light breeze, their scents mingling with those of freshly mown grass to give the air a delicate and unmistakable perfume of golf. At the range, which spilled downhill from the hilltop tee, perhaps a dozen men were beating balls. From the narrow crescent of grass, the broad curve of the river sparkled in the sun as it swept past the angular lines of the old clubhouse. There were some tennis courts off in the woods to the right, and I could see the blue slash of the club's swimming pool over near the clubhouse. With school back in session, the pool was largely deserted, except for a pretty young lifeguard who was stacking up the chaises.

I wandered down the tee to an empty hitting station, next to two guys who were hitting balls with stern purpose. I put down my bucket, strapped on my golf glove and began some stretching exercises designed to loosen up the big muscles of my back. One of the men next to me was lecturing the other about the golf swing, and I quickly discerned that the two were partners for the weekend's tournament.

The one doing the lecturing was a small man with a stocky, well-defined build, somewhere in his late forties. It was obvious from his lithe, trim shape that he spent some time in the gym. He had jet black hair long on the sides and in back, but cut short on top and in front, and he used lots of wet goop to keep it in place. He was dressed all in black: slacks, golf shirt and highly polished shoes. His golf shirt was open at the neck, displaying a thick, twisted strand of gold chain that hung down onto his thick, black hairy chest. As he lectured his partner earnestly, I noticed his deep-set eyes, framed by a prominent forehead and a large, aquiline nose. His narrow pointy chin stuck out defiantly as he made his points, gesturing with sharp-edged hands. With his well-muscled upper torso, he looked like a black-topped fireplug, short but powerful.

His partner, on the other hand, was an older man wearing a sweat-stained baseball cap beneath which a few stray strands of wispy white hair escaped. He was at least a foot taller than his partner, and outweighed him significantly. He had broad shoulders and a prominent beer gut, and his clothes seemed to sag on his soft frame, especially his pants, which clung desperately to his waist. He wore thick glasses with lenses that were tinted slightly darker than normal. I couldn't see his eyes, but I could tell by his body language that he was getting slightly annoyed with the incessant and energetic lecture he was getting on the basics of a sound golf swing from the black-clad fireplug. He stood there patiently, resting both hands atop the butt of his club, and tried to listen and nod at all the right places.

The fireplug was expiating on the importance of a full rotation in the backswing, demonstrating the turning motion in exaggerated movements. "You gotta turn, Fred," fireplug was saying. "Turn your back to the target. Then, coming through, lay your head on the pillow. On the pillow, Fred. Like that."

He demonstrated for Fred. The backswing turn was good, but what he did with his head during the swing was something I had never seen before. He seemed to be trying to stick his right shoulder into his right ear while hitting the golf ball. It was a move I don't recall reading in Hogan's book, "Five Lessons."

Fred nodded, raked a ball from the pile at his feet and whacked at it. It didn't look to me like Fred bothered much about either turning his back to the target or laying his head on his pillow. He just swung at it, and watched as the ball skittered off to the right.

"Watch your angles, Fred! The angles!" Fireplug yelled. "You released way too early. Hogan says you gotta keep those angles until the very last second!"

"Vitus," Fred said with a noticeable sigh. "I haven't got the faintest idea what you're talking about, and in case you haven't noticed, I ain't no Hogan."

I chuckled out loud at the exchange. Vitus the fireplug heard me and shot a dark look at me.

"None of us are," I said with a friendly smile.

Vitus pulled himself up to his full height, which still didn't come up to my shoulders. "If you don't mind," he said icily, "We're working on our game here."

My smile faded. Prick, I thought. "'Scuse me," I mumbled and went back to my stretching. I wasn't going to let the guy spoil a beautiful day. Golf is not a physically demanding game, but it's also not an activity that God had in mind when He designed the human body. So I always loosened up before I began striking balls, otherwise I would feel it the next morning. And with four days in a row of golf ahead, I didn't want to put undue stress and strain on my back or legs. Heck, even Jack Nicklaus used to spend an hour a day stretching and loosening. Just another thing me and Jack have in common.

Once I felt loose, I started swinging with my sand wedge. It's a heavier club than the others, so that too helped me stretch out. I started by hitting some half shots, not worrying about how far the ball was going, or even in what direction, but simply trying to develop a smooth tempo and make good contact. Most golfers go out to the practice range, pull out a driver and immediately start trying to hit the ball 300 yards. Big mistake. One must work up to hitting full shots, slowly and carefully.

Once I had a rhythm going, I stretched out the swing to three-quarter and then full swings. Then, I switched to a seven-iron and, again, began by hitting little half-shots, and some knock-downs, trying to keep the ball low and in control. I tried to keep the tempo slow and smooth, always slow and smooth. Effortless. Trying to "not try." After a bit, I began to focus on the 150-yard marker planted down the hill, and began to try and hit the ball somewhere in that vicinity.

I get into my own little world on the practice range. Hitting balls is both fun and therapeutic. As I get into a practice session, everything around me begins to fade out. The world slowly dissolves and disappears as I concentrate only on my tempo, my swing, and the ball. McNamara and his entire brass band could march up behind me and launch into the Washington March and I probably wouldn't notice. I would be thinking about my tempo, looking at the golf ball sitting on a little tuft of green grass, and trying to make that ball get in the way of my swinging club. And doing so with some deep, inner part of me that's primal and unknown.

I had moved from seven- to a five-iron and then on up to my three-iron, which I was using to crack some nice controlled draws down the hill where they landed and stopped near the base of a tree some 200 yards away, when I finally noticed Vitus and Fred had stopped their own practice and were staring at me. Vitus had his arms crossed across his burly chest, and his bushy eyebrows were knit in a thoughtful expression, while ole Fred slouched beside him, his mouth open as he watched my last shot bore high through the air and down the hill.

When I stopped, Vitus spoke. "You've got a beautiful swing, sir," he said. Fred nodded his agreement.

"Oh, thanks," I said. "I just can never get my head to stay on the damn pillow."

I was, of course, trying to be facetious, and at least Fred got it. He chuckled softly, and nodded at me, smiling. The fireplug, however, didn't react. He strode up to me and stuck out his hand.

"Vitus Papageorge," he introduced himself. His grip was hard, and he scrunched my knuckles together hard, just short of being painful. Maybe he had got it after all. "I don't think we've met, and as the club president here, I know pretty much everyone. What flight are you in?"

I confessed that I had no idea. I was aware that the field of golfers had been divided into various divisions, according to the combined handicaps of the partners, but I didn't know where Jack and I had been placed.

"Well, who are you playing with?" Vitus asked, looking at me as if I were a total idiot.

"Jack Connolly," I told him.

"Oh," he said, and blew out a breath in a rushing sound of disapproval. "Well, I certainly hope you can keep him reined in. He has been known to act out, and I hope there won't be any such incidents this year."

I didn't reply. As true as his observations might be, I thought it was a bit classless to say so out loud. Unless one was a prick.

"Well, then, you must be Hacker, handicap 3," he said, eyeing me with suspicion. "You will be playing in our flight. Fred and I have won our flight the last two years running. Isn't that right, Fred?"

Fred sighed and nodded. I was about to introduce myself to the man – his partner had rudely ignored him – when Papageorge cut in again.

"Where, exactly, is your handicap established, Hacker?" he demanded. "You have an awfully smooth swing for someone with a three handicap."

"Hingham," I said, the name of the club where I played perhaps three times a year.

"Indeed," Papageorge said, his eyebrows moving up and down rapidly. "Well, if you don't mind, I may ask Teddy McDaggert to make a phone call just to verify that. Just to ensure that the playing field is level, of course."

Having just been accused of cheating, I said nothing, but merely leveled a cold gaze on this most unpleasant little man.

He picked up one of my irons and hefted it, swinging it back and forth.

"I wanted to ask you. Where exactly in the swing do you release your hands? You've got such a nice swing, I thought you might ..."

He paused, fully expecting me to jump in with the answer. His head was cocked to the side in anticipation, his small body drawn up, his legs spread authoritatively. I recognized the posture as that of a chronic over-achiever, one used to asking questions and getting immediate answers. Never mind that he had just insulted both my friend and me.

I laughed. "To tell you the truth," I said, "I really don't know. If I tried to think about what my hands were doing while I was swinging a golf club, I'd probably fall over on my head. All I do is start the swing slowly and throw 'er in automatic, if you know what I mean."

I saw Fred nodding in understanding. Vitus, however, peered at me for a long moment, his beetled eyebrows knit, his lips pursed unpleasantly, his darks eyes staring out at me.

"C'mon Fred," he said finally. "Let's go get some lunch. The problem with most guys who think they're good is they never want to share with others. Selfish."

He turned on his heel and strode off towards the golf house. I stared at his retreating back in stunned disbelief.

"What did I say?" I wondered aloud. Fred picked up his clubs, looked at me sadly and shrugged as if to say "who knows?" and turned to follow his partner.

I shook my head and turned back to my practice. First impression confirmed, I thought. Major-league prick. I tried to regain my tempo, but it had gone. I stubbed one, hit a quacker of a duck hook with the next, and blocked the third shot dead right. I sighed, stopped a minute to look out at the quiet river flowing silently past the island, and then picked up my clubs and headed back.

SIX

My partner was still deep into his card game up-stairs in the locker room, and his pile of chips had grown quite a bit larger. Somebody had ordered a tray of sandwiches and some chips, so I grabbed a ham and cheese and asked Roland to bring me an iced tea. Jack looked at me with an expression that hovered between amused and aghast. I ignored him and sank into a nearby leather chair. Jack did a double-take.

"Anything wrong?" he asked as he sorted his hand.

"Just met a wonderful fellow," I said. "Somebody named Vitus . . ."

'POPPYCOCK!" said about six voices in unison. They all began to laugh uproariously.

Jack threw some chips into the center of the table as his ante. "So you met old Vitus, eh?" he said. "Legend in his own mind."

"Asshole," grunted one of the other card players.

"Dickhead," chimed in another.

"Aww, he's not so bad for a total fuckwit," said a third.

"Popular guy, huh?" I asked.

"What do you expect," Jackie said, "He's the club president."

"Really?" I said. "That guy won an election?"

The card players laughed.

"We decided that since Papageorge knows everything about everything already – just ask him and he'll tell you so – we might as well let him have all the fun of running the club," Jack said. "Frankly, it couldn't happen to a more deserving guy. So he gets to preside over committee meetings four nights a week, and deal with all the petty little problems involved in running a place like this. In return, he gets a parking space right outside the door that helps feed his ego. Dr. French here," – he nodded across the table – "is of the opinion that in about another six months, that ego will get so large that it will explode, scattering Poppycock's brains all over the 18th green."

Jack picked up his second batch of cards, looked at them sadly and folded, swearing softly under his breath. He pushed his chair back, stood up, yawned, stretched and left the room.

"What does the guy do when he's not running the Shuttlecock Club?" I asked.

A short, stocky man with a bristling crew cut, took the nasty stub of a cigar out of the corner of his mouth and, waving it in small circles, answered.

"Guy's a zillionaire," he said. "He's a bank president up in Nashua. Married the former bank owner's daughter, guy put him to work as a favor and about five years later,

Vitus engineers a takeover and forces his wife's father into retirement. Poor bastard never saw it coming, and died six months later of a massive coronary. Few years later, Vitus dumps the daughter, marries this hot young chickie."

The guy stuck the cigar back in his mouth, threw a few chips into the pot and asked for two cards. Then he continued his story.

"The bank's been making millions for years – southern New Hampshire has been growing in leaps and bounds, and Papageorge's bank has pulled in all kinds of business loans, mortgages, corporate work...you name it. He didn't stop there," the guy poked the cigar for emphasis. "He also invested on the side, on his own, or so he says. Whatever...he's got a golden touch. Guy owns car dealerships, apartment houses, strip centers...you name it. When the goddam politicians come to New Hampshire for the presidential primaries, Vitus Papageorge's ass is the first one they have to kiss when they drive over the border."

Jack walked back into the room, smiling from ear to ear.

"Got us a game," he announced. "You and me against Vitus and good ole Fred. We tee off in ten minutes."

The card players all groaned. Jackie smiled even wider at the reaction.

"You did that on purpose, didn't you? I accused him.

"Oh, hell, yes," he grinned. "I thought you ought to get the full Monty, as it were. It's always quite the experience, playing our Pissant Prez. It's why no one in the club will play with the son-of-a-bitch."

There was a good deal of head nodding around the card table.

"Guy cheats like a bastard," said one.

"Will do anything to make a withdrawal from your Hip Pocket National."

"Stay with him if he hits it into the woods. His best club is the foot wedge."

"Five to one he throws a club by the third hole."

"What an asshole."

Jackie just laughed. "C'mon Hack-Man," he said. "Let's go watch this mother operate up-close-and-personal. It'll be a gas!"

"Did anyone ever tell you you're a sick puppy?" I wondered. But I followed Jackie and his booming laugh down the stairs.

While we waited under a canopy of oaks on the first tee for the group ahead of us to clear the fairway, Jack and Vitus negotiated the terms of our little match. I went over and finally introduced myself to Fred, whose last name was Adamek.

"Twenty-five a side OK with you Connolly?" Papageorge barked, swishing his driver back and forth impatiently.

Jack had his three-wood out, and he thought about it while he took off the head cover, walked onto the tee, took an address position and made a practice swing. He swung as hard as he could, dug a foot-long trench out of the tee, and stumbled from the momentum of his follow through. Vitus watched Jack's performance through narrowed, disgusted eyes.

"How 'bout a hundred?" Jackie slurred, grinning lopsidedly at Vitus.

Papageorge's bushy eyebrows rose imperceptibly but he quickly nodded. "Done," he said. "Ten bucks for birdies, greenies and sandies? Automatic press on two down?"

Jack was swishing his club back and forth again, pretending to pay attention to his elbow position at the top of his backswing. "Huh?" he said confusedly. He swung his eyes around and focused on Vitus. "Oh, yeah, fine, whatever," he said.

Papageorge looked at me. "Is this OK with your partner?" he asked.

"Fine, fine," Jackie said, before I could interject. "And yours?"

We all looked at Fred, who had turned an interesting deep red. "Well, actually, …" Fred started, when Vitus cut him off.

"Fred agrees," Vitus said. He turned to me.

"I assume you're still claiming to be a 3 handicap?" he said unpleasantly.

"I'm not claiming anything," I said. "That's what my handicap is. You wanna call my club and confirm it?"

"Well," Papageorge said. "As a matter of fact, and just so we understand each other, I intend to have the tournament committee check your handicap prior to tomorrow's start of play. And if I see any indication today that your alleged handicap is bogus, I intend to inform the committee of my observations. You are on notice."

I could feel my face getting hot. "Notice of what, you goddam little wea —"

Jackie grabbed my arm and pulled me away from Vitus Papageorge, who was very close to taking a Callaway to the noggin. "Leave it," he said to me, sotto voce. "He's just trying to get your goat. It's part of his shtick. Just play the game, kick his ass and leave the rest to me."

I took a deep breath and exhaled. I nodded at Jackie, who gave me a smile and a wink. Vitus looked at us both.

"Fred and I will be walking," he said archly. "I do not believe in golf carts. Except for the revenue they bring the club, carts are an abomination. Golf is a sport, not something meant to be played from a sitting position. I play the game for its exercise value. I hope you understand."

"Whatever turns you on," I said to him. I looked over at Fred, who did not seem pleased with his partner's announcement. Fred Adamek looked like a cart kind of guy.

"Furthermore, we will be playing strictly according to the USGA Rules of Golf," Papageorge said. "We play the ball down here at Shuttlecock. None of this rolling it over, mulligans or giving yourself putts. I firmly believe the game should be played according to the rules. Otherwise, what's the point?"

I heard Jackie snort quietly behind me. Vitus pulled a scorecard from his back pocket.

"Okay, Mr. Hacker here is a three. Or so he says," he said, making some marks on the card with his pencil. "We will therefore stroke off him. Connolly is a 10, I'm a 12 and Fred here plays off 15. So, I'll get nine strokes and Fred will get twelve. Correct?"

He looked at us, eyebrows arched.

"And Jackie gets seven," I reminded him. "Do we get a scorecard too?"

Papageorge peered at me. "It's a free country, Mr. Hacker," he said. "But I will keep the official card of the match." He looked down the fairway, where the foursome in front was approaching the green.

"Right," he said. "We can hit. Go ahead, Fred. Play away."

Jack and I exchanged a glance. Papageorge had simply appropriated the honor for his team. Not exactly cheating, but also not exactly the way the Rules specify for the beginning of a match, which usually begins with a coin toss or some other means of determining the first team up. Obviously, Vitus' version of the Rules were somewhat different than those published by the U.S. Golf Association.

The first hole at Shuttlecock is prime Donald Ross. Just 290 yards long, it appears to be a simple and easy start to the round. The fairway is wide open, the entrance road cutting across some 200 yards off the tee, and only a tall oak off to the right, a small nest of bunkers across the road down the right, and an out-of-bounds fence way off to the left, alongside the narrow branch of the river that creates the island provided any danger from the tee box. So unless one completely choked, it was pretty hard to find anything but fairway. But there, the fun began. The green was small, raised about four feet, and crowned, calling for a delicate and precise approach shot. Anything short would roll back down the upsweep, or catch a deep bunker on the right. Anything too hard would roll off the back, or one of the sides, into deep rough. That was the genius of Donald Ross. One could hit almost anything off the tee, from driver to five-iron, but even from 70 yards away, the hole could exact a six as easily as a three.

Fred hit a weak tee shot that didn't make it across the road. Vitus stepped into his drive, releasing his hands at just the right moment and his head found the pillow, and his ball carried straight and long. Jack and I looked at each other again. We had to give away nine strokes to him?

Jackie motioned at me to hit first. I had my three-wood, figuring a straight drive was more important than a long one here. I made solid contact and the ball ended up just 30 yards from the green.

"Attaboy," Jackie cheered.

"Nice shot, Hacker," Fred said, smiling at me.

Vitus stared off down the fairway.

Jackie teed his ball and made a lurching swing at it. The ball skidded down the left side and caught up in the thick rough under the trees. "Damn," he muttered.

Vitus and Fred set off down the fairway together, trailed by their caddie, a young kid wearing floppy socks, old sneakers, shorts and a T-shirt. He carried both bags, and seemed to be struggling with the weight, especially Papageorge's large staff bag. Jackie and I got into our motorized abomination.

"Do you always play for this much money?" I asked, a bit concerned.

"Money, s'money," he waved his hand in dismissal. "It's not how much, it's how the game is set up. He thinks I'm blasted, so he's concentrating only on you."

"But Jack," I said as we drove down the rough, "You are blasted."

"Oh, yeah," he said. "I forgot. Good point."

We found his ball, which was sitting down in the thick rough. He pulled out his wedge and hacked it about fifty yards down the fairway. "Damn it," he said, getting back into the cart. "You gotta pick us up for a few holes until I get my swing grooved."

I shook my head sadly. "Whatever happened to that smooth Connolly swing I used to know?" I asked.

He laughed. "That was many years ago, Hack," he said. "Age, work, booze and broads … they all take a little something out of you."

"Based on those two swings, either you're 150 years old, you own your own distillery or you've screwed half the women in America."

He laughed, but it took him three more swings to reach the green. Fred dumped his approach shot in the front-right bunker. Vitus decided to try a run-up shot, and nipped his ball so it scooted up the fairway, slowed as it swept up the rise in front of the green and stopped about 20 feet from the hole.

"Nice shot!" I called to him. He ignored me.

I took my sand wedge, trapped the ball perfectly and watched as my pitch bounced once beside the pin, took a hop forward and then stopped dead. Fifteen feet. Vitus walked past me on his way towards the green. He never looked at me or acknowledged my shot. Major league prick. Fred tried to explode out of the bunker, but caught it fat and it stayed in the sand. He cursed, smiled and hacked the next one out.

Both Vitus and I missed our birdie putts, and we headed to the next tee all square. We had to wait a minute or two until the fairway ahead cleared.

"So, Fred, what line of work are you in?" I asked, making conversation.

"I'm in the construction business," he said, swishing his driver back and forth.

"Based on the figures I've seen, that's a questionable statement," Vitus interjected snidely.

I laughed, thinking Papageorge was making a joke. But then I noticed that Fred wasn't laughing. Or even smiling. He glared at his partner.

"Hey, c'mon," he said with an edge to his voice. "There's a recession going on, in case you haven't noticed. Trouble with you bankers is you think life goes on in a vacuum. Well, it don't. Some months it's pretty damn hard just to make payroll."

"You borrow the money, you're supposed to pay it back," Vitus said curtly.

"We can hit now," Jackie said from the cart, where he was sitting with his feet propped up, beer can in hand. Shuttlecock's second is a longer and more difficult hole than its first. A high ridge extends down the left, with the fairway beginning on the plateau above it. But any tee shot that goes left gets thrown down the ridge, blocked out of view of the green by a stand of tall trees. A good tee shot up onto the plateau leaves a long-to-midiron approach to a sloping, well-bunkered green.

Three of us hit pretty good tee shots up onto the plateau. The exception was my partner who hit four trees with his first three swings, picked up his ball, rummaged around noisily in the cooler for another beer and sank heavily back into the cart. "Play hard, pard," he said and popped the tab which made a loud hissing sound. Vitus had been standing over his approach shot, and backed away, shooting an angry look across at Jack. He ignored Vitus and downed about the half the can in one swallow.

Vitus was about 170 yards from the green, and had what looked like a seven-wood in his hand. He made a nice pass at the ball and it flew straight at the green, landing just short and bounding up the hill to the back tier, stopping maybe 10 feet short of the hole. Jack and I watched the great shot in silence.

"By the way," Jack said calmly, "Did I mention that dickhead over there is the biggest sandbagger in the club?"

"No," I said, "I don't think you actually did pass on that semi-important little factoid."

"Doesn't dickhead get a shot on this hole?" he asked.

I looked at the card. "Yup," I said.

"Aha," Jackie said, and drank some more beer.

"Aha?"

"Well, I don't want to put any more pressure on you," Jack said with a soft burp. "But whenever Poophead has a stroke, he damn near always makes either a par or a birdie. Uncanny, isn't it?"

"So what you're saying is that I'd better hole this seven-iron?" I asked.

"Wouldn't hurt," he said.

I didn't hole it. I hit a nice shot, but left myself a 25-footer for birdie. Hit a nice putt, too, but hell, even the pros miss half the time from six feet. The odds are even longer from 25 feet.

Vitus took a long, long time lining up his birdie putt. He studied the damn thing from every angle, even though all he had to do was two-putt from ten feet for his par-net-bird to win the hole. It occurred to me that he was perhaps rubbing it in. Finally, he stood over the ball and stroked it towards the hole. It almost went in, catching just a corner of the hole and rimming around the edge. I was about to tell him "nice putt" and concede the next when Vitus Papageorge went totally and completely ballistic.

"Gawwwwwwddddddddd-DAMN-it ALL!" he screamed. He took two giant strides to the left, bent over from the waist until his face was parallel to the ground and screamed again. "DAMN it !... DAMN IT! DAMN...DAMN...DAMN! I can't believe that ball stayed out! GAWD-damn-it-all TO HELL!"

He held his putter up to his bulging eyes and glared at it in unrestrained fury. His face had now turned a dangerous shade of red, and his black hair had fallen forward over his eyes. I was beginning to think that Vitus Papageorge was quite mad, in the certifiable, call-the-guys-in-the-white-coats kind of way. It was shocking to see him react this way. After all, he still had won the hole with an excellent par four. Yet here he was throwing a force-five tantrum. I looked over at Jackie, who was standing on the edge of the green, his arms crossed, smirking.

"That's good, Vitus," Jack said, referring, I think, to the two-inch putt Papageorge had left and not about the performance we had just witnessed. "You guys are one-up."

We headed for the third tee while Vitus stomped around the green talking about the injustice of that last putt, until he realized nobody was left listening to his fervid ranting. Fred already had his ball teed and let fly with a pretty good rip down the middle. Adamek was not a bad player. He just had the typical handicaps of his age: a lack of flexibility and upper-body strength. But I could tell he'd once been an strong athlete and a pretty good golfer.

Vitus, still muttering and red-faced, finally climbed onto the tee, waggled angrily and made a hasty swing. The ball went straight up into the air and fell with a heavy plunk no more than a hundred yards away. He let out a mighty yell – a primal screech – reared back and hurled his driver down the fairway after the ball.

"Whoa," I said as I watched his club helicopter end over end, before it landed, dislodged a chunk of turf and bounced a couple times. I hadn't seen a temper like this since I was 10 years old and playing in the Wallingford town tournament, junior division. Even then, allowing for the immaturity of youth, it had been unforgivable behavior. I still remembered the time when I was a kid when, after missing a short putt, I had thrown my putter in frustration across the green. I had been playing with my uncle, who walked over, picked up the offending club and snapped it neatly in two across his knee. "There," he'd said, "That'll fix it." It did. I haven't thrown a club since.

Vitus stomped off the tee, muttering and kicking at clumps of grass. I was about to say something to him when Jackie caught my arm and shook his head quickly. Although the man deserved a lecture, if not a left cross to the jaw, I held my tongue. We played on.

Jack hit two abysmal worm-burners to get within shouting distance of the green, then one beautiful chip to about four feet. He made the putt to halve the hole against Fred, who managed a routine par. Vitus and I made bogies, me after hitting my approach just over the green to a place from which I couldn't get it up and down. Donald Ross strikes again.

I stood there watching while Fred putted out.

"Hey!" I said suddenly. "You putt left-handed!"

"Great powers of deduction there, pard," Jack said sarcastically.

I did feel a little stupid, but I hadn't noticed that while he played his full-swing shots right-handed, Fred putted from the left side. "Have you had the yips?" I asked as we strolled over to the fourth tee. "I know some guys on Tour have tried putting lefty to smooth out the stroke."

He laughed. "Naw," he said. "I'm actually a natural lefty. But when I picked up the game as a kid, there weren't many left-handed clubs available. So I learned the game from the right side." He shrugged. "My first putter was a Bullseye model with the flat blade, and it just felt right to putt with it lefty. So I did. And I've played that way ever since."

The fourth hole at Shuttlecock is a pretty par-three over the narrow slice of river to a well-bunkered green on the mainland side. The river had carved out a deep ravine over the centuries, so the water wasn't in view. An old steel-girder bridge, just wide enough for a golf cart to squeeze through, lay across the channel. While we waited for the group in front of us to putt out, Vitus and Fred walked to the front of the tee and looked over at the old bridge. Fred pointed and said something, and Vitus began shaking his head. They turned and walked back towards us.

"I'm telling you, it can't be done that way," Fred was saying, his face reddened. "You gotta repour the footings, and the steel has to meet state specifications. It's the law, Vitus. Our price is the best I could come up with, and I've already cut it to the bone."

"Your estimate is just way beyond what the grounds committee has budgeted," Vitus said. "It simply must come down if you want the contract. That's all there is to say about it."

"Hell, Vitus, I'm not making a goddam dollar on this job," Freddie started to protest angrily, but he stopped quickly when he saw Jack and I listening.

"Right," Vitus said quickly. "It's still our honor I believe. Play away, Fred."

Fred bunkered his tee shot, but the rest of us made it onto the putting surface. As we drove our cart across the rickety bridge, I asked Jackie what that was all about.

"They gotta replace this bridge," he said, motioning at the rusting girders above and around us. "Been here since about the 1940s. Guess Freddie wants the job. Guess Vitus wants to make him sweat for it."

When Vitus and Fred, who continued their heated discussion as they walked across the bridge, trailed by their caddie, reached the green, Fred took a sand wedge and climbed down into the front bunker. He skulled his sand shot over the green, and waved his hand in surrender. Vitus putted first and just missed on the low side. He cursed loudly again and tapped in for his par. I was next and ran my putt past the hole about two feet. I marked.

"They're pretty quick, pard," I told Jack as he lined up his putt. He nodded. His putt looked good all the way, but at the last moment it veered slightly to the right and skirted past the hole, finishing just three inches away. We groaned in unison. Jack walked up and scooped his ball away. "I hate this game," he sighed.

"Good try, though, Pards," I commiserated. "Makes mine good." I leaned over and picked up my coin, slapped Jack on the back and we headed for the next hole.

Vitus was standing on the edge of the green, scorecard and pencil in hand, shaking his head sadly. "I'm sorry gentlemen," he said. "But neither my partner nor I conceded either one of your last putts. So according to Rule 3-2, the hole is ours. We're now two-up."

I stopped dead in my tracks, unbelieving. Jack, amazingly, kept on walking. As he passed Vitus, he turned his head and said quietly "That's real bullshit, Vitus."

"Rules of Golf, Connolly," Vitus snapped. "I informed you on the first tee that we're playing strict Rules of Golf. If I don't concede you must putt out. You didn't putt out, you lifted your ball. You should know the Rules, especially in a tournament. You may thank me, come Sunday afternoon."

I looked at Jackie appealingly, hoping he'd give me the nod that would permit me to knock the sanctimonious shit out of this insufferable little man. But he just shook his head sadly and kept walking back to the cart. I looked around for Fred, hoping his sense of decency would assert itself, but Fred, having chased his ball across the green and into the woods, had his back to us, pissing against the trunk of a large oak. Vitus stalked off to the next tee.

I slammed my putter back into my golf bag with an unrestrained fury, and added a kick to the cart tires for good measure. I plopped down on the bench seat of the cart and Jack Connolly and I stared at each other. He handed me a cold beer. Together, as if on cue, we burst out laughing.

"Let's kill this motherfucker," Jack said.

"Onward," I nodded.

SEVEN

A nger is a useless emotion on the golf course. It just tightens muscles that should be loose. It clouds judgment. It takes you out of the present and the task at hand, and puts you in the past, filled with recrimination, or the future, filled with dread. It releases endocrines into the bloodstream that cause a chemical reaction remarkably similar to that caused by a healthy snort of cocaine. Except for the rush, of course.

So I didn't get angry. I got serious.

Vitus had a stroke coming on the par-five fifth, a shortish hole that played up a long hill. Sure enough, he played three conservative and steady shots to reach the green in regulation. Forcing my mind and body to relax, and focusing on the task at hand, I crushed my drive and watched it fly and roll nearly 300 yards straight down the middle. I followed that shot with a clean two-iron that flew up the hill and bounded onto the green, stopping just under 20 feet below the hole. Fred and Jack had their usual problems: sideways drives and stubbed irons.

Vitus rolled his approach putt up close to the hole, maybe 18 inches short. He looked at me, but I said nothing. As far as I was concerned, the son-of-a-bitch was going to have to putt everything out for the rest of the round. He marked.

I took a few extra seconds to study my putt. It was straight uphill, with just the hint of a break to the right near the end. I nailed it solidly and watched it drop cleanly into the center of the cup for an eagle and a win. Jackie gave me a thumbs-up and one of his patented Connolly grins, and as we walked back towards the sixth tee, Fred came over and slapped me on the back.

"Great playing, Hacker," he said. "I can't remember the last time I saw an eagle. Beautiful!"

I thanked him. He seemed like a nice man. Unlike his partner. Vitus, as usual, didn't say anything. He walked up to the tee with his scorecard and pencil in hand. "I had a net birdie there," he said. "What did you take?"

I laughed, recognizing the man's shameless gamesmanship. I had played with assholes like Vitus many times, even on occasion during my short stint on the PGA Tour. There are all kinds of ways to get under someone's skin, and Vitus was trying them all.

"Three," I said, and he wrote it down.

"Go ahead, Fred," he said, putting the scorecard back in his hip pocket. "Play away."

"Excuse me," I said, "We won that hole. If I remember the Rules of Golf correctly, that means we get the honor on the tee."

Vitus just looked at me and shrugged. "No need to get snippy," he said reprovingly. "Just trying to keep play moving along. I abhor slow play. Detracts from the enjoyment of the game, in my opinion."

Nobody stroked on the sixth hole, a short par four, so I made a routine birdie: nice drive, wedge to six feet and drained the putt. Vitus and Fred made pars; Jackie made another "X" when he couldn't get the ball out of a greenside trap. We were back to even in the match.

Jack cracked open another beer back in the cart. "Keep it up, pards," he said, "We're doin' great!"

"What do you mean 'we,' Kemosabe?" I cracked.

Jackie actually made a contribution on the par-five seventh, as he managed to make a par-net-birdie to hold off Vitus, who did the same. I let my drive drift too far to the right and got caught behind some trees guarding the dogleg, and had to scramble to make par, while Fred made a bogey. Eight was also halved: my four against Vitus' five-net-four.

We came to the ninth at Shuttlecock with the match even and a hundred bucks on the line. Every Donald Ross course I've ever seen has a hole like the ninth. It says par-three on the card, but those who play it week-in and week-out know that it's really a par three-and-a-half. Ross loved long par threes. This one was 220 yards, playing from an elevated tee box to an elevated green. In between was a rocky gully that swept upwards steeply in front of the green. There were woods to the right and a swampy marsh to the left. Long, shallow bunkers protected the bail-out area to the right of the green, and the left side was death: bunkers, trees, rocks and mounds. The hill in front of the green was closely mown, so a ball that didn't quite get up and over the lip of the hill would run all the way back down to the bottom, at least twenty yards away.

It was still our honor. I tried to work a two-iron in from right to left, but it caught one of those greenside bunkers to the right of the green. Jack bumped his shot down to the bottom of the hill in front of the green. Fred hit a high pop-up drive, but it landed on a rock in the gully and leaped forward, coming to rest near Jackie's ball.

Vitus was the last to hit, and his three-wood started right and stayed right, fetching up in the thick and heavy rough beyond the bunkers. I looked at the scorecard and saw that both Fred and Vitus stroked on this hole, so if the prick could get his shot up and down for par, they'd probably win the hole and the front nine.

The hole was cut in the back of the green, just ten paces from the back edge. Behind the green was a row of young junipers and behind that was the snack shack, where golfers could order a hot dog and a beer. On this course, as at the Old Course in St. Andrews, the ninth green was about as far from the clubhouse as one can get.

Fred and Jackie headed off into the gully together, each armed with a wedge and a putter. Vitus walked around the high road above the gully, and the caddie lugged the clubs up the hill, over the green, and dropped them on the back fringe before disappearing into the snack shack to get himself something to drink. I drove our cart around the path to the green.

Fred flubbed his first chip, and his second ran just to the edge of the green before losing its momentum, stopping and running almost back down to his feet. He looked at the ball despairingly, sighed, and picked it up. Jack hit a nice chip that stopped in the middle of the green, maybe 30 feet from the hole.

My ball had landed in the first of two bunkers, a bit further away from the hole than Vitus' shot, which had carried over the sand. Walking past his ball, I was glad to see that it had nestled down in the deep stuff. Good, I thought to myself, he'll have trouble getting it out of that lie with any kind of control or spin. Could go anywhere.

Then I caught sight of my ball, and my heart sank. It had hit the soft sand and plugged. The old and dreaded fried egg. The ball was nestled in its pitch mark, surrounded by the ring of displaced sand. Because I was still a long way from the hole, I couldn't explode the ball out of that lie – with that ring of sand surrounding the ball, my club would slow down as it neared the ball and I'd probably leave it in the bunker. Instead, I'd have to close the face down, dig it out with a hard blow, and hope it didn't run all the way off the other side of the green. My chances of getting it close ranked somewhere between slim and none.

I dug in and tried to make the swing, but the ball actually came out softer than I imagined, and it landed and stopped well short of the hole. I had probably 25 feet for par. Two putt range. Well, I consoled myself as I smoothed the sand with a rake, at least Vitus will have a tough shot too.

I turned to watch him make his important chip. My mouth dropped open in amazement. Vitus' ball was now sitting atop a soft cushion of grass. Unless there had been a major earthquake at Shuttlecock in the last two minutes, which I hadn't felt, some unknown force had moved Vitus' ball from its position nestled deep beneath the thick grass to its current soft and lovely lie. I suspected the foot wedge, and could not believe the chutzpah of the man.

As Vitus prepared to hit his shot, I bit down hard on my back teeth. For all his sanctimonious crap about the honor of the game and playing by the rules, the truth was that Vitus Papageorge was a cheater. He knew nothing about sportsmanship, gentlemanly behavior or anything else that made golf such a great and genial game. I decided the man had gone way beyond the category of world-class prick. He was now All-Universe.

From its new and improved lie, Vitus caught the ball cleanly, with a bit of spin. It bumped onto the green, checked slightly and began to roll out towards the hole. I watched it with sinking heart as it headed straight for the flag. Vitus began to run towards the green, holding his wedge high above his head, readying for a triumphant celebration.

But at the last second, the ball veered imperceptibly and caught just an edge of the hole. The power lip-out gave the ball enough added momentum to keep it rolling past the flag, where it caught the slight downhill crown and kept rolling on and on, trickling finally off the back of the green and bumping up against one of the golf bags that the caddie had laid in the fringe.

"ArrrrrRRRRRRR-SHIT!" Vitus screamed. Turning his body in a coil, he threw his wedge in a beautiful, arching parabola over the juniper trees and out of sight. We heard it land with a crash on the roof of the snack shack, and someone inside yelled "What th' FUCK?"

"Oh. Wonderful shot, Vitus," Fred said, ignoring the post-shot hammer throw. "You got robbed. That was in all the way."

"Yeah, great effort, Vitus," Jack said with a smirk. "I hope you didn't put a hole in the roof. I'd have to make sure you got assessed for the damages."

Papageorge didn't respond. His face red and angry, he stalked over to his ball, jerked his golf bag upright, and yanked his putter out. He squatted down and began to study his putt, just a shade over ten feet away from the hole.

I didn't say anything. I took a minute to finish raking the bunker smoothly. As I walked onto the green, Jack was watching his par putt skim by the hole. He walked over and knocked it in the hole backwards. "I putt, I miss," he said apologetically.

I still didn't say anything. My ball lay on the green where it had stopped after my bunker shot. I walked over and picked it up, and kept going towards the snack shack. Jack made a gagging sound of disbelief. Vitus was also staring at me in amazement.

"You are conceding the hole?" he asked, unable to keep a tone of gloating out of his voice.

"No," I said. "We won the hole."

"What?" Vitus stuttered. "That's preposterous. You and I both lie two and I have a stroke here. How do you figure? I'm sorry, but you picked up your ball. That's a concession. The hole is ours. . ."

His face was red again, and his eyes darted sideways at me. I suspected he was worried I was going to call him for moving his ball into a better lie in the rough. But that would lead to a loud and angry argument, since no one actually saw the transgression, and it would end up being my accusation against his word of honor. So I just let him stew for a few long moments.

"I think it's Rule 19-2," I finally said. "The one about stopping or deflecting a ball in motion. Your chip shot rolled into your golf bag. That's a deflection caused by your own equipment. Two-shot penalty in stroke play. Loss of hole in match. Rules of Golf. You lose. Sorry about that, chief."

Jackie nodded thoughtfully, turned on his heel and led me through the junipers to the shack. Vitus Papageorge, probably for one of the few times in his life, was struck absolutely dumb. I didn't look at him, but I could feel the emanations of hatred rolling off this tightly wound little man.

The explosion, when it came, was a doozy. First, Vitus took his anger out on the offending golf bag. He slammed it to the ground and kicked it a few times, then he turned it upside down, dumped out the clubs and hurled it against a tree, shouting obscenities at the top of his lungs the entire time. Then he started kicking the clubs around on the green. I wasn't sure, but I think there was some froth about his mouth. When he got tired of screaming and kicking, he set off in search of someone else to blame. Storming into the snack shack, he zeroed in on the poor caddie. The kid was sitting on a bench, sucking on a Coke, minding his own business. Vitus burst through the door breathing fire and blowing smoke, and began screaming a line of sputtering, saliva-punctuated curses and threats at the boy.

Fred cut him off before I could. "Stop it, Vitus," he said, grabbing the angry man by the arm and getting in his face. "Leave the boy alone. It wasn't his fault. It was just one of those things. You're the one who wanted to play by the all-fired rules, so just shut the hell up."

Fred's quiet little speech was effective. More effective, probably, than what I had in mind, which was a snot-stomping thrashing of the man. Vitus started to argue, but then he looked into Fred's eyes and saw something there that snapped him out of his rage. Fred let go of Vitus' arm, and Papageorge shook himself, once, twice. Then, he turned on his heel and stalked off towards the next tee.

The young caddie was sitting as still as a rock, blood drained from his face, his eyes big and round and beginning to fill with tears. He didn't have the slightest idea of what he had done to inspire Vitus' tirade.

Jackie went over and squeezed the kid's shoulders. He reached into his pocket, pulled out a twenty-dollar bill and handed it to him.

"Here, kid," he said. "Combat pay. You just earned it."

EIGHT

The back nine went much the same as the front. On those holes where Vitus had a handicap stroke in his favor, he was unbeatable. He drove it down the middle, knocked his approach shot onto the green and two-putted for his par-net-birdie. Mr. Automatic.

Vitus and Fred won three holes that way, but on two other holes, where Papageorge didn't have a stroke, I managed to make birdie, and on the long, uphill par-3 17th, my besotted partner somehow managed to run his chip into the hole for a two. It took him a few seconds to figure out why I was cheering.

Vitus' temperament was unchanged as well. On those holes where he played well, he kept silent and to himself. He never once congratulated another player – not even his partner, Fred – for a good shot or commiserated over a missed putt. When he spoke, it was only about his own game and its fortunes, the good putt that he had just stroked or the overhanging tree limb that had prevented him from getting his shot closer to the hole. And I counted three screaming tantrums, five helicoptered clubs and one tee marker neatly drop-kicked into a thick patch of poison ivy. He sent the caddie, the poor kid, in after it.

One of his screaming fits came on 13, where he had a long, 80-foot putt for birdie. His putt, rapped with authority, looked better and better as it rolled closer and closer to the hole. But it stopped less than two inches shy of the goal, and Vitus let loose, with both voice and putter, which went flying off in the direction of the next tee. He put together a very imaginative combination of "fucks" and "shits" in a voice loud enough to carry all the way back to the clubhouse. Jack waited until he was finished stomping around.

"Yeah," Jack said dryly, "I know how you feel. I always get mad when I miss those 80-footers, too."

At first, Vitus thought he was getting a sympathetic message. "Well, God-DAMN it!" he started in again, face red and angry. "It was IN all the God-DAMN way …"

That's when he noticed his partner's shoulders jumping as Fred laughed silently at his foolishness. Jack and I wore big grins.

Vitus harrumphed, stalked over to the hole, bent down and snatched up his ball angrily.

"That's good," Jackie and I said in unison. Fred laughed out loud.

So we came to the 18th all square again. Vitus and Fred needed to win the hole to win the back nine and halve the match. My heart sank when I saw the scorecard. Naturally, Vitus had a stroke on the hole.

The last at Shuttlecock is a damnable hole. It's a short par-five, but trouble lurks along virtually every yard. The tee shot must be threaded through a narrow chute of trees to find not just the fairway, but the right-hand side of the fairway. For that's the only place from which the second shot can be advanced up a steep hill to find the narrow fairway that curves slightly to the left. The left corner is guarded by several large, overhanging trees, so any tee shot that finishes left of center is virtually blocked, and requires the near physical impossibility of hitting a low hook from a hanging lie. Once over the crest of the hill, the fairway drops sharply back down to the right, with a nest of trees and thick rough waiting for any pushed shot, and drops down a hill to a huge green complex surrounded by pot bunkers and closely bordered by the entrance road, which is out-of-bounds.

It's possible to reach the green in two shots, but it requires a perfectly placed tee shot, followed by a precision fairway wood that threads through the S-curve of trees, catches a good bounce on the downhill side and rolls between all the bunkers. No problem! Most players therefore elect, or are forced, into playing the hole in three shots, but that final approach, with its sharp drop in elevation, is no picnic. Depth perception is always thrown off by the drastic downhill change in elevation, and the roadway and parking lot beyond lurk with the promise of many penalty strokes. And the green is the largest on the course, so a slight miscalculation in the approach can result in a 100-foot putt. Three-putts from 100 feet are commonplace. Especially when, like ours, the match is tight and there is a hefty wager riding on the outcome.

My tee shot, despite my best efforts to keep it from going left, drifted that way, and while the hill threw it back to the right a bit, it was not in the best position to tackle the corner. Jack, who had cracked the last beer on the cart in celebration of his birdie and rare contribution to the fortunes of the team, jammed his drive deep into the woods on the right. I could tell by the nonchalance with which he greeted this turn of events that he was pretty much cooked for the day. He went back to the cart, sat down and drank about half the beer. "A veritable golfing machine," he sighed.

Freddie grounded one up the middle, safe, but a long, long way from home. Vitus made an awkward pass at his drive, trying to let the club release freely but attempting to steer it at the last second. His ball ended up going right, landing in the fairway and then bouncing hard right into the rough and underneath the limbs of a tall pine. Not dead, but not in good shape.

Fred's second shot was another grounder that ran almost to the crest of the hill, still a good 200 yards from home. Vitus tried to hack his ball up and over the hill, but the rough was thick and his backswing was restricted by the nearby tree. His ball skittered forward just 30 yards.

Thwock! He slammed his club against the offending tree trunk and the club snapped neatly in two pieces. The part with the clubface went spinning off into the woods. The caddie started dutifully after it.

"Leave the GODDAM thing," Vitus screamed. He threw the grip end after the first, kicked the ground hard enough to dislodge a toupee-sized divot, and stalked off after his ball. If Vitus had a dog waiting at home, I hoped the poor thing had Blue Cross.

I had a bad angle for my second. Because the fairway dove sharply to the left, with those trees protecting the corner, I'd have to hit a career three-wood with a sharp drawing action to get it close to the green. And with the fairway sloping below my feet, I knew the percentages for success on that shot were poor. If I tried it and missed, I'd likely end up down off the right side of the fairway, in that tree-and rough-encrusted jail.

So I pulled out my seven-iron and, playing the ball back a bit in my stance, hands forward, I hit a little knock-down punch shot up the hill and with a bit of running draw to take it around the corner. All I wanted was a safe shot that stopped in the fairway somewhere. From there, I'd take my chances with an eight- or nine-iron and a putt.

Poor Fred, who was trying so hard, skanked a three-wood almost dead right, where it rattled around in the trees and dropped out of sight. He was out of it. Vitus, still with his stroke in hand, also hit a safe iron up and over the hill. He and I would be pretty close, but I lay two, and he was three with his stroke. When Jack—who had ricocheted one even deeper into the forest and quit— drove us over the hill, I saw our two balls, no more than three yards apart. It was Vitus and I for all the marbles. The game was on!

Jack parked over in the left rough opposite our two balls. I walked over, saw that I was away, and looked at the lie. Perfect. Slight downhill stance, but nothing difficult. I checked a nearby sprinkler head for the distance. 148 yards to the center. The pin was back right, so I added another 15 yards. But the hole was cut precariously close to the back edge of the green, no more than 10 steps further to the ashphalt surface of the road. And we were way up the hill, easily 50 feet above the green level.

I thought about all this. Downhill, with a bit of wind blowing left-to-right. Don't want to challenge that pin, because anything that drifted to the right might carry onto the road, out of bounds, and give Papageorge the hole. But I didn't want to play too safe, because it was a big green and I didn't want to leave myself 50 feet for birdie, which was what I figured I needed to win against Vitus the all-star sand-bagger.

I pulled my eight-iron, figuring a nice, solid swing would get the ball up to, but not over, the pin. Vitus, Fred and the caddie were standing about 15 yards behind our golf cart, in the left rough. I thought it a bit odd that Vitus wasn't over near his ball, getting ready to play, but I pushed those thoughts out of my head and went into my preshot routine. I stood behind the ball and pictured the shot I wanted to hit. I saw a little patch of sunlight on the shade-dappled green, and decided that was where I wanted the ball to land: perhaps 20 feet short of the pin and just to the left of it. Hit that patch and the ball should release nicely towards the hole. With my target selected, I took a deep breath to relax, walked up to the ball and lay the clubface down behind it, pointing down the target line I had selected. Then I placed my feet along that aiming line. Took one more relaxing breath. Waggled once. Twice. Looked at the target one last time. Thought: "slow and easy." And let it rip.

It was a pretty good shot. Guarding against that dreaded out-of-bounds on the right, I pulled it slightly and missed my patch of sunlight to the left by about 10 feet. The ball bounced forward once, then checked on the second bounce and spun to a quick stop. Looked like maybe 25 feet. Not bad.

"You da man," Jackie said from the cart. I laughed as I walked back towards him. He gave me a tired, slightly unsteady, thumbs-up.

Then I saw Vitus, out of the corner of my eye. He had wandered even further into the rough behind our cart, and was bending over, picking a handful of grass and tossing it into the air, to judge the wind speed and direction. But why was he doing that way over there, a good twenty yards away from his ball? He began walking towards that ball now, slowly, on a line that would take him past the rear of our cart. Where I was putting my club back in the bag. Where he could see which number iron I had just used. Which would help him make his own club selection.

I saw all this in an instant. I have seen all the tricks in the book in my years in competitive golf, and in watching and reporting it. I've seen them try everything from the patently illegal to the borderline unethical. I could have done a number of things to prevent Vitus from learning the little piece of data he wanted. I could have kept the club in my hand and away from his prying eyes. I could have leaned over the bag and blocked his view that way. I could have looked straight into his eyes, so he'd know I knew what he was up to.

But I didn't. Instead, I tried something I'd heard Tommy Bolt once used on a similarly snoopy opponent. Quickly, I put my club back in the bag, snatched my towel and began polishing the clubface. Vitus stepped up, stuck out his hand and said "That was a very good shot, Mr. Hacker. Especially under the pressure."

I smiled at him happily and shook his proffered hand. "Thanks, Vitus," I said. "I stepped on it pretty good. Wasn't sure if I had enough club."

I watched his eyes and saw them dart down into my bag to catch the number of the club I was wiping. I saw his quick, half-smile of triumph. The All-Universe prick had stolen my signals.

He continued on to his ball, where his caddie was waiting, and I walked around the cart and sat down next to my partner. He was looking at me strangely. "What the fuck was that all about?" he asked wonderingly.

I smiled at him. "Just watch," I said.

Vitus had been studying his shot. Finally, he turned and pulled a club out of his bag. He took about four practice swings. He knew the importance of putting this shot — his fourth — on the green. If he could get it close, he could still make a five-net-four, which might be enough to win. My thirty footer was certainly no gimme. But even if he could get it on the green and two putt, it was likely that we'd halve the hole. That, at least, would save his team a $100 bet for the back nine. His goal was to try and get his ball inside mine.

Finally, he stood over the ball, wound up and let the ball fly with his short and powerful swing. It was a beauty. He had flushed it. The ball took off into the beautiful blue afternoon sky, sailing high into the air, a tiny white dot of hopefulness. From where we sat, it looked to be tracking the flagstick all the way.

"Oh, baby," Vitus breathed softly to himself when the ball was in mid-flight. "Be the stick. Be tight, BABY!"

Finally, the ball began to descend. We all watched as it fell from the heights. We watched as it came down right over the pin. And over the green. We all watched as the ball smacked down with a sickening click on the asphalt surface of the road, bounced high into the air again, and kept on bouncing crazily down the road and in among the cars parked in the shady lot beyond.

"Holy Mother of God," Fred exhaled, after watching the disaster unfold. "What the hell did you hit, Vitus?"

Vitus Papageorge was frozen at the top of his follow-through, posing, waiting for the ball to drop next to the hole. He began to shake his head in disbelief, as if trying to shake out the cobwebs from an unexpected right cross to the chin.

"It was …I can't … I don't …" He tried about four sentences at once, and none of them made it out. His brain was fried. "A four," he finally croaked. He looked at his partner in agony. "A four-iron. I thought … he hit …"

He looked at me. I was smiling enigmatically. Jackie broke out in loud guffaws. He waved his hand. "Tough luck, Vitus," he chortled. "Great match. See you guys inside. We'll buy!" His brays of laughter echoed across the fairway as we drove down the hill and back to the clubhouse. "That was beautiful, Hack-Man," he said, pounding his fist on the steering wheel. "A-One Magnifico! How the hell did you do that?"

"I thought he'd been clubbing off me," I said. "He usually went one or two clubs down. So when I saw him trying to sneak a peek up there, I started cleaning off my six-iron. I had just hit an eight. I figured that if he thought I had hit a six, he'd go up to his four. I think even a five would have gone OB, but I was hoping he'd take enough club. He bought it hook, line and Top-Flite. Hit it pure, didn't he? Hope it didn't dent someone's Mercedes."

Jackie howled and howled. I told him, as we unloaded our clubs, about the Tommy Bolt inspiration. Terrible Tommy had been one of the purest ball strikers in history who could make a ball curve any which way he wanted, and stop it on a dime. The story I'd heard was that he'd seen his opponent clubbing off his iron choices, so he let the guy see him take his five-iron out on a shortish par 3. Bolt then used his considerable skill to manufacture a shot to put the ball on the green, even though a normal club selection might have been the seven or eight. He just put an extra cut on the ball, or hit an upsweeper than fell far shorter than his normal five-iron shot. His opponent, unsuspecting, also hit a five, but his landed forty yards over the green.

Neither Vitus nor Fred showed up in the grille for the after-the-round drink we'd offered. But that was OK. Jackie and I had one or two extra in their honor.

NINE

We celebrated our victory for the next hour. In between drinks, he explained the format for the Shuttlecock Invitational. The tournament was scheduled over the next three days, and the field had been separated into ten flights of eight two-man teams each, and each flight would crown a champion team over the weekend. The teams in each flight had been selected so that the players were all roughly in the same handicap range: the lower flights were made up of pretty good, low-handicap golfers, while the ninth and tenth flights had teams of choppers and hackers. But that meant that, based on handicaps anyway, each team in each flight played at pretty much the same skill level. Each team would play a nine-hole match against the others in its flight: two nine-hole matches on Friday, three on Saturday and two on Sunday.

Scoring was by modified match play: the goal was to win each hole with the lowest score, but each match would consist of nine full holes because it was the cumulative score that counted. Each outright win of a hole was worth one point, and each team got one-half point for halving a hole. At the end of the weekend, the team with the most points in each flight would win: there would therefore be ten winning teams, and ten runners-up.

Jack and I had been assigned to the third flight. My three handicap and Jack's 10 put us in a flight where the combined team handicaps ranged from 10 to 14. Of course, since we were playing nine-hole matches, our handicaps were halved, so I was playing off 1.5, and Jack at 5 for the purposes of the tournament. Further, the tournament committee, to guard against sandbaggers, or those who inflate their handicaps so they can win more easily, had decided to automatically reduce everyone's handicap by 10 percent. So I'd be playing off 1, and Jack off 4. Quickly scanning the list of players in our flight, I saw that I'd be giving away strokes to everyone. But, I thought, that's only fair and it's what handicaps are supposed to do: level the playing field among players with disparate skills so we could have a competitive and interesting match. At least Jack would get three shots per match, which he could certainly use. Especially since his real handicap was his general state of inattention.

Scanning the list of players in the third flight, two names immediately jumped out: Vitus Papageorge and Fred Adamek. We were scheduled to play them in the second match on Friday. This worried me. Not only did I never want to play golf with that All-Universe Prick ever again, I knew that the revenge factor would be high. Jack and I would be in for a tough match.

I pointed this out to my partner, whose eyes were red and tired. He just shrugged and said "Let's go eat."

First, we went upstairs to the locker room and took a long, hot shower. It's a funny phenomenon, but the world's best showers are often located in the most run-down, aging and decrepit-looking locker rooms, just like the ones at the Shuttlecock Club. I have personally tested this theory all across the country, and it's always true. I've showered at many of the fanciest new clubs, the ones that drip with prestige and wealth, that have deep-pile carpeting, hand-rubbed African mahogany lockers, animal heads on the walls and plush sofas everywhere for lolling on ... and the showers are always poor. Water pressure is low, the shower heads are stingy, and the hot water runs out too fast. But at the great old clubs, like Shuttlecock, the locker facilities are crappy, with threadbare linoleum floors, metal lockers that open with a clanging echo, and paint that's peeling off the walls and ceilings. But the showers are magnificent: big shower heads that drench one in an endless supply of steamy hot water, with dispensers that release dollops of shampoo and body gel that foam up quickly. One never wants to get out of such a pleasurable place, but there were huge, thick towels waiting. Talcum powder for feet and crotch. Deodorant for the pits. Hair dryers. Brushes. Throw-away razors. Sure, the locker room at Shuttlecock was old and drafty and the décor would make the editor of Architectural Digest retch, but for a bunch of male golfers, it is nirvana.

Showered and dressed and feeling spiffy, we strolled across the lawn from the golf house to the main clubhouse in a deepening twilight. As we neared the main door, a long, silver Cadillac limo swung around the corner of the building and glided to a stop in front of us. The headlights pinned us and we had to step out of the way as the driver pulled up right in front of the door. The car sat there, growling at idle. The windows were tinted so we couldn't see inside in the fading light of day. No one got out.

Suddenly, the back door flew open and Vitus Papageorge clambered out. His hair was wet and slicked back, and he wore a yellow linen blazer, black pleated tropical-weight woolen slacks, tassel loafers, a blue pinpoint Oxford shirt with white collar and cuffs and a yellow paisley tie. Dapper.

And angry. He slammed the car door shut, and started to enter the clubhouse ahead of us. But then he turned on his heel and stalked back to the limo, walking around to the driver's door. Jack and I heard the soft whine as the window wound down.

"Goddamit, O'Grady," Vitus snapped in an angry, hissing voice. "I pay you goddam good money. I expect you to get your fat ass out of the car and open my door. Do you read me?"

The driver did not answer. I saw a tiny red glow from behind the tinted glass, and then a cloud of bluish smoke billowed out of the window and wreathed the fuming Papageorge. We heard the whine as the window wound up again.

"We'll talk about this later, damn you!" Vitus pounded on the window with frustration, and stalked around the car and into the club. Jackie and I followed, and exchanged a look and a shrug of the shoulders. It seemed not to be Vitus' day.

Inside, we followed the sound of a hundred happy men to the banquet hall, where the pre-tournament stag party was in full swing. Take a hundred golfers, generous portions of scotch and vodka and beer, add the promise of a glorious weekend of golf on a fine old course, throw in a prime rib dinner with baked potatoes, and leaven within the comfortable atmosphere of a genial group of self-assured and over-achieving American men, and you will get a cacophonous but happy sound.

Jack and I fought our way to the bar, and then found two seats at one of the tables set up around the large hall. Huge banks of picture windows provided views of the Merrimac as it flowed silently past the island. As soon as we sat down, a waitress presented us with deep bowls of clam chowder, thick and creamy.

"Specialty of the house," Jack told me as we tucked in with relish.

"Actually," I said, "I think it's a state law that clam chowder be served at all important Massachusetts functions."

After we finished our chowder, Jack introduced me to the other Shuttlecock members sitting at our table. On my left was Dr. Walter Bainbridge who was chief medical officer at Lowell General Hospital. He was a rotund man with a shiny bald pate that reflected the spots inset into the ceiling high overhead. He wore a pair of small reading glasses perched on the end of his nose and smelled faintly of bay rum. He was wearing a blue blazer over a blue-and-white striped shirt, open at the neck, and a pair of gray flannel slacks. His handshake was firm and he seemed a genial sort. His partner, a surgeon from Boston, shook my hand and went back to attacking his slab of roast beef. I wanted to ask what his cholesterol number was, but restrained myself.

Across the table was Charlie Stansfield, a local insurance agent, in his mid-40s, whose hair was starting to resemble more salt than pepper, and his brother-in-law, a guy named Eric, who lived outside Philadelphia.

"Hacker?" Charlie said when he was introduced, "Golf writer for the Journal?" I nodded. "Heck, I read your stuff all the time! Tell me, is Tiger not the best there ever was? I mean, really …"

It was a question we get a lot these days, and with good reason. So I was prepared.

"Well," I said, as everyone at the table stopped eating to listen to my opinion, "I think the best one-sentence way to answer that is what David Fay, the USGA's executive director, said. 'We are all lucky,' he said, 'to be alive at this point in history to watch Tiger Woods play golf.'"

Everyone nodded wisely.

"The hell with that," Dr. Bainbridge interjected in a deep basso profundo voice. "Tell us about all these blonde models he gets to boink."

Everyone laughed and I was about to tell the one good Tiger Woods nightlife story I had in my arsenal, when the squeaking of an amplified microphone being turned on caused the room to fall silent. At the head of the ballroom, Vitus Papageorge stood behind the wooden podium. He could have used an extra tread, as his head barely cleared the upper rim.

"Gentlemen…gentlemen…your attention please," he called out, and waited until he had everyone's attention. The room finally fell silent. "As the president of the Shuttlecock Club, it is my honor to welcome you all here for the 55th annual Shuttlecock Invitational Member-Guest tournament." He paused dramatically, apparently waiting for applause, but there was none. In the sudden and awkward silence, somebody called out "whoopee!" which drew a few chuckles, and then my partner, sitting next to me, let out a horrific belch, which echoed across the room. Gales of laughter erupted, but Vitus' face screwed up in taut disapproval.

"Excuse you, I'm sure," he snapped, and held up his hand for quiet.

"Classy, as always," I murmured to Jack.

"Thank ye kindly," he giggled.

When he had our attention again, Vitus launched into a long and rather detailed explanation of the rules of the tournament, pointed out the board where the flights had been posted and reiterated that everyone was responsible for knowing their tee time and whether they were starting on the front or back nine. "There will be no excuses or exceptions," Vitus lectured, waggling his finger. "You must be on the tee at the appointed time, or you will be disqualified. We have a full field as usual, and the only way we can ensure that all matches finish in daylight is to observe strict starting procedures and to enforce strict rules concerning pace of play. To that end, I can assure some of you that if you dawdle as you usually do, you will be assessed penalty strokes and/or loss of hole. Is that understood?"

"Yes, Master," someone called out in a Transylvanian accent. Boos and catcalls filled the air.

"Go ahead and make fun," Vitus continued, "But you'll be thanking me later."

"Aw, stuff it," yelled someone from the back of the room. Laughter welled up again. It was a tough crowd.

Papageorge held up his hand for quiet. "Now then," he said, looking down at his notes. "As you are undoubtedly aware, the U.S. Golf Association has officially notified all member clubs that any gambling and wagering activities officially or unofficially sponsored by this club are not allowed." More boos. "However, I am also aware of the long traditions of the Shuttlecock Invitational, and what you gentlemen decide to do on your own is your business." Loud cheers. "I will therefore leave the premises shortly so that whatever you want to do can be safely accomplished without the knowledge or interference of your club president."

That got a standing ovation. Vitus Papageorge was not the type that enjoyed being the subject of sarcasm, but he managed a silly grin, waved his hand and disappeared through the French doors at the entrance to the banquet hall. The room returned to its high decibel hubbub as the assembled golfers went back to their drinks, their dinner and their conversations.

"What an ass," said Charlie Stansfield. "I don't know anyone who likes that guy."

"Why is he the president of the club, then?" I asked.

Stansfield shrugged. "It's a thankless job," he said. "You gotta referee every damn disagreement, make decisions that leave someone mad as hell every time, and generally spend a lot of your time screwing around with stuff that's totally meaningless. On the other hand, you get a parking space right in front of the clubhouse, your name on the plaque of past presidents in the lobby, and, I guess, you get to know everyone else's business."

"So you think it's basically a power trip for Vitus?" I pressed.

"It's gotta be," Charlie said. "He's a bank president and a successful real estate investor, so he's got all the money he could want. I think he just likes running things and telling other people how to run their lives. I sure wouldn't do it."

I turned to Dr. Bainbridge sitting on my left. He had been listening quietly while working on a dish of apple pie a la mode.

"What do you think?" I asked him.

Bainbridge finished the last forkful of pie, carefully wiped his lips with his napkin, and set it down next to his plate. He motioned for a hovering waitress to bring him some coffee. I noticed that Jackie had quietly left the table, and was standing over by the bar, fresh drink in hand, chatting happily with a few other well-soused members.

"I respectfully disagree with my friend Stansfield here," Bainbridge rumbled, finally. He turned and peered at me over his narrow spectacles perched at the end of his nose. "I've had my eye on Papageorge ever since he joined the Shuttlecock Club some 15 years ago," he said. "He has always been the most disagreeable sort, and that's unusual in a club like this. Most of the people here are fairly easy going and get along with each other. After all, the Shuttlecock Club is a country club, a place where people come for recreation. We bring our families here, our friends and business associates. We come to play golf and tennis, to dine, and to relax with other people of similar interests. Certainly, like any organization, this club needs someone to run it. Someone to make sure the bills are paid and the grass is mowed. But it's hardly a major undertaking, and the amount of power, as you termed it, is hardly significant."

The waitress brought a silver pitcher of coffee and began pouring it into the white cups. Bainbridge waited until she had gone before picking up again.

"Not long after he joined Shuttlecock, Papageorge let it be known that he was willing to serve on the club's finance committee," he continued. "Everyone agreed that having a bank president on the board of directors would be a good thing. Of course, we had other bankers from Lowell and even Boston on the board before, but he was new and brought a fresh new perspective. At least, that's what we all thought.

"It was just three or four years later than Papageorge ran for, and won, the position of club president," Bainbridge said, stopping to blow on and sip his coffee. "I remember thinking it quite unusual for such a new member to quickly rise through the ranks. The Shuttlecock Club, like most other private country clubs, can be a rather stuffy old place, and generally speaking, presidents are elected from a rather short list of well-known old families that have been members here forever. I also recall that the president just before Vitus not only didn't run for re-election, but resigned from the club altogether soon after the election. It was Harding Wolcott, wasn't it, Stansfield?"

Bainbridge looked across the table. Charlie Stansfield nodded slowly.

"I think you're right, Walter," he said. "I'd forgotten old Harding. But you're right. He left the club and I think he and his wife pulled up stakes and moved down to Florida."

"I thought that was quite unusual as well," Bainbridge continued. "The final odd occurrence was that two years later, when it was time to rotate in a new president, the nominations committee announced that it could not find anyone willing to serve as club president. They'd asked everyone, they reported, and no one would commit. So, they recommended that Vitus continue on for another term. Two years later, it happened again. He's now on his fifth term."

I laughed. "Just like FDR, huh?"

Bainbridge chuckled. "Quite so. As I said, I've had my eye on the man for a long time. Indeed, a few years ago, I even volunteered to run for election to the board, just so I could keep a bit closer watch on Papageorge. But I was defeated in the election."

"Not surprising," Charlie Stansfield said. "Vitus has pretty much hand-picked the members of the board. I wouldn't say they are his friends, since he doesn't really have any friends. But he lets his wishes be known, and his wishes get elected."

"Just so," Bainbridge said. He fell silent and sipped some more coffee.

"Well," I said, "Some of the best clubs are run by dictatorship. Augusta National springs to mind, as does Pine Valley, Seminole, a lot of them. Sometimes it's better if everyone knows and understands that all important decisions will be left to the top guy. Management by committee is not always a good thing."

"I quite agree," Dr. Bainbridge said. "But there should be some mechanism in place for checks and balances. Vitus seems to have surrounded himself with yes-men, and no-body else is really quite sure how the club is operated."

"Isn't there some kind of annual report, or published audit?" I wondered.

"Certainly," Dr. Bainbridge rumbled. "There's an an-nual meeting to which all members are invited and very few bother to attend. It's usually at the end of January when many members have high-tailed it down to Florida and the rest have no desire to drive out here on a cold night. Vitus' finance committee sends out an annual accounting, which shows incremental increases in both revenues and expenses, and every three or four years an increase in dues."

"Except for the surprise of a couple years ago," Stansfield chimed in, shaking his head.

"What happened?" I asked.

Stansfield took a sip of his coffee and grimaced. "It still ticks me off," he said. "There was an incident with a burst pipe one winter, the kind of thing that happens in old buildings all the time. All of a sudden, Vitus announced that the sewer system had been determined to be old and decrepit. Didn't meet the city code, somehow, after sixty years of trouble-free flushing. Had to be dug up and replaced. Cost a bloody fortune, and every member was hit with an assessment to pay for it."

"Jeez," I said. "How much?"

"The project was priced out at four million dollars," Dr. Bainbridge said, fingers drumming on the table. "Every member had to kick in four grand. It caused an uproar in the club, but Vitus was adamant and the city officials backed him up. It was either replace the sewer system or close the club. I know at least four fellows who dropped out, and I'm sure Stansfield does too."

Charlie nodded. "It was really hard on some of the younger guys, with families and educations to pay for," he said. "We tried to get the assessment stretched out over five or ten years, but Vitus said it had to be done in two. I think the club lost something like 40 members."

"It couldn't be too hard to replace them, I'll bet," I said. "Place like this must have a long waiting list to get in."

"Took less than six months," Bainbridge said. "Vitus kicked the initiation fee up another ten thousand and the new members were begging to pay."

"And where did all that new money go?" I wondered.

Dr. Bainbridge nodded at me sagely over his spectacles. "Excellent question," he said. "The annual report says there is a new long-term capital improvement fund, with a current balance of $2.5 million. But nobody knows what the long-term improvements are. There have been rumors about new tennis courts, an enlarged pool and a major remodel of this building to add a health club and meeting space."

"And they say we need to replace the steel bridge over the river between four and fourteen," Stansfield chimed in.

"I have also heard that the main bridge, where you drove in today, has been surveyed by the city and the rumor is they are going to condemn it as unsafe. That would quickly eat up the capital fund and then some."

"Well," I said, "Isn't it lucky that your club president runs a big bank?"

"Yes," Dr. Bainbridge said. "Isn't it?"

I paused a minute before asking my next question. "Do you think there's a cause-and-effect?"

Walter Bainbridge looked at me over his spectacles again. "Are you asking me that question as a reporter for the Boston Journal?" he said.

I laughed and held up my hand in protest. "No, no, not at all," I said. "I'm just a lowly sportswriter, and I'm here for fun, not on business. This is all strictly off the record. Unless you've got proof that the guy is a crook. In which case, dish."

Everyone at the table laughed.

Bainbridge sipped more coffee and fell silent again, his fingers tapping softly on the tabletop. He seemed to be having an internal debate, and finally decided.

"Your question is not outside the bounds of reason," he said. "Papageorge has cut a wide swath here in the Merrimac Valley and has earned a reputation as both a hardnosed dealer and someone just a bit shady. His banking empire, for instance, was reported to be under investigation during the savings and loan scandals of the 1980s, but no suits were ever filed and nothing was ever said in public."

"Yeah, and the guy Papageorge was supporting was elected to the U.S. Senate from New Hampshire," Stansfield said. "I'm sure that didn't hurt."

Bainbridge nodded, his lips pursed. "There is nothing illegal, of course, with donating money to a candidate for elective office and receiving some aid and assistance from that candidate once he is elected to public office. That's how the game is played, isn't it? Still, once his bank was safe, Papageorge really began building his little empire in southern New Hampshire. Again, there were whispers that the bank foreclosed on certain properties that later ended up in Vitus' personal portfolio. Or that competing banks and credit unions that suddenly found themselves in hot water with regulatory agencies, leaving the path open for Vitus' bank to step in and take over. But again, no charges have ever been filed and no one has ever accused Papageorge of doing anything illegal."

"But what kind of scam could he run here?" I wondered out loud. "I can't imagine this place generates enough cash to make it worthwhile to steal."

Walter Bainbridge winced. "Please, Mr. Hacker," he said. "I have not implied in any way that Vitus Papageorge has stolen any funds from the Shuttlecock Club. Even though most members here find his personality, er, somewhat challenging, I don't think anyone for a moment considers that he might be a common criminal."

"I apologize," I said. "I leaped to conclusions. But it seemed as though you were headed in that direction."

"Not at all," Bainbridge said. "There is simply no way for Vitus Papageorge or anyone else to cook the books."

"That's what they said about Enron," I said dryly.

Jack Connolly staggered back to the table and demanded I come with him to have a drink. I shook hands all around the table and joined him. He introduced me to more of his pals, and for the next hour, we stood around the bar and talked about golf. They were interested to hear some of my stories from covering the PGA Tour, the little weekly dramas of victory and defeat that I got to witness close up. We talked about new courses we'd played, vacation spots in Florida, whether or not Phil Mickelson had replaced Greg Norman as the greatest choking dog of all time, considered the question as to Colin Montgomerie's needing to wear a brassiere, and invented some very creative ways to torture the members of Augusta National into resigning en masse and letting real people run that tournament. In other words, we had ourselves a boozy, brawling good time of standing around and letting the testosteroned good times roll.

I tried not to drink too much, knowing I would regret it in the morning. But boys will be boys, and after an hour or so, the call of nature and a desire to remove myself from the smoky atmosphere of the Shuttlecock's main bar drew me away from the crowd. I found a men's room down the hall and while I stood at the urinal and offloaded, I studied

the framed print of a turn-of-the-century English gentleman preparing to whack a golf ball. The pictured golfer wore
a heavy tweed jacket that seemed to be much too tight to
allow a free-swinging motion of his arms, a necktie that
must have been most uncomfortable in a hot midsummer
sun, plus-fours with woolen knee socks that must have
itched, and he had the club wrapped around his head in an
odd, broken-elbow backswing that I imagined would have
led him to miss the ball completely seven times out of ten.

Coming out the men's room, I decided a bit of fresh air
was important to my future health and well-being. I stumbled
down the hallway and pushed out a door that led to the
back patio. Pillars of square, rough-edged granite held up
the roof of the porch that overlooked the swimming pool
terrace and the dark river beyond. It was a deliciously clear
night with that tang of autumn, that first forewarning of the
coming winter. The sharp bite of cool air quickly cleared
my fuzzy head. The sky was filled with stars and lights from
the homes along the river were reflected in shimmering bands.
I could smell apples ripening on the trees, the sweet decay
of crops gathered in, the end of summer.

I took in several deep draughts of cold air, watching
my breath in a cloud of vapor. I wandered down to the far
end of the porch, where delicate scents from the nearby
garden wafted in the air. There were no lights on the pool
terrace, save for some dim illumination that came faintly
through the windows of the dining room inside. I could see
the shadowy shapes of the pool furniture and heard a faint
gurgling from the pool's water filtration machinery.

Just below the porch was a narrow strip of lawn bordered by a high wall. As my eyes grew used to the darkness,
I became aware that someone was standing there. Two
someones, in fact. A male and a female. Locked in embrace.

Passionate. What the younger people ineloquently call "sucking face."

Without knowing exactly why, I stepped back behind one of the broad stone pillars as the couple broke apart with a soft gasp. Moving my head forward I could still see them, but only in the shadows.

"Oh, babe, you don't know what you do to me," the man said softly. I glimpsed his hands moving softly over her body and then pulling her into another tight embrace. The woman reached up and pulled his head down to her lips, her hands a ghostly white in the darkness. I caught a glimpse of long, blond hair before the man's head moved as they clinched in another long, soulful kiss. I heard soft little moans and mews and rustlings as they explored various erogenous zones together.

I was caught somewhere between embarrassment and prurient interest. I didn't mean to be a Peeping Tom to the happy couple, but I also didn't want to move away suddenly and get caught eavesdropping. Then again, they didn't know me, I didn't know them, so what the hell.

A car's horn suddenly split the night air with an insistent bleep. The kissing couple leapt apart at the sound. The man stood there while the woman did some quick, squirming adjustments of hair and dress. The horn sounded again.

"Leta?" A voice rasped in the night air. It sounded familiar, but I couldn't quite place it. My brain, despite the refreshment of the cool air, was still fuzzed. "Leta? Where are you?"

"I gotta go," the woman below me whispered. "How do I look?"

"Like a zillion bucks," the man whispered back. "When can I see you again?"

"I'll call you, doll-baby," she said, and reached up for a final soft kiss.

Honk. Honk. "Leta?"

She ducked down to her left, behind the wall, dashed across the concrete apron by the pool and trotted up the stairs through a gate that led out to the parking lot. Her swain and I watched her go. Then, he turned quickly and melted into the darkness, heading around behind the clubhouse. He was either going to walk all the way around the back, past the kitchen, or maybe use a rear entrance I didn't know about.

"Where the hell have you been?" rasped an angry male voice from the parking lot. I suddenly recognized the voice. "I have a goddam golf tournament in the morning! I need to get some sleep!"

I stepped quietly back down the length of the porch and peered around the corner. A big white limousine chugged softly at idle in a pool of light thrown off by a floodlight. The blond woman was bending over, getting into the car. From behind, I could only see a shapely body sheathed in a blue knit dress, trimmed at the waist and hemmed with black stripes. Long legs, shimmery white stockings, low slung black heels. Her posterior, as it disappeared into the limo, was nicely rounded.

Vitus Papageorge climbed in behind her and the door slammed angrily. The engine revved up and the car moved off slowly out of the pool of light and into the darkness.

Now I did feel like a Peeping Tom. Sordid. Soiled. "Country club life," I thought as I turned to go back inside. The John Cheever special. Grown-ups acting like hormonal kids. Too much booze, too much money, not enough sense. Bob boinking Carol boinking Ted boinking Alice. Stolen kisses under the stars on cold autumn nights, dreams lost in crystalline bottles of gin, innocence and integrity kicked away like undergarments for a few cheap thrills.

And somebody was putting the horns on Vitus Papageorge. As despicable as he was, I managed to feel just a tad sorry for him. Just a tad.

"I think this calls for a drink," I said out loud, to no one. And I went inside the clubhouse to find one.

TEN

The tournament began Friday morning. Our flight wasn't scheduled to tee off until late morning. Ted McDaggert had utilized a computer to schedule all the matches – ten flights, eight teams in each flight – and while some flights had three matches scheduled the first day, our group was in a 2-3-2 schedule over the three day weekend. That gave me time to sleep late at Jack's house, pour some extra strong coffee down to offset the alcohol consumption of the previous evening, and make a few phone calls.

I called Suzy Chapman at the PGA Tour's press room in Endicott and got a report on my intern. Tony Zec had checked in, been assigned a workspace in the press tent and had managed to avoid getting mugged, rolled by the caddies in cards, arrested for drunk driving or sneezing in anybody's backswing. In fact, he was sitting there at this early hour watching the scoreboard as the has-beens and never-weres of the PGA Tour were dew sweeping in search of the paltry thousands available at the B.C. Open. Suzy punched me through to him.

"How's it going, kid?" I asked.

"Great!" came his enthusiastic reply. "Harrison Frazer is three-under after six."

"Stop the presses," I said. "What else ya got for me?"

"Well, I covered the caddie tournament on Tuesday," he said. "I wrote up the piece."

"How long is it?" I asked.

"Four thousand words, give or take," he said.

I groaned silently to myself. If any newspaper anywhere in the country were to consider running such a piece — which they wouldn't, especially during football season— it would run maybe five graphs, max. Two hundred words. But I didn't want to burst this kid's bubble. He seemed to be having a great time, and he was providing me with some cover for the weekend.

"OK," I sighed into the phone. "Here's my email address…cut it down to a thousand words, send it in and I'll take a looksee. In the meantime, I want you to file a daily update on the tournament. Try to keep it to maybe five hundred words. Eliminate all the flowery b.s. and just give us the facts, OK?"

"Right," he said. I could hear him taking notes. *No bullshit. Just facts.* Ah, to be young and impressionable.

"And keep your ears open for some interesting tidbits. There's always somebody complaining about something, or changing club sponsors, or planning to play in the next three tournaments to try and make the 125 money-winning list. Read the local paper – it's usually a good source of leads. Capisce?"

"Got it," Zec said, scribbling furiously.

"Send me your stuff every night by 7 p.m." I finished. "I'll look it over and try to get it into the paper. Can't guarantee there'll be room – it's football season and my fuckwit boss seems to think that the report on the Holy Cross game is more important than whether or not Harrison Frazer is gonna win the B.C. Open. "

"Got it, Hacker," he said. I laughed to myself. Kid's on the job for one day and we're buddies and pals.

I called home and got Mary Jane.

"How's Mister Shit?" I asked. "He miss me at all?"

"Ducky is fine," she reported. "But he crapped in the corner of the dining room, which puts him on the endangered species list around here. Hasn't he ever been introduced to the concept of a litter box?"

"How," I asked, "Do you think he got his name?"

"Oh, great," she groaned. "When are you coming back?"

I laughed. "Think of it as an opportunity to teach Victoria that having pets is a responsibility," I suggested.

"I'm thinking of it as a weekend spent picking up cat feces," she snapped. "You'd better be home on time Sunday night or I'm feeding Mister Doo-Doo something extra-spicy and putting him back in your apartment."

"Right," I said. "Love to Victoria."

"Bite me," she said and hung up.

I took a long, hot shower, thinking about the Shuttlecock Club and the tournament ahead. Jackie eventually rolled out of bed, looking disheveled and refused to speak until he'd had three cups of coffee. Eventually, he came back to the land of the living, and we got to the club at about eleven, and changed into our Blues Brothers uniform for the day. Or, at least I did. Jack sat in front of his locker and moaned a little, so I went to hit some balls to loosen up. After twenty minutes or so, I went back up to the locker room to find my partner. He was sitting slumped in front of his locker, dressed only in underwear and socks, looking a bit pale.

"Mornin' pards," I said cheerfully. "Ready to kick some major butt?"

He looked up at me with bleary, bloodshot eyes. "Gimme a Bloody Mary," he groaned. "My head's killin' me."

I looked at him sadly, shaking my head. "Do I hear you saying 'Play hard, pard?'" I asked.

He nodded, holding his head in his hands.

"Well, screw that," I said sternly. "I'm not gonna carry your sorry ass around this course all by myself. Go take a shower and I'll find some hot coffee."

He moaned again, but he did what I told him. When he got back from his shower, his skin flushed to a more healthy shade of pink, I handed him a steaming mug. I stood there until he drank it.

"Wow," he said. "I can feel my toes again. I think I'm gonna live!"

Jack was back. The man had amazing recuperative powers. Knowing he would now be halfway contributive to the team effort, I left him to get dressed and went out to the practice green to hit some putts. Vitus Papageorge was there, lecturing poor old Fred about how to read a putting green. I ignored them and worked on feel and speed. I could feel the licks of competitive fire begin to alight somewhere deep inside. It had been a while. I play a lot of golf every year, charity events, media days, occasional friendly rounds with friends. But those are just outings, relaxing days when the results really don't mean anything important.

But a tournament – even just a fun event like the Shuttlecock Invitational – is different. As a professional, playing on the Tour, I learned how to get myself "up" for every round. How to block out the distractions. How to make my body relax and focus on the task at hand. How to visualize every shot before I hit it. How to make every shot count. How to make myself believe that every shot I faced could be made flawlessly, with the result I wanted. On the Tour, I made myself think and do. And it worked enough that I came to believe I could do that every single time, with every single shot, whether a 290-yard booming drive, or a tricky three-footer for par.

But that had been years ago. I couldn't do that now. Didn't really want to, in fact. Because to get to that higher level of concentration and confidence requires total devotion to the game. It requires months of practice, and endless repetition. That's what the professional game demands. But I was no longer a professional golfer. I was a journalist. When I left the Tour, I had to reprogram myself, once I started playing the game again, to enjoy golf as just a game, a pastime, a recreational event. I had to learn how to play for fun and relaxation, for the fellowship of my friends, for the fresh air and the birdsong, and for the occasional pleasure of hitting a ball squarely on the screws and having it obey my command.

Did I want to win my flight in the Shuttlecock Invitational? Sure – winning is always more fun than losing. But my main goal for the weekend was just to have a good time. Enjoy the experience that was Jack Connolly, one of my oldest and dearest friends. Meet some nice folks. Have a few laughs. Quaff a few brews. Try to make some difficult shots when I had to, sink a few putts. Play the game with something on the line. That's what I wanted. Winning some silver-plated little trophy was secondary.

So, while I could still feel those competitive little flames inside, I didn't try to fan them, or stoke them either. I concentrated only on working on my putting stroke, and trying to get a feel for the fast Shuttlecock greens. And I stopped to feel the warm fall sunshine on my face and enjoy the feeling. I putted for about five minutes, and then picked up my practice balls.

Vitus Papageorge, who apparently had been watching, stared at me in disbelief. His face was shiny with sweaty exertion, and his whole body seemed strained with effort. "That's all?" he said to me. "You've only been practicing for a few minutes."

"Vitus," I said nonchalantly, "When you're a world-class athlete like me, you don't need a lot of practice."

I couldn't help one final look back as I strolled off the putting green. He was staring at me, his thick, dark eyebrows knitted together in envy and fury.

He was an odd, odd man.

I went back upstairs and collected my partner. Together, in our matching outfits, wide-brimmed white Panama hats and wraparound shades, we made quite a stir as we walked together down the stairs, through the members' grill and out onto the first tee. There were wolf whistles, catcalls, and loud laughter all around. I think the psyche job was working.

Our first opponents were a local furniture-store owner and his brother-in-law from Cleveland. First-hole tournament nerves were in evidence as we teed off and my partner had to make a tough up-and-down from the front bunker to halve the hole after I sculled a sand wedge over the green and made a bogey.

As we waited to tee off on the second, Jack reached behind the seat of our cart and flipped open a cooler he had stashed there. He pulled out a cold beer, hissed it open and took a deep draught as I just looked at him. He plunked it down in the cup holder.

"Jack," I said, "Do you really need that?"

"Hell," he said. "I won the first hole. How much more do I gotta do?"

I had to laugh.

It was a good close match. The member was a friendly, gregarious sort who had been a member at Shuttlecock for years. He told me of the pre-war days when the club had made most of its money from the slot machines in the clubhouse, and of the big flood of 1936 when the river had covered most of the island and threatened to wash away the entire city of Lowell. I was giving away strokes to everybody, of course, and they played us tough for the whole match. I finally managed a birdie on the long seventh to get our team to one-up, and Jack and I held them off on the last two holes to win.

We shook hands all around and enjoyed a cold beer and a thick, juicy hot dog on the picnic tables set out underneath the trees behind the ninth green snack shack. The other teams in our flight were coming up behind us.

Vitus Papageorge and his partner Fred were in the foursome that came up the ninth behind us. As he had the day before, Vitus sprayed his drive to the right, into the rough. Fred and one of their opponents were in the valley down below the green, while the other fellow caught one of the bunkers next to the green. Vitus chipped on to about eight feet and the others followed suit, none closer than 20 feet from the hole. All three missed their attempts for par, leaving the green to Vitus.

The little man stalked his putt, walking around the green looking at the break from every possible angle. Then, he asked both Fred and his caddie for a read. One of his opponents, who had been standing on the back edge of the green while all this was going on, finally turned and walked away.

"Fuckin' asshole," he muttered under his breath.

"How do you guys stand?" asked the furniture store owner.

"Oh, they're one up. They've got the match," he said.

"Vitus get a stroke here?" I asked.

"Oh, hell yes," the guy said, shaking his head. "I don't know why he's taking so long. All he's gotta do is lag it up and we'll give it to him, for Chrissakes."

"He'll make it," I said. "He likes the dramatic effect."

"Asswipe," the guy said and went inside the shack for a beer.

Vitus, of course, drained the putt. When the ball rolled over the lip and disappeared from view, he let out a victorious shout, jumped into the air and pumped his fist to the sky, like Tiger Woods winning another major. When he landed, his spikes gouged out some marks in the surface of the green. But Vitus, naturally, didn't notice. He continued to jump around in a self-congratulatory dance.

Fred shook the hands of the opponent standing next to him and they walked off the green together. Finally, Vitus noticed he was celebrating all by himself and stopped. He motioned to his caddie to return the pin to the hole, handed him the putter and strode off, his shoulders pulled back and his head held high in a patrician pose.

ELEVEN

A s it turned out, the team of Vitus and Fred were our next opponents. They barely had time to order a beer and hot dog before one of the older club members who was serving as tournament marshal for the weekend came running over from the tenth tee. "Papageorge versus Connolly," the geezer called out, looking down at his clipboard. "On the tee please, gentlemen."

Vitus pulled his driver out of his golf bag and headed down the path towards the tee. His partner followed while their caddie, struggling under the weight of the two bags, trudged off in the other direction down the fairway to stand at the corner of the slight dogleg to watch for shots that might drift into the woods.

My partner loaded up his cooler with a fresh supply of beer and ice, stored it securely in the back of our cart and drove us down to the tee. The back tee of the tenth was a raised affair in a sunny clearing in the thick surrounding woods. The course superintendent had planted low-growing evergreens and some colorful annuals in beds on the side of the raised tee.

"The Connolly team has the honor," the starter intoned in a deep baritone that reverberated through the clearing. "Please keep the pace of play moving, gentlemen. The field has backed up a bit."

Jack and I shook hands with our opponents and wished them good luck. Fred smiled and said "play well," but Vitus, naturally, said nothing. "Go ahead, pards," I said to Jack. "Show us the way."

Jack hit a beautiful pull hook that started down the left side, just missed the first big overhanging pine, and then ducked hard left into the woods. The caddie, who had dropped the two bags at his feet, ran a few steps to his left and then bent at the waist to watch the ball as it ricocheted among the trees. The kid looked back at us and raised his hands as if to say "I dunno."

"Damn," Jackie said, pounding his driver on the tee. He turned and gave me one of his patented Connolly grins. "Play hard, Hack-Man!"

I sighed. I had my three-wood – getting the ball into the fairway here was much more important than banging it a mile – and laid into it. The ball started down the right side, well away from the overhanging trees, and drew back nicely into the middle of the fairway, running to a stop just past the corner. I'd have about 155 yards left. "You da man!" yelled my partner.

Fred led off for Team Papageorge. He hit a nice drive that faded just a bit at the end, but stayed in the short grass on the right side. Vitus was next, and I saw him take a quick look at my three-wood. He was holding his driver. He teed his ball, swished the club back and forth a few times, staring down the fairway. He stopped, looked over at me again and then began waving.

"Boy! Bring me the bag!"

A simultaneous groan broke from the rest of us on the tee as the kid bent over, picked up Vitus' bag and began trotting back toward us.

"Isn't there a five-minute rule on tee shots?" Jackie asked facetiously.

"Vitus," the starter protested. "We're already running behind. Why don't you hit the club you got?"

Papageorge spun on his heel and glared at us. "I have the right to select the proper club," he snapped. "It's not my fault the boy was standing way down there. It can't be helped."

He stood there, arms crossed defiantly, until the breathless, sweating caddie ran gasping up the hill onto the tee and plunked the bag down next to Vitus. Papageorge replaced his driver and pulled out his three-wood. As usual, he was clubbing off me. I thought for a moment about calling him on it, especially with a witness at hand, but decided to keep quiet. The whole thing smacked of gamesmanship anyway – Vitus was undoubtedly trying to get us riled up before we'd even started.

"Don't forget to start it down the right side," I called out. Jackie burst out laughing. Vitus threw a dark glance over his shoulder.

"I beg your pardon?" he said darkly.

"Nothing, Vitus," I said, motioning for him to play away.

He should have stuck with the driver. He swung at the ball with his three-wood and sent a high pop-up weakly down the fairway. It carried just 150 yards and bounced around in the rough short of the fairway before finally coming to rest.

"Finally," the starter said with a sigh. "Get the hell out of here, would ya?"

Jack and I headed for our cart while our opponents began walking off the front of the tee. As they walked, I heard Vitus berating his caddie for poor positioning. I sighed. Some people are born to make life difficult for the rest of us.

Our nine-hole rematch was as closely contested as our practice-round competition had been. Every time Vitus had a stroke on a hole, and I was giving him four, he either won or halved the hole. I upheld the honor of our team three times, and on the par-3 17th, my partner knocked it on the green and then sank a roller-coaster of a 30-footer for a birdie and the win. Seventeen seemed to be his hole.

Again, we went to the last hole all even. But this time, the match ended differently. I put a tad too much draw on my tee ball, and it landed on the left side of the fairway, where I was blocked by trees from getting my next shot all the way around the corner of the dogleg. I had to chip to the top of the hill and had a three-iron to get home. I hit it well, but it came up short and right of the green.

Vitus, meanwhile, with a stroke in hand, played the hole in regulation: straight drive, iron over the crest of the hill and an easy wedge into the middle of the green. He didn't look into my bag for club advice, this time.

Jack and Fred were out of it, having had various adventures of the chopping kind. Figuring I had to make my chip for a birdie to tie Vitus' sure par-net-bird, I hit the ball firmly and watched as it just missed the flagstick and rolled some ten feet past.

Vitus had about 25 feet for his birdie. He looked at it from every angle, and then hit a miserable putt, leaving the ball a good five feet short. He began cursing and stomping around, but I ignored him. I suddenly had new life. If I could make my ten-footer for a par, and if Vitus missed his knee-knocker, we could escape the match with a half-point.

I gave it my best shot, but the greens at Shuttlecock are renowned for their subtle shadings, and my putt just skimmed past the left edge of the hole. Bogey. I turned to Vitus and stuck out my hand. "Yours is good," I said. "Nice match. You guys played well today."

He was shaking his head. "No," he said. "I'm going to make this putt." And he began to study the line of his five-footer. I was nonplussed. I had just given the jerk the putt and the match, and he had turned me down. That had never happened to me before and I really didn't know quite what to do. I was pretty certain that once an opponent concedes a putt, a hole or the match, that's it ... game over. I looked over at Jack, who was standing watching on the edge of the green, and he just shrugged his shoulders.

I recalled the scene on the ninth green a couple hours earlier. Vitus' victory dance. The great white hunter celebrating his kill, daubing the blood of his victims on his body in ceremonial fashion for all to see. Except, of course, no one else was paying attention to this little victory except Vitus.

I picked up the flagstick and watched quietly as Vitus stalked his putt from every angle. I watched as he crouched behind his ball, held up his putter between thumb and fore-finger to plumb-bob the line, and finally approached his ball. I watched while he swooshed the putter back and forth carefully down the line, then carefully wiped the putter blade on his pants leg. I watched as he went into his crouch over the ball, setting the putter down carefully, adjusting it minutely, taking his last look at the hole, and then back at his ball. I watched as he took the putter back slowly and then smoothly accelerated into the ball.

The ball ran straight for the back of the cup. Until it ran into the side of my foot. I took a quick step forward, kicked his ball away and jammed the flagstick back into the hole.

"Wha—?" Vitus cried out, amazed. "Hey!"

I turned and looked him in the eyes.

"I gave you that putt, you insufferable showboating bastard," I said to him in a quiet undertone that only he could hear. "According to the rules of golf, the hole and the match are yours. You don't get to rub it in. And let me tell you something else. I will give this game up before I ever play another round of golf with you."

I turned and stalked off the green. I could feel the anger making my face a dangerous shade of red. Vitus could do nothing but stand there sputtering. I shook Fred's hand and Jackie took one look at my face and said "OK, pards, it's time for some serious inebriation."

We went upstairs to the men's locker bar and joined the coterie of sunburned yet happy men who had gathered there to swap tales of disaster and triumph, putts that stayed out and those that fell in, drives that bonked off trees and ended up in the middle of the fairway, chips that scurried into the hole and two-footers inexplicably left one-foot short. All part and parcel of what makes golf such a damnable yet intriguing game.

Jack made the effortless switch from beer to bourbon, and after a couple of quick ones, I gave up on trying to keep up with him. At one point, he pulled me into the corner and asked what I had said to his honor, the club president.

"I told him he was an insufferable bastard and that I would never play his sorry ass again," I said.

Jackie looked into my eyes and nodded. "You shoulda kneed him in the 'nads," he said. "Or something that woulda left a mark."

He went back to drinking and talking while I went to take a long, hot shower. It felt magnificent. The hot spray washed away the lingering sweat of the day as well as the last traces of anger at Vitus Papageorge. That match was over and in the books. If there was a God, and He enjoyed hitting one on the screws as much as the rest of us, I'd never have to speak to that insufferable bastard for the rest of the weekend.

I dressed, and rather than try to interrupt my partner and drag him off to dinner before he was quite ready, I went downstairs and outside to the big scoreboard that had been set up near the putting green. The results of the day's matches had been posted, flight by flight. I pushed out the screen door and almost flattened a woman who was coming in at the same time. Our bodies squashed together before we could stop, and then we leapt apart, laughing and apologizing simultaneously. The first thing I noticed was her long blond hair, spilling prettily down onto her shoulders. Then her bright blue eyes and deep red lips, and a soft scent of perfume. I was too much of a gentleman to do a full-scale scope of the bod, but I could tell it was nice. Male peripheral vision.

"Whoa," I said, "Excuse me, I'm sure! Don't know why I'm in such a hurry to read the scoreboard. Nothing but bad news up there!"

She trilled her own embarrassed laughter and her hands made a couple of quick passes to straighten out her clothes. It was a movement that registered as strangely familiar.

"Oh, dear," she said, "No harm done. But if we ever meet again like that, we might have to elope!"

She gave me the once-over, so I did the same. She was in her late thirties, I guessed. Her face had a sharp profile, with thin lips, a pointed nose, high, sharp cheekbones and a smallish chin. There were some telltale lines beginning at the corners of her eyes, and in addition to her red lips, she wore a lot of mascara and blush. She was wearing a simple white sleeveless blouse, a thin gold chain around her neck and a pair of red-and-white striped shorts. A few large twin-kling things on her fingers.

I felt her doing the top-to-bottom scan on me too, and watched as her eyes widened slightly and a smile played at the corner of her lips.

"Maybe I should go look at the scoreboard, too," she said. "I guess I should find out how my husband did today." I motioned for her to proceed and fell into step as we walked over to the putting green.

"And who is your husband?" I asked politely.

"Vitus Papageorge," she said. "Have you met him yet?"

I laughed. My laughter helped cover my sudden flush of recognition. Now I knew where I had seen that smooth-ing gesture before. In the dark out by the pool the night before. Vitus' lovely bride, smooching with a stranger.

"I should say so," I said. "He beat us on the last hole today."

"Oh, dear, I am sorry," she said, putting her hand lightly on my arm. "If you want to say bad things about him, go right ahead. I've heard them all."

I laughed again, and she joined in, a high trilling that was anything but unpleasant. We studied the day's scores, side by side.

"Oh, you must be Jack Connolly's partner," she said, her eyes darting across the score sheets. I introduced myself and she said "I'm Leta. Leta Papageorge." We shook hands. She let her soft hand linger for an instant longer than nor-mal in my hand. "What a lovely man Jack is," she said. "So uninhibited, so alive! Of course, having all that money helps."

"As you should know," I said.

She trilled her laugh again. And reached over and touched my arm again. She was a touchy-feely one.

"I like you, Hacker," she said. "I like a man who says what he thinks." She moved closer to me, bumping me with her shapely hip. "How'd you like to buy me a drink? Tell me some more unvarnished truths?"

I was a bit taken aback. A little flirting is one thing, but Leta had shifted rapidly into seduction overdrive. And there was already someone else who had gotten up close and personal with the club president's wife the night before. My male ego was flattered, of course, but I had enough common sense left to know that this one was trouble.

"Thanks," I said, "But I've got to go get some dinner into my partner. We've got an early start tomorrow. Nice to meet you, Mrs. Papageorge."

I left her standing there, underneath the ancient old oaks and the dwindling light of the day.

TWELVE

I found Jack upstairs and told him I was hungry. He took a quick shower, poured his bourbon into a plastic "to-go" cup and followed me out to the parking lot. There were less than a dozen cars left. Night had fallen and dew was already gathering on the grassy surfaces around us. In September in Massachusetts, the heat of the day ceases with the last ray of sun, as if someone had thrown a switch. The air had turned from balmy to cold. I shivered.

"I'm driving," I told my slightly inebriated friend. He concurred without an argument. Jackie could hold his booze better than anyone I had ever known. He was loose-limbed but still pretty much in control. But he was in no shape to operate a motor vehicle. Especially in Massachusetts, where the jack-booted government thugs who patrol the state's highways love to throw people in jail for registering even the smallest number on the breath-o-meter.

"Head downtown," Jack said. "I know a place."

I drove off the island and followed the river downstream towards the city of Lowell. As we neared the city, the river broadened out. We passed a flag bedecked marina on the bank and saw a flotilla of small sailboats tied up on the docks. A mile or so downstream, I could see a crude-looking wooden dam arching across the river in front of an old brick bridge. Water splashed over the boards in several places, crashing down on the dark rocks below.

"Pawtucket Falls," Jack said, looking out the window. "From this point, the river drops something like 250 feet in elevation in less than a mile. By building that dam and then a series of canals running off it, they were able to harness all the power of that falling water to run the turbines that powered the textile machinery. Pretty remarkable piece of engineering for the early 19th century."

I smiled at the slight note of pride I heard in Jackie's voice. A bit of hometown boosterism was showing through, even in my worldly and sophisticated friend.

He navigated while I wended my way into the heart of the city, an old, decaying warren of brick factories, warehouses and cobblestone streets. We passed four-story tenements, dilapidated storefronts and huge, Gothic granite churches covered with dark soot and decades of grime. We passed through bustling Hispanic neighborhoods filled with colorful bodegas and the smells of hot frying food, and through quieter areas where the signs were in Asian scrawl. As we finally reached the downtown, the brick buildings looked cleaner and newer, and some of the main streets glowed in the light of old-fashioned gas lamps.

"City of Lowell was one of the armpits of the nation twenty, thirty years ago," Jack said. "The textile mills all went

South two generations ago and the place just began rotting away. Then Ted Kennedy brought the Feds in with a barrel full of urban renewal dollars and someone had the bright idea of turning downtown into a living museum of the Industrial Age. Whole blocks down here are part of a national urban park, showing off the birthplace of the American industrial revolution. You can tour the mills, ride a boat through the canals, do the museum of textiles. They kinda skip over the parts about the mill girls losing hands and fingers in the machinery, but what the hell. I can't complain. It brings business to town and keeps my presses humming."

We zigged and zagged on one-way streets until we finally found a parking space on a narrow lane. We locked up and strolled back down the block to the restaurant. The place was called A.G. Pollard and Sons, and inside it was a classic loft space, all weathered wood and exposed brick. Candles on the tables threw pleasing patterns on the rough brick walls, and the thick pine floorboards creaked nicely as we walked towards the bar, where a pianist was playing soft chords.

"This used to be a warehouse for a local department store," Jackie told me as we ordered drinks. "Steaks are good here and the bartender is a buddy."

"I'm sure he is," I said. "You probably are single-handedly putting his daughter through college."

He laughed. We sat at the bar and asked for menus. Our drinks arrived and we ordered rib eyes. Rare. With the works. Jack took a sip, sat back and sighed.

"I really hated losing to ole Shit-for-Brains this afternoon," he said. "How come you didn't play better?"

"Up yours," I retorted wittily. "But let me tell you something interesting that happened earlier tonight."

I told him about my encounter with Leta Papageorge. And my feeling that she had been hitting on me. Jackie laughed, took another sip from his bourbon and reached into the basket of roasted peanuts the bartender had placed in front of us. The tradition was to throw the empty shells on the floor, adding to the atmosphere of the place. I wondered if the janitors appreciated the tradition as much as everyone else.

"Ah, yes, the lovely Leta," he smiled. "Woman is something else."

"Sounds like you've had, er, some experience in these matters."

"Please, Hacker," he protested, laughing. "I do have some standards."

"If you do, I've never been able to figure them out," I said.

"Well," he said, "I wish I could say that she singled me out on account of my boyish good looks, sparkling personality and the rumors concerning my length and girth, but the truth is that I think Leta Papageorge has hit on just about every person who's male and breathing at the Shuttlecock Club at one time or another. Come to think about it, I'm not so sure we can rule out all the women, either. Some of our best girl golfers are, shall we say, a bit on the lumpy and mannish side, if you catch my drift."

"Drift caught, you misogynous bastard." I said. "Let's talk about Leta."

"Well," he said, "She's got this incredibly sexy mole on her left . . ."

"No, no," I interrupted. "What's her story?"

Leta Papageorge, Jackie told me, while he motioned for two more drinks, was Vitus' second wife. The first Mrs. P had been a dumpy woman with thick and heavy eyebrows who had introduced him to her banker father, had his babies, kept his house and been unceremoniously dumped for a younger and sexier version after 15 years of marriage. I winced at Jack's inelegant and mostly sexist descriptions of the unfortunate first Mrs. Papageorge, but knew the story. Successful businessperson struggles when young, makes it big, dumps the faithful helpmate for the young trophy.

"He needed an ornament, something that would look good on his arm when he went to important functions," Jack said. "Especially when the presidential candidates showed up on the dinner circuits every four years."

He paused and sipped his cocktail.

"In return, Leta got a gold card or two, nice big house, new car every two years, regular vacations in Europe. The usual. Kids not allowed, of course. Vitus had been there and done that. But it turned out that Leta had one or two smarts in addition to her long blond hair and nice ta-tas."

Apparently, Jack said, Leta had some good political instincts. People liked her, especially male people. Vitus was the quintessential mover and shaker, a big operator with the big bucks of his bank to give him some importance. But it turns out Leta was a sharper thinker, and someone who could size someone up quickly and know what buttons needed pushing to get that person to do Vitus' bidding.

"So Vitus must have liked having his trophy wife turning out to be smart too, huh?" I asked.

"I think he hated it," Jack said, swirling the ice around in his glass. "He doesn't like not being the main man. You could see that on the golf course. There's only room for one ringleader in his circus. I've heard that things are not altogether happy in Vitus City. Especially lately. The word is that some of Leta's friends are encouraging her to run for office, the state senate up there in New Hampshire. Word is, Vitus hit the ceiling when he heard about it."

"Uh-oh," I said. "Could be trouble."

"Yeah," Jackie said. "Don't think that marriage is headed for the love-and-kisses hall of fame. He's still got his trophy, which he drags out when he needs her. She's got the gold cards, the house and the cars…but she's also got a lot of internalized anger."

"So she runs around sleeping with all the boys she can," I said,

"Hey," Jackie shrugged. "Girls just wanna have fun."

"And Vitus?"

"Probably does the same. I would."

"Whatever happened to love, cherish and obey 'til death us do part?" I sighed.

"Oh, crap, Hacker, please tell me you don't still believe in that never-ending romantic bullshit," Jack snapped.

I shook my head. "'Mingled things are more pleasing than single things,'" I quoted at him. "'A chord moreso than a single note.'"

He held up his hand to ward me away. "I don't even wanna know," he said.

I told him anyway. "St. Thomas of Aquinas."

The bartender brought our steaks out, so we stopped talking and ate. It was nice, here in this bricky room, glowing in the candlelight, the pianist tickling the ivories in the background. Yeah, I thought to myself, I do still believe in that romantic crap. I think we all do. Mingled things *are* sweeter. But Leta and Vitus Papageorge? Not exactly a chord that resonated with anyone.

After our steaks, Jack led me down the street and across a bridge that spanned one of Lowell's dark and narrow canals. We crossed a busy street and entered a bar called Old Werthan's. Jack was immediately recognized and greeted warmly by at least half the patrons in the place. We stood at the long, mahogany bar with its traditional brass footrail and Jack ordered us a couple snifters of brandy.

"This used to be a great dive," he said. "Draught beer for twenty-five cents. Ten cents for a hot dog boiled in beer. Town's alcoholics got here at 10 a.m. sharp every day and stayed until closing. Was a rite of passage as a teenager. trying to come in and get served. That and getting laid by one of the hookers out back. Lunch hour, the place would be crawling with politicians."

He stopped and surveyed the place, looking a bit wistful. "Then they wrecked it," he said. "Put in some ferns, knocked out a wall, added tables and chairs. Added a menu, for God's sake. Too bad. Used to have some character."

We sipped our drinks in silent homage to the memories of Old Werthan's.

"Tell me, Hack," Jack said, leaning back against the bar. "You ever miss playing on the Tour?"

"Honestly? No," I said. "There were, of course, parts of that life which were, and still are, immensely attractive."

"Money. Women. Free golf balls," Jackie began ticking off his fingers. I laughed.

"Yeah, well, I was thinking more of a sense that you were one of a select few on the planet who had the game. A sense of some accomplishment that, even if you never won a tournament, was real. And important."

"So why'd you quit?"

"Well, the process of getting to the Tour was automatic," I said. "Played junior golf with success to get a college scholarship. Played college golf with success to try and see if I really had enough game for the pros."

"And you made it," he said. "I didn't."

"No, you didn't," I said. "Did you really think you could?"

He shook his head a bit sadly.

"Naw," he said. "I knew I wasn't good enough. But I had to try."

"Exactly," I said. "You had to try. I had to try. It was the next step in the process. A follows B follows C. We never stopped to ask ourselves if we really wanted to take the next step. It was just automatic. Of course we wanted to play on the Tour. Who wouldn't?"

I stopped and sipped my drink. The brandy burned going down.

"So I made it on Tour and the next step was trying to win, get exempt, keep my card. That kept me busy for the next three years, so I never had to actually think about what I was doing. Finally, I went off by myself for a few weeks. Funny, I had started to turn the corner, started to play really well. I had finished in the top ten two out of three weeks, started to pile up some bucks. Things were looking good, finally. But instead of being incredibly happy, I was incredibly depressed. Way down in the dumps."

"You needed to get laid," Jack said.

"Maybe," I laughed. "But I just went off for a couple weeks by myself and took a little internal inventory. Began to think about things differently for a change. And what I decided was that I really didn't want to be a professional golfer anymore. Sure, it was fun. I got to travel all over the place, made lots of good friends, met nice people. Made enough money to keep doing it. But it wasn't enough. Something inside told me it was wrong. So I decided to quit. Everyone thought I was nuts. Maybe I was. "

"Getting laid woulda been easier," my friend observed.

"Maybe so. But I did manage, finally, to figure out a way to live the Tour life vicariously by writing about it in the newspaper. And I haven't really looked back since."

"So now here you are, sitting in a tired old bar in a tired old city with a tired old friend, without a scintilla of fame or fortune." Jackie shook his head sadly. "What an idiot."

"But a generally happy idiot," I told him.

He nodded and held up his glass towards me. We clinked. Cheers. No matter what decisions we had made in our lives, right or wrong, we were still friends.

We drank silently for a while, listening to the music coming from the jukebox at the end of the bar. "Who we got tomorrow?" I asked. "I hope you're planning to show up, finally. I don't think we can afford to lose another match."

"I dunno," he shrugged. "You never know with these things. Somebody will always come out of left field on you, knock off the leaders and tighten things up. Of course, Vitus will be there. Son-of-a-bitch is always right there."

The door opened and two not-so-young and not-so-beautiful women came in, giggling to each other. One had a bouffant blond do and wore a faux leopard-skin jacket. The other had a black mini, red spandex top, black pantyhose with a dark seam down the back and straight black hair, with puffy bangs in front. They looked over at us and giggled again. I felt Jackie come to attention beside me and my heart began to sink. I was ready for bed. Jackie wasn't.

"Know what, Hack-Man?" he asked.

"What?"

"I'm sick and damn tired of talking about Vitus Papageorge."

And he lurched off down the bar in the direction of the two non-lovelies. I sighed. It was going to be a long night.

THIRTEEN

We left Jack's house, a modern stone-and-glass construct on a bluff overlooking the Merrimac River just east of the city, early the next morning. I'm not exactly sure what time we had left Old Werthan's, but I was quite sure that neither one of us had logged in the recommended eight hours of slumber. We had three matches to play, the first beginning on the 10th tee at 7:35. We stopped in at a Dunkin' Donuts shop for some coffee, since I don't think Jack knew where the kitchen in his house was located.

"How do you feel?" I asked, as we drove back up the river, inhaling a few jelly doughnuts and sipping the hot, black brew.

"Not bad," Jack said, licking some sugar off his fingers. "But I still can't understand what went wrong with the ladies last night. It seemed like a sure-fire tap-in there for a while."

"I think you lost 'em when you invited them back to the house for a game of naked leapfrog," I told him.

"But that's what everyone was thinking," he protested.

"Maybe so," I said, "But the female animal generally responds better to a more subtle, less graphic approach."

"Oh," he said, and thought about it for an instant or two. "Well, screw it. I haven't got time to play games."

I glanced over at my friend. His hair was tousled and unruly, half of the collar of his polo shirt was sticking up in the air, and neither his shirt not his trousers had seen an iron in months. He rummaged around in the waxy donut bag and pulled out another piece of breakfast. Glancing up, he gave me one of the famous Connolly incandescent grins. I had to laugh.

"You never plan on growing up, do you?" I chided.

"What the hell for?" he asked. "What's in it for me if I do? Life is for the living, Hack-Man. You gotta grab it by the balls and hang on for dear life."

He took a huge bite out of his donut and fiddled with the radio, looking for the morning news.

When we arrived at the club, I found a parking spot close to the clubhouse. Jack rummaged around in my backseat and pulled out a garment bag he had stowed there as we were leaving his house.

"What are we wearing today?" I asked.

"Purple," he said with a grin. "It's the color of passion. You need passion on the golf course. It's one of the seven chakras. Very important."

We went upstairs and changed into the day's uniform. Bright purple slacks, silk shirts streaked with a pattern of green, yellow and more purple lines, and purple visors emblazoned with the words "The Brothers." Jack followed me into the bathroom to stare at our reflection in the big mirrors over the line of sinks.

"Awesome," he said, "We can't lose in these. We exude passion."

"We look like a couple of hungover grapes," I said.

"Whatever," Jack shrugged. "I need a Bloody Mary to get the blood flowing. You?"

I shook my head and went downstairs. There was a breakfast buffet set up in the main grille, and I grabbed some orange juice and made a plate of fresh fruit. I saw a copy of my newspaper lying on a table and sat down to see what was in the sports section. One of Teddy McDaggert's assistants came out of the pro shop waving a slip of paper at me.

"Mr. Hacker … you got a phone call," he said.

I looked at the note. Tony Zec had called from Endicott, New York. Right on schedule. The kid was good at following orders.

I went into the phone booth at the back of the grille and placed the call. I got through to the pressroom at the B.C. Open and Suzy Chapman answered on the second ring.

"Press room," she said in a tired, early morning voice.

"Suze … don't you ever go home? Does Tim Finchem know how many hours you put in for the Tour?"

"Hacker," she said wearily. "Finchem doesn't know shit from shinola about anything other than smoozing either the players or the bigwigs who got bank accounts in the Cayman Islands. He could care less if I work seven hours a week or seventy."

"So," I said cheerily. "Going well up there is it?"

"Swimmingly," she said. "First round got delayed by two hours of heavy rain. Just barely got the second round in yesterday, although the last three groups had to finish in the dark. Which meant I had to be here, oh, I'd guess about 20 hours. I hate golf."

I laughed. "How's my young intern doing?" I asked.

"Oh, you mean Warren Beatty Jr.?" Her voice dripped with sarcasm. "He's doing pretty good, I think. Hasn't sneezed on anyone's backswing. Yet. Actually, he's a nice kid. Reminds me of my little brother, a little. Except for all that acne."

"Is he there?"

"I think he went out to the practice range to talk to some of the guys," she said. "Want me to have him call you he gets back?"

"Nah," I said. "I'm gonna be busy most of the day."

"I'm sure you are," she said. "Remember to take it back slow."

I laughed again. "Tell him I'll call tonight. O-seven hundred."

"That's what it is right now, you dumbshit," she said. "You probably mean nineteen hundred. Seven o'clock pee emm in civilian?"

"Oh, right," I said. "I was a draft dodger. What you said."

"Ten-four," she said and hung up.

I went back and finished my breakfast. Frank Donatello had given the B.C. Open all of three inches of wire service crap, and run an inch of the leaderboard. That covered the first ten golfers. But the hapless Patriots got six pages of breathless coverage, in which our readers learned everything about every player up to and almost including the names of their kindergarten teachers. It would have been more interesting if we published the names and reputed side effects of the steroids each member of the team was taking, but I guess that wasn't in the cards.

With another cup of strong black coffee inside, I felt half human again. I walked into the pro shop to pick up some balls for the day. Teddy McDaggert was standing in the doorway the led back to his little cramped warren of an office, just off the back of the shop behind the counter. He was leaning against the door jamb, staring at nothing.

I walked up and greeted him. "Mornin' Ted," I said. "Coupla sleeves of Titleists please."

He didn't answer. Still staring off at nothing, he slowly raised a hand containing a cigarette to his lips and took a deep pull. I couldn't help but notice that his hand was shaking. He blew the smoke out in a long, slow cloud.

I waved my hand in front of his face.

"Yo! Earth to McDaggert! Customer needs service. Come in please!"

He started upright, his face beginning to color red, and he grinned at me sheepishly. "Sorry, Hacker," he said. "Guess I'm not awake yet. Whaddya need?"

I repeated my order and he bent to get the balls out of the glass counter, putting the cigarette in his mouth to free up his hands.

"I didn't know you smoked," I said. "Those things'll kill ya."

"If this place don't," he answered. "One way or another, I'm goin' toes up someday anyway." He put the balls on the counter, I slipped him some bills and he turned away. I looked at the back of his head for a moment, then shrugged and turned away. Teddy looked like he had just lost his best friend. I shrugged and put it down to tournament stress. Couldn't be easy running this three-day circus, trying to make everyone happy and having Vitus Papageorge looking over your shoulder the whole time. I glanced at my watch and, seeing that I had only about ten minutes before we were due on the tee, decided against going to hit some balls. I figured I had time to hit a few putts and that's it. Not as good as warming up properly, but what the hell. Guy's gotta adjust to the circumstances. And it was going to be a long day, anyway.

I went outside and began to scan the long line of golf carts to find the one that held our clubs. To save time and energy, the crew just kept the golf bags on the carts at night and drove them back into the cart barn to plug them in to the chargers overnight. I couldn't see my bag, and walked up and down the line for a minute. Finally, I caught the attention of an older teen holding a clipboard that looked like he was the caddie master.

"You got Connolly's cart somewhere?" I asked the kid. "We're going off ten in about fifteen minutes."

The kid checked the list. "They should be out here," he said. "There might be a couple wagons still in the barn haven't been wheeled out yet. I can run down and look."

"Don't bother," I said. "You got stuff to do here. I'll go. I just need my putter."

The kid pointed to a wooden shed behind a hedgerow at the back of the parking lot and I strolled across the asphalt. It was another gorgeous early fall day, and the sun was burning off the early morning chill. A light breeze ruffled the leaves in the trees. It was going to be a perfect day for golf.

The cart barn was an old wooden structure with a pitched roof, stained with age, with two large swinging doors on either end. Pine needles draped on the roof and spilled out of the gutters on the side. One of the front doors was open, but it was still dark and gloomy inside. I could see the metal framing overhead, which held the big electrical transformers from which the plug-in wires dangled. I walked in the open door, and saw the shadows of some carts parked at the rear. Because there were no windows, it got darker and darker inside as I walked deeper into the shed. The air was hot and stagnant and slightly acrid. A low humming sound from the electrical chargers filled the barn.

Halfway back into the barn, it became pitch black. I turned around and walked back towards the open door. I looked on both sides and finally found a bank of light switches. I flipped them to the on position. There were maybe ten carts still parked at the back, still connected to their thick yellow umbilicals dangling down from the overhead framework.

I walked back. About halfway down the length of the barn, I stopped. Walking and breathing. Behind the last cart, something was hanging from the overhead grid. Something dressed in golf clothes. Something with a thick yellow electrical cord wrapped tightly around its neck. Something that was obviously dead.

All I could see was the back. One arm hung limply by its side. The fingers of the other arm were tucked underneath the electrical cord, frozen in a terrible and unsuccessful battle to loosen the noose. The body began to turn slowly. And slowly, inexorably, the purple face of Vitus Papageorge swung into sight. His open eyes bulged and his tongue hung out of his silently crying mouth in horrible rictus. The diamonds in the rings on the hand that had been scratching at his neck twinkled cheerfully at me in the artificial light. But there was no light at all in his eyes.

I don't know how long I stood there, staring, frozen in place. I don't know how long it was before the kid with the clipboard came whistling through the doorway behind me.

"Found your clubs?" he asked cheerfully.

Then he saw what I was staring at.

"Holy Christ," the kid said. He dropped the clipboard in a clatter and started forward as if to try and save Papageorge from his fate. I stuck out my hand and grabbed him.

"Go and have Teddy call the cops," I told him, trying to keep my voice calm and steady. "Nobody should be allowed in here until the cops get here. Go tell McDaggert. Now."

"Holy Christ," the kid said again. Then he turned and ran out.

Bedlam broke out quickly in the quiet environs of the Shuttlecock Club. Murder will do that. Throw a professional-size monkey wrench into anyone's day. The kid came running back to the cart barn with Teddy McDaggert at his heels. Ted took one look at Vitus dangling from the rafters of his cart barn, said "fuck" rather softly under his breath and turned and ran out again. I'm not sure, but I'll bet the PGA of America operations manual doesn't have a chapter on what to do when the president of your club is found hung by the neck in the cart barn. Teddy would have to wing this one. The kid stayed and gazed at the body of Vitus Papageorge as it continued to twist slowly on the electrical cord.

Pretty soon, a crowd of gasping, whispering onlookers gathered at the door to the cart barn, trying to peer inside. For some reason, people tend to whisper in the presence of death. Don't know why. At this point Vitus Papageorge certainly could care less if they whispered or shouted. And I can't say I gave much of a damn about it either.

Jack Connolly pushed his way through the crowd and came and stood beside me. Together, silently, we watched Vitus hanging there. He stopped twisting. Thankfully, he stopped with his face to the back wall. I was getting tired of looking at those bulging eyes and ugly tongue.

"Hmmm," Jack said after a minute. "Looks dead."

"Yup," I said.

"You didn't do it, did you?"

"Nope," I said. "You?"

"Nope," he said. "Good idea, though."

We were vetting some emotional steam, of course, but I glanced over at Jackie and saw that he was doing what I had first done. He was studying the scene, trying to see if he could figure out what happened. How it happened. It's a reporter's first instinct at a crime scene. Piece together the story. Find the beginning and work it through to the end. Who, what, when, where and how. That way, you don't get caught up in the raw emotion of death, bloodshed and violence and the various unspeakable ways in which human beings often treat each other.

I don't know what Jackie saw, but I noticed that Vitus' body hung some three feet away from the back of an empty golf cart that had been pulled forward, out of line with the final row of carts at the back of the barn. I noticed his huge staff bag filled with shiny clubs leaning against the back wall of the barn, next to a smaller, slightly care-worn bag of clubs that probably belonged to Fred Adamek. Since they were walking, their clubs wouldn't have been strapped into a golf cart. There were three other golf carts still parked in a neat row, the yellow electrical cords still hooked up to the overhead transformers. One of those carts held my clubs and Jackie's.

"Looks like he was propped up on the back of that cart, the cord wrapped around his neck and the cart was then driven forward, leaving him dangling," I said.

"Umm," Jackie nodded agreement. "Just like a hanging in the Wild, Wild West."

Behind us, I heard Teddy McDaggert chasing the onlookers away from the cart barn. "Cops on the way," he said. "Stay away from the barn. Don't want to mess up the crime scene." Teddy had obviously been watching all the cop shows on TV.

When he got the other golfers out of the way, he shut the two swinging doors on the front of the barn. The overhead fluorescent lights that I had switched on now provided the only illumination.

With the doors closed, the air got closer and hotter almost immediately. And something changed in the air pressure, causing Vitus to swing around one more time, facing us.

"Do you see something under his eye?" I asked Jackie, pointing.

"The right one?" he asked, peering. "Looks like the beginning of a mouse."

"Could be where someone slugged him," I said.

"Maybe knocked him out so they could string him up," Jackie nodded.

"So who do you think?" I asked.

"Shit Hacker," Jackie sighed loudly. "Could have been almost anyone in the club, plus maybe a thousand people in both Lowell and half the state of New Hampshire. I don't know too many people who actually liked the son-of-a-bitch."

"Cops should have fun with this one," I said.

"Yeah," Jackie said. "Which reminds me. I ought to go call this one in. We might actually want to run something in tomorrow's newspaper."

"Sure it won't offend any advertisers?"

"Up yours," he snorted and left the barn.

I glanced at my watch. 7:45. I still had about four hours before the first deadline for the early blue-star edition of my newspaper. Which would be just about enough time for me to come up with an explanation for Frankie Donatello as to why I was playing golf at the Shuttlecock Club in Lowell when he thought I was covering the PGA Tour in Endicott, New York. But rather than call the city desk right away, I decided to hang around for a bit and see what happened next.

I heard a faint siren in the distance and listened as its insistent whoop-whoop got louder and louder. The first car skidded to a halt outside the cart barn and the doors flew open again. A uniformed cop came through first, his gun drawn and held down by his side. A short and plump man with dark hair, black slacks, white shirt, black shiny shoes, sticking a plastic case holding his shiny gold badge into his breast pocket, followed him. The uniform cop went over to Vitus, looked at him for a moment, then felt for a pulse in the carotid artery. He glanced over at the short guy standing next to me and shook his head once, briefly.

The short guy blew out a breath, short and loud. He turned to look at me.

"Tierney," he said. "Lowell PD. Who're you?"

"Hacker," I said. "Guest here. Came in to find my clubs. Found him hanging there."

"Was he dead?" Tierney asked.

"Well, he wasn't exactly doing the cha-cha," I said.

Tierney gave me the hard look cops do so well. I guess it was a little early in the morning to smart off. The uniformed cop was speaking softly into his shoulder-mounted microphone. Calling in the crime, requesting the medical examiner, photographer, crime-scene unit. Maybe ordering some coffee and doughnuts, too.

Tierney turned to Ted McDaggert. "What's your story?" he barked.

"I'm Ted McDaggert, the golf pro here. This is the annual member-guest tournament here...all weekend. This guy..." he nodded at the dangling Vitus, "Is ... was ... the club president. Name is Vitus Papageorge."

"The banker?" Tierney asked. I noticed the uniform cop had whipped out a notebook and pencil and was taking all this down.

"Yeah," Ted nodded. "I was in the pro shop when my caddie master came running in to tell me Hacker here had found a body in the cart barn. I came to see, then called it in."

Jack Connolly strolled back into the barn as if he was dropping by Cumberland Farms to pick up a gallon of milk and some crullers. "Mornin' Leo," he said to the short cop in a pleasant, lilting tone.

Tierney looked at Jack and his eyes got narrow. "Shit," he said. "We got enough trouble here without the goddam press getting in the way, too. Especially a lace doily like you. Outta here."

"Fuck you, Leo," Jack said, just as pleasantly. "Have you met my partner here? Hacker's with the Boston Journal."

"Holy crap," Tierney exploded. "Billy, get these asswipes outta here. Get their statements. Then, tape off the barn. Nobody goes home until we talk to them. That goes double for you two idiots," he said, glaring at Jack and me. "I don't care what amendment to the Constitution you throw at me, you're both material witnesses and you don't get off this island until I say so. Got it?"

Jackie gave him the upright, one-finger salute and we walked outside the barn and stood there waiting to be interrogated.

"He doesn't seem to like you," I said.

"Well, most of the Lowell cops don't," Jack said with a smile. "We've kinda hammered the police union about all the political promotions and cheating on the tests and stuff. They seem to think I'm some cop hater or something."

"Are you?"

"Oh, hell yes," Jack said. "Cops these days are greased more than an old Ford in the pits at Darlington. Not that I blame them, really. If I had people trying to stab, spit on or shoot me every working day, I'd wanna get a little extra for the trouble, too. But it's the political crap that offends me. Anyway, there are still a few good ones, and I think Leo Tierney is actually a close as we get these days to an honest cop. He comes from a long line of cops. It's in his DNA."

While we stood there in the bright morning sunshine, we watched a round little man in an ill-fitting black suit come running down the sidewalk from the main clubhouse. As he drew nearer, I noticed his well-gelled, slicked-back hair, his jowls that bounced as he ran, and the two pinky rings that glistened in the sun. He nodded rather frantically at Jack as he passed us and bustled into the barn. He was halfway through the door when we heard his outrushing exclamation of horror.

"And that would be?" I asked my partner.

"Herbert Incavaglia, our club manager," Jack said. "Obsequious little twerp who kisses up to everyone. In fact, I think that's Herbie's main job description: Kiss up to all members. He's particularly good at berating the staff in public. You know, snaps his fingers and demands loudly that the waitress go immediately to the kitchen and tell them Mrs. Pennington wants her garlic-mashed potatoes instead of these cold au gratins. Stuff like that. There aren't enough drugs in the world that would enable me to do that job."

"Bet his nose was solidly welded to Vitus' butt," I said.

"Oh yeah," Jack said. "Vitus hired the guy. Some of us think that Herbie tattled to Vitus whenever he heard someone making critical or negative comments."

"Hmmm," I said thoughtfully.

The uniformed cop came out of the barn, took us over near his squad car and flipped open his notebook. Licking

the end of his pencil – why does anyone do that? I wondered – he looked at me and said "Start at the beginning." I
suppressed my urge to smart off to the guy, or make his life
difficult, and just told him our story. What time we arrived
at the club, what we did, and how I came to walk into the
cart barn looking for my putter and discovering instead the
corpus delecti.

"Corpus what?" the cop said, writing furiously.

Jack and I looked at each other and tried not to laugh.
"Never mind," I said. "Change it to 'body.'"

"Right," the cop said. He looked at Jackie. "And you?"

Jackie stuck his thumb in my direction. "What he said,"
he said.

The cop nodded. "Tierney says he'll want to talk to
you his own self later on. Don't leave before he does."

We solemnly swore not to make a break for the border.
Crossed our hearts and hoped to die. The cop nodded, satis-
fied, flipped his notebook closed and turned to get the yellow crime scene tape out of the trunk of his squad car. We
strolled back into the main grille, where most of the contestants in the Shuttlecock Invitational had gathered. Most of
the men wore shocked looks, and some seemed disappointed.
I guessed they were the ones who had had good days on the
course yesterday and were leading their flights. Now some
dead guy was keeping them from competing. Murder can
throw a double bogey into anyone's day. I didn't think Vitus
Papageorge's was off to a good start, either.

The assembled group of golfers had obviously been
talking about the events in the cart barn, and everyone fell
silent when Jackie and I walked in. Apparently, everyone
knew that I had discovered the body, and they had seen us
getting the third degree from the cop even if it was only the
first degree. Still, a hundred pair of eyes stared at us. I let
Jackie make the first move.

"Well, hell, boys," he finally said. "Somebody get me a drink and I'll tell you what I know."

There was a rush to get a cocktail into my partner's hand, and the members crowded round to hear Jack's story. He began to spin out a good yarn, embellished with some Gothic flourishes, obviously in his element as the center of attention. I drifted away from the crush and headed off to the telephone closet. I dialed the city room.

"Journal news," said a bored voice. I recognized the voice of the day shift rim editor, Howard Purcell.

"Purce?" I said. "Hacker."

"Hack-Man!" he chirped. "How's things on the links?"

"Deadly," I answered and quickly filled him in on the events of the morning at the Shuttlecock Club. Purcell listened silently, and I could hear his pen scratching furiously as I relayed what I knew about the victim.

"Yeah, Papageorge was a player in the Merrimack Valley," Purcell said. "Known to have a heavy hand in politics. Probably a thousand guys up there woulda liked to wring his scrawny little neck."

"Listen, Purce, can you do me a small favor?" I asked. "Donatelli thinks I'm covering the PGA tournament upstate New York. I sent an intern instead so I could play in this tournament. I'd work this one for ya, since I'm here and all, but I gotta do it on the Q.T."

"I hear ya, Hacker," Purcell said. "I think Angela Murphy is in Lowell this morning, filing something on the city manager getting indicted for corruption. Gee, go figure, huh? Corruption in a Massachusetts city government? I'll track her down and send her over."

"Thanks, Purce," I said. "I owe ya one."

"More than one, pally," he said, and rang off.

Next, I called the press room in Endicott and got connected with Tony Zec. He told me that Jeff Sluman was now leading by two shots over Brad Faxon heading into the weekend. Be still my heart, I thought. We talked over some story lines for a few minutes and I told him to email me his stuff by six that night, so I could look it over and resend it down to the sports desk. Might as well keep the charade going as long as I could.

I walked back into the grille about the same time that Teddy McDaggert came in from his pro shop, carrying a clipboard and looking even more frazzled than normal. His face was flushed and sweat gathered at his brow. A yellow pencil was stuck behind his ear where it disappeared into the curly regions of his hair.

"Okay, gentlemen, if I can have your attention, please?" he called out in a wavering voice. The room slowly fell silent. When he had our attention, McDaggert began talking.

"First of all, you are all obviously aware of the tragic events of the morning," he said. "This is a terribly sad day for the Shuttlecock Club and for all of us who knew and were touched by Vitus Papageorge." He paused, his hands shaking a bit. I waited for someone to make a snide comment, but the assembled crowd was as silent as death.

"I have talked to police detective Tierney who tells me that he wants to talk to everyone who had arrived at the club this morning before 8 a.m., which is probably most of you," McDaggert continued. "I have given him a list of all participants in the tournament, and he has requested that no one leave the premises today before one of the Lowell police officers has a chance to interview you and check your name off this list." He held out his clipboard.

"Because of this, and because the Lowell police will need several hours to examine the crime scene, we've decided to cancel today's rounds. We'll try and start up again tomorrow, once I figure out a way to rejigger the board so we can try and have a competition. Thanks for your under-standing and patience. Just hang tight here until the police are ready."

"Do you think that's the best plan, Teddy?" a quiet voice said from the back. We all turned. It was Dr. Bainbridge.

"The tournament committee has discussed it, Walter," McDaggert said. "We all think that Vitus would have wanted us to continue the Invitational. We need to keep out of the police's way for a few hours and let them do their job. Later, we can sort things out."

There were murmurs throughout the room as the con-testants looked at each other and began talking. There were obviously divided feelings. McDaggert finally raised his hands and called for attention again. The debates stopped.

"It's only fair, I think, to let you guys decide," he said. "If you don't want to continue, that's OK with me. But I think we should honor Vitus Papageorge's life and keep play-ing the game he loved. If you agree, then I'll reschedule the matches to begin early tomorrow morning."

The room was silent for a few moments, then, with a roar of approval, everyone began to applaud. The decision made, there was a rush for the bar, as the golfers in the room girded themselves for a wait to be interviewed. Oth-ers filtered into the locker rooms or upstairs to the card room. I followed Ted McDaggert as he walked back into his small office at the back of the pro shop, where he picked up a walkie-talkie and began barking orders. One of his assis-tants began working at the computer, trying to get two days worth of tee times rescheduled into one. Another one was glued to the telephone, trying to call all the members who had late tee times to let them know the day's events had been cancelled. Ted let out a deep sigh.

"Strange morning, huh?" I said, trying to sound sym-pathetic.

"One that'll live in infamy," Ted said, smiling weakly.

"How are you doing?"

"What?"

"Well, you must have worked pretty closely with Vitus over the years," I observed. "This thing has gotta hit you pretty hard. You holding up?"

McDaggert rubbed his chin, his eyes closed for a moment. His hands were still shaking slightly, I noticed.

"Hell, Hacker," he said finally, his voice thin and high. "Papageorge was one of my original backers when I tried the Tour years ago. He helped me get this job. I've known him for years. I ... I guess I'm kinda shook. But I got a job to do here, y'know? Hundred guys waiting for me to tell 'em what to do."

His voice trailed off and his eyes came back from some point out in space and turned on me. I saw some pain, some fright, some uncertainly. And something else too. The eyes of the condemned? I reached over and squeezed his shoulder reassuringly.

"Okay," I said quietly. "Let me know if I can do anything to help."

He nodded, then reached under the counter and found a pack of cigarettes. With a trembling hand, he shook one out, lit it, took a deep drag and let the smoke out in a billowing rush.

FOURTEEN

I went upstairs to the locker room to find my wayward partner. He was in the card room, sitting in one of the oversized plush chairs, cocktail at hand, lost in thought. I asked Raymond to bring me a cup of coffee and sat down next to him.

"Well," I said, "That was an interesting morning. What have you got planned for the afternoon? A car crash or a bank robbery?"

He laughed, took a sip of his drink. "Hey, never a dull moment here among the country club set. You'd rather be writing dull stories about golfers?"

"Touché," I said as Raymond brought me my coffee. "But unfortunately I can't go for the Pulitzer on this one since my dumb ass boss still thinks I'm in upstate New York."

"Ah, the tangled webs we weave," Jack smiled at me.

I nodded and sipped some coffee.

"So," I said, "Who do you think dun it?"

"Elementary, my dear Hacker," Jack said in his best affected-Brit accent. "I don't have the first clue. That's what I've been sitting here thinking about. The problem is, there are maybe a thousand people who had good reason to string ole Vitus up. Maybe more."

"Yeah," I said, "But there weren't a thousand people who were here this morning. More like a hundred or so. It's gotta be someone who's still on the island."

"Unless they high-tailed it before the body was found," Jack pointed out.

"Or swam across the river," I added.

Jack made a face. "Phew," he said, "Then the cops would just have to smell him out." He paused and sipped at his drink. But his eyes were bright and alert. The events of the morning had obviously captured his attention.

"Here's what I think," he said. "A lot of people hated his guts. But there's a pretty big leap between hating someone's guts and actually killing them."

"True enough," I said. "Murder is usually a crime of passion. Something that tips the scales from good old-fashioned hate to actually acting on it. It can be a threat to someone you love, or a threat to something you love, like money, a job, a Callaway ERC II driver."

"Oh, yeah," Jack laughed. "That's it...Vitus was trying to steal someone's driver."

"Let's take the lovely Leta, for example," I said. "She somewhat engenders the concept of passion."

"Somewhat," Jack said. "Like with about half the membership here at Shuttlecock."

"At least one of whom I saw playing tongue tag with her last night," I said, and told Jack the story of my inadvertent voyeurism the night before.

"Do tell?" Jack said, raising his eyebrows. "Any idea who the lucky guy was?"

I shook my head. "Too dark," I said. "And I was trying to keep out of their way."

"So," he said, "Mystery Kisser goes to the head of the class. Suspect number one."

I held up my hand. "But it could be coincidental. And, in truth, the fact that Leta was fooling around with someone here at the club, not an uncommon occurrence according to you, is not really a good reason for someone to kill Vitus. Better reason for Vitus to kill the guy, or maybe even Leta."

"She coulda asked our Mystery Man to off her husband," Jack mused. "She'd then inherit all his money."

"But it seems that she has the full use of it anyway, as long as she drapes herself on his arm when he needs her," I said. "It doesn't quite add up to me."

"Who else?" Jackie asked.

"Well, I thought about the chauffeur," I said.

"We did hear Vitus chewing his ass out last night, didn't we? Maybe it was the chauffeur who was fooling around with Leta."

I shook my head. "Nah. He was in the car with the engine running when I saw Leta and the Mystery Kisser down by the pool. And I don't think getting reamed by your boss, especially a boss like Vitus who seems to use reaming as his main management tool, is enough of a reason to kill the guy. Still, I'm sure the cops will find out where he went after dropping Vitus off here this morning. If he even drove him to the club."

"Hmmm," Jackie stroked his chin. "I might have one of our young hotshots at the paper do a little digging. See what turns up."

"Of course," I said, "Vitus also had a rather strong reputation as a hard-nosed businessman who liked to step on people's toes. Maybe somebody felt ripped off and decided to do something about it."

Jack shook his head again. "That widens the field again," he said. "And I still don't think somebody could have snuck in here this morning, done the deed in the cart barn and snuck out again without someone noticing. Nor would Vitus have willingly gone into the cart barn with someone he thought might have reason to do him harm. It's gotta be someone he knew, someone from the club."

"Or someone he wasn't afraid of. Isn't old Freddie a customer of his bank or something?"

"You really think Fred is a cold-blooded killer?" Jack asked.

We looked at each other and simultaneously said aloud: "Nah."

"Maybe he got tired of Vitus telling him how to swing the golf club," I said, and we laughed.

Just then, a uniformed cop stuck his head in the door. "Tierney wants to see you guys, pronto," he said.

"Thanks Officer Krupke," Jack said, "We'll be right down."

The cop eased his 250 pounds into the locker room. "He said now and I think he meant it as in 'immediately and without delay,'" the cop said. "And the name's O'Malley."

We sat there and looked at his imposing figure.

"Alphonse?" I said, motioning to my partner.

"After you, Gaston," he said, and we got up and walked out the door.

The Lowell cops had been busy in the hour or so since they had arrived on the scene. When Jack and I wandered out behind the golf clubhouse, the entrance to the cart barn had been cordoned off with the familiar yellow police-line tape, and a large white RV painted on the side in blue letters that spelled "LOWELL PD – CRIME SCENE SQUAD" had parked near the barn. We could see the flashes of a photographer's strobe coming from inside the barn, where Vitus' body no doubt still dangled from the electrical cord.

Officer O'Malley led us to the back of the RV, and we climbed in a doorway, up three stairs and into a tiny room, about five feet square. The room was painted bureaucratic green, and had a narrow table bolted to the floor at which sat Detective Leo Tierney, who was studiously reading his notes from a small, flip-up notebook. There was even a small, mirrored rectangle on the back wall behind Tierney's head. Jack sat down in one of the two plastic chairs opposite Tierney while I made an elaborate show of checking my teeth for stray detritus in the little mirror. I thought I heard a muffled chuckle from behind the glass and sat down, feeling pleased with myself. Officer O'Malley closed the door behind him and assumed the position: standing against the wall, hands folded in front of him, eyes locked straight ahead, seeing nothing.

"Quite the set up, Leo," Jack said. "Do the taxpayers know how much this joy wagon set them back?"

"Funded by a special state and federal grant," Tierney said, not looking up from his notes. "And the taxpayers seem to want to do something about the rising crime rate in the city."

"While the cops seem to want to play with all the expensive toys money can buy instead of actually walking a beat and arresting bad guys," Jack countered.

"So go write an editorial," Tierney replied. "I know better than to argue with someone who buys ink by the barrel. I'm trying to catch a murderer here."

"And how's that going?" I interjected.

Tierney looked at me and smiled. "We're following several promising leads," he intoned in perfect police-ese. "And anticipate a quick arrest of the perpetrator."

We all chuckled.

"Now," he said, "If we can stop our little game of cops and reporters, maybe you can tell me what you know."

I retold my story again, from the time I had gone in search of my putter until I discovered Vitus hanging from the ceiling. Jack chimed in that he had been upstairs in the private lounge "getting his game face on" – I had to laugh at that – and had been standing in the pro shop with Ted McDaggert when the cart kid came running in with the news.

"What did he do?" Tierney asked, jotting down things in his notebook.

"I think he said 'fuck,' and called 9-1-1," Jack said. "Then he ran out to the barn."

"You sure?" I asked. "He called the cops before he came out?"

Jack nodded. "He made a call and then ran out there. I went looking for you. Didn't want you to miss all the fun. When I couldn't find you, the cart kid told me you were already out in the barn."

Tierney made a note. "How well did you guys know the deceased?"

I sighed. "I played golf with him twice this week and swore never again," I said. "Vitus was an asshole."

"I've known Papageorge since he joined the club more than ten years ago," Jack said. "What my partner means is that Vitus had a well-earned reputation as a self-inflated, overbearing, pompous, tempestuous and holier-than-thou person who often cheated at golf."

"Sounds like the technical definition of an asshole," Tierney said.

We nodded.

"Interesting how a guy like that can be president of the club," Tierney said. "Especially for ... how many years?"

"About six I think," Jack said.

Tierney let that number hang in the air in the little interrogation room, where the air was suddenly close and clammy.

"Don't blame me," Jack said. "I never voted for the son-of-a-bitch. Then again, I never voted."

"Kinda interesting, isn't it?" I said. Tierney looked at me, tapping his pencil against his front teeth. "How can a guy who is universally disliked maintain his hold on power, if being president of the Shuttlecock Club means having power?"

Tierney nodded and raised his eyebrows. "Yeah," he said. "How?"

I shrugged. "Could be the Mussolini Excuse – he kept the trains running on time. Took care of all the messy business stuff and let the members just be members. There are plenty of golf clubs run that way, you know."

"Or," Tierney said, "He coulda been greasing his own wheel."

"Hard to do," I said. "He had a finance committee and six hundred members looking over his shoulder. Makes it tough to sneak cash out the back door. And that's assuming there is a lot of cash to sneak. Clubs like this tend to run budgets pretty close to break-even."

Tierney looked at Jack. "You're the member here. Any hint of funny business?"

Jack shook his head. "Not that I'm aware of," he said. "But to be honest, I never paid too much attention to the financial side of the club. They sent out an annual report that I never read, and had an annual meeting, which I never went to. Most guys are only interested in the operations of the club if the greens are dying or the price of drinks in the grill go up. Other than that, most of us don't give a rat's ass about who runs the place. Far as we could tell, Vitus paid the bills and everything was hunky dory."

"Yeah," Tierney said. "And Vitus Papageorge probably liked it that way too. He was a sharp one, from what I hear. And he ran a bank that had some troubles with funny investors in the past."

"Funny how?" I asked.

Tierney shrugged. "Go read your own newspaper," he said. "Feds were looking at him for laundering, false reporting, bunch of stuff. Never made it stick. He skated, but barely, from what I hear. Helped that he was a major fundraiser for the junior senator from New Hampshire. Now the guy is offed in a cart barn. I just find that interesting."

Jack and I sat there silently, but I could tell Jack's little grey cells were whirring as fast as mine. It was more than interesting, and the strings that dangled off the body of Vitus Papageorge, swinging gently in the cart barn of the Shuttle-cock Club, now seemed a tangled mess. But it was a helluva story.

Tierney dismissed us with a wave of his hand, and Officer O'Malley came out his deep REM state to open the door to the RV for us. We walked silently back across the parking lot, into the clubhouse and upstairs to the private lounge. Jack motioned to Roland, who disappeared to his secret lair and quickly emerged with two cocktails. Jack drank most of his with one swallow. I sipped at mine.

"Velly intellesting, Hacker-san," Connolly said. "I'm gonna go home and get out my game of Clue. I think Colonel Mustard's gotta show up any second now."

"Yeah," I said, nodding wisely. "I think I got it narrowed down to about 50 possible suspects now. I think I'll stick to golf writing. Fewer headaches. Less dead bodies, too."

Jack raised his glass in agreement. Dr. Walter Bainbridge walked in, looking as frazzled as everyone else that morning at the Shuttlecock Club.

"My God," he exclaimed, throwing himself into one of the leather chairs and running his fingers through his graying hair. "What an unbelievable turn of events!" Roland appeared soundlessly from the back room, but Bainbridge waved him away. Jack looked at him sadly.

Bainbridge looked at me. "I heard you were the one who discovered the body," he said. "That must have been awful. Do you need anything? I might have some medication in my locker …"

I smiled at him. "Thanks," I said, holding up my glass of bourbon. "This is helping."

"Don't blame you," he said. "Must have been an ugly shock."

"So whaddya think, Doc?" Jack piped in. "Who did it?"

Bainbridge sighed deeply. "I cannot imagine," he said. "It's beyond the pale. I mean, certainly Vitus was not well liked. He was, well, *difficult* I guess is the nicest word one can come up with. But for this to happen…" He shook his head again.

"The cops seem surprised that someone so difficult could keep getting elected as president of the club," I said. "I have to admit, I've wondered about that too, and I only knew the guy for a couple of days."

Bainbridge nodded wisely. "Well, it's true that he could rub some people the wrong way," he said. "Especially out on the golf course. He was so competitive. He just couldn't understand that not everyone was wired the same way. But as the administrator of the club, most people agreed that he took a thankless task and did it extremely well. I mean, the club is in excellent working order. McDaggert runs a good golf operation, the dining room makes money. He brought in that fella Incavaglia, who's been an excellent manager."

"Where'd he come from? I asked.

"Herbert?" Bainbridge scratched his head and thought a moment. "Someplace in Boston, I think," he said. "It was a downtown club of some kind. I can't recall. But he's done a bang-up job. The staff is well-trained, and the house is ship-shape."

"What about that sewer thing?" I pressed. "That was a surprise."

Bainbridge sighed. "Yes, a very costly project," he said. "But how can you blame anyone? This club is more than 125 years old. It figures that the infrastructure will need upkeep as years go by. Who could have predicted that the sewer main would crumble?"

"Hoo boy, remember the smell?" Jack chimed in. "When that pipe burst and flooded the basement, no one could go near the place without retching!"

"Nasty," Bainbridge agreed. "Nasty bit of business. But Papageorge stayed on top of it, got the emergency repairs done and then helped finance the construction project. It was quite extensive. As usual, when you start digging up hundred-year-old plumbing, there are always expensive surprises."

A soft but insistent beep went off. Bainbridge reached down and pulled his pager off his belt. "Damn," he said. "Gotta call the hospital." He strode off in search of a telephone.

"Did you notice?" Jack asked, when Bainbridge had left.

"What? That the good doctor, who a night or so ago was rather harshly critical of old Vitus now considers him the Jack Welch of Shuttlecock? Yeah," I said.

"Kinda funny, huh?"

A group of men came into the lounge and drafted Jack into a game of poker. He looked at me, but I shook my head. Cards were never my thing. Roland the white-suited attendant came in and took drink orders. I stood up, stretched and walked over to the windows that looked down on the first tee and the putting green. I saw a familiar figure standing under an oak, talking on her cell phone and waving her hands.

I caught Jackie's eye and told him I'd be right back. He smiled happily. He had a fresh cocktail at his elbow and a pile of chips in front of him.

I walked down the stairs, through the pro shop and outside and reached the woman just as she said "Right, OK, call ya back," into her phone. Angela Murphy worked for the *Journal's* state desk. Her beat was covering the cities and towns of Massachusetts, always a fascinating study of public miscreants, shameless nepotism, major and minor malfeasance and, all-to-frequently, downright corruption. She was somewhere around 40 years old and as severely sexless as a woman can get. Her slightly graying hair was pulled back tightly from her forehead and pinned securely in a bun at the back. A pair of thick glasses balanced at the end of her nose. She was short, round, dressed in drab khaki-colored shirt and slacks, with sensible brown shoes, and a large brown leather carry-all bag slung over her shoulder. She looked — and was — serious and no-nonsense, with that professional journalist's studied look of skepticism, cynicism and heard-this-before at all times.

"Angie," I said in greeting. "Wassup?"

"Oh, hi, Hacker," Angela Murphy said. "Purcell told me you were here."

"Yeah," I said. "Doing some deep background for a series on the country club life in northeastern Massachusetts."

"Or just screwing around with the boys for the weekend," Angie smiled poisonously at me.

"Yeah, well, whatever," I said. "Lucky you were in the neighborhood to get the call."

She nodded, and I saw briefly in her eyes a flash of excitement. After a dozen years of wading through pages of public audits, environmental studies, and tax-law proposals, and hours of ass-numbing small-town council meetings, a real, live, hard-news murder story was something new for her, and although her professional reserve and carefully constructed detachment would never let her admit it, I'd bet she was excited.

"Were you here this morning?" she asked me.

"I discovered the body," I said. "Lucky me. What are the cops saying?"

She flipped open her notebook. "Victim was seen arriving at the club this morning at approximately 6 a.m.," she said. "He had one of those whatchamacallits…?

"Tee time?" I prompted.

"Right, a tee time scheduled for 7:55 a.m. That's a gap of almost two hours. Is that normal? Getting here two hours before you're supposed to play?"

"Well," I said, "For a dumb little tournament like this, most guys roll in with just enough time to swallow a couple aspirin with coffee for their hangover, and maybe hit a few warm-up putts. Papageorge took himself kinda seriously as a golfer, so I'm sure he was planning to beat balls for at least an hour."

"Hmmm," Angie said, and she scribbled something into her notebook. "Time of death has not been established yet, but it fell sometime between 6 a.m. when he got here, and 7:25 a.m. when his body was discovered … by you."

"How'd he get here?" I asked.

Angie looked confused.

"He often had a chauffeur drive him around," I told her. "Liked to look like a big shot. I wonder if he was driven here, or if he drove himself this morning."

"I dunno," Angie said. "I'll ask. What else you got?"

I smiled. I was now the source.

"Guy was not very much liked," I told her. "Ran the club here with something of a heavy hand. Tinpot dictator type. Rubbed a lot of people the wrong way."

She began writing furiously.

"Apparently, he was also something of a mover and shaker in the area, politically and business-wise. You probably know more about that than I do."

Angie nodded, still scribbling. "Yeah, he was a hard-nosed SOB," she said. "Got things done, but ruffled a lot of feathers doing it."

"Interesting thing is that he kept getting re-elected as president of the club, even though everyone I've met here pretty much thought he was an asshole," I said. "Nobody really has a good explanation for that. He apparently appointed all the members of whatever board of directors the place has, hired the club manager, the golf pro, probably the head chef and the course superintendent, too, for all I know."

"Little empire all his own, huh?" Angie said. "He stealing all the money?"

"That was my first thought, too," I nodded. "But I can't figure out if there was any money to steal or how he might have done it. Despite the old money types that belong to a club like this, it's usually operated pretty close to the bone. Usually isn't a lot of spare cash lying around for anyone to abscond with. And he didn't abscond. He was hanged."

"I'll check around, see if I can find anything," Angie said.

"There's one thing," I said. "Couple of years ago, the pipes burst in the place. Shit hit the fan, literally. By the time they were through, they had to install an all-new sewerage system. Big project. They ended up hitting all the members with a big assessment to pay for it."

"I'll bet they did," Angie said. "Nobody is supposed to let a drop of poop or anything else into that river." She nodded her head in the direction of the Merrimac. "There are federal, state and local clean-water commissions guarding this river, and each one of them has a thousand pages of regulations, permits and applications for variations, easements, public hearings …"

"Stop," I said, holding my hands over my ears. "I'm getting a bureaucracy migraine."

"Welcome to my world," Angie said and flashed me what passed for her version of a grin.

"With all that bureaucracy, there must be a paper trail," I said.

"And you want me to go dig it out, I suppose," she said, her fleeting grin turning into an equally unenthusiastic frown.

"You're right," I said. "Probably nothing there. I'll get my friend at the Lowell paper to see what he can find."

"The hell you will," she snapped. "It's my story. I'll do my own reporting."

"Fine," I said. "Just trying to help."

"Yeah," she said. "Like a fish on a bicycle. Was Papageorge married?"

"Yeah," I said. "In fact, I've met her. Younger. Blonde. Attractive. Allegedly active in a John Cheever-esque way here among the clubby set."

Angie frowned and stopped writing. "You do her?" she barked at me.

"Angie," I protested, holding my hands up to stop her. "What an indelicate question to ask a colleague. I am shocked…shocked! But no, I cannot say I have had the pleasure."

She shook her head. "Then I ain't gonna go there. Maybe she had hot pants, maybe all these pencil-neck geeks around here just wish she did. Until someone official says her sex life had something to do with this guy's murder, I ain't going there."

"How honorable," I said.

"Yeah, well, it's the oldest trick in the book," she said, her face getting a little red. "Young, good-looking wife. Older, hard-nosed husband. Everyone immediately assumes she's some kind of slut, only married him for the money, fucks everything that's not tied down, and is prime suspect numero uno when the guy gets dead. Well, I'm not buying it."

"Slow down," I said, holding up my hand again. "I agree with you. Even though I might have something a bit stronger than hearsay or malicious gossip to suggest that she might have been fooling around –" She started to protest again before I hurried on – "There's no good motive for *her* to kill *him*. Be more the other way around."

"Was Papageorge having an affair?" Angie asked.

"Dunno," I said. "Good question. That'd create a motive."

Angie nodded, and glanced over my shoulder at a gaggle of Lowell cops gathered around a police car. "Look, I gotta go see if these geniuses have any further information to divulge," she said. "I'll ask about the chauffeur and let you know if I find anything out about the sewer mess. Thanks."

"Okay," I said. "If I learn anything else, I'll call."

She started to walk away.

"Hey Angie," I called, remembering something. She stopped and looked at me.

"Does the name Herb Incavaglia ring any bells with you?"

She thought for a minute, eyebrows furrowed, chewing on her pencil. "Nope," she said.

"Okay, thanks," I said, waving my hand. She gave me one of her quick smiles, a mere twitch of her lips that carried zero warmth and just a smidgen of gratitude, and strode off quickly. Walking back into the clubhouse, I almost collided head-on with Fred Adamek, who was pushing out the door. Freddie! I had almost forgotten about Papageorge's long-suffering partner. He was wearing a thin blue blazer, an oxford dress shirt and a wide necktie. His whitish shock of hair was wet and plastered down on his round and motley head. He carried a small athletic bag in one hand and his golf shoes in the other.

We stood for a moment looking at each other. What do you say to a guy whose partner has been murdered? I reached out and put a sympathetic hand on his rounded shoulder.

"Geez, Fred," I said. "This has been quite a day, hasn't it?"

He nodded, his eyes grateful. He shrugged his heavy shoulders.

"Hell of a thing," he said, shaking his head. "Hell of a thing."

I pulled him outside and out of the way of people streaming into and out of the door to the grill. "Got a minute to talk?" I asked.

"Guess so," he said, casting a longing look at the parking lot. "I was heading home. The party's over."

"Drink?" I asked.

He shook his head. "Nah," he said. "I'm tuckered out. Cops made me stick around all morning. Telling my story, over and over. I need to get home and get some sleep."

"What did they want to know?" I asked.

He threw his hand up. "Oh, just where was I and when did I see Vitus last and what did he say and stuff like that." He pushed his thick glasses back up his nose and sighed.

"I got here pretty early this morning," he said, launching into his story again. He had obviously been on automatic pilot most of the day and didn't need much prompting for the story to come spilling out one more time.

"Vitus wanted us to get to the practice range first to get some work in," he continued. "He was a great one for working out the kinks. Anyway, when I got here, he was already here, on the putting green. Said he had been waiting for me! This was about 6:15 this morning! Keee-rist! He was an intense little son-of-a-bitch!"

Freddie looked up at me and smiled. I smiled back encouragingly and he went on.

"I came upstairs and changed into my shoes and went back down. He met me outside here, gave me a bucket of balls and a few of my clubs. Told me to go work on my wedge. He was going to get his three-wood out of his bag back in the barn and meet me up on the range."

Fred stopped and rubbed his head wearily. I nodded to keep him talking.

"That was it," he said. "That was the last time I saw him. I went on up to the range, and hit the entire bucket. There were a couple other guys up there and we got to talking and I finally noticed that Vitus hadn't showed up when the bucket was gone. I went back to the clubhouse to look for him. He wasn't in there having breakfast. He wasn't upstairs in the lockers. He wasn't in the crapper. "

He shrugged his shoulders again, mournfully.

"I figured he'd find me eventually. I came back down to the grill, got some coffee and a doughnut and was sitting over by the windows, reading the sports pages. Next thing I know, I hear somebody run in and say 'Vitus Papageorge got strangled out in the cart barn' Then there were the sirens, the cops . . ."

He stopped and looked up at me with suddenly teary eyes. "Hell of a thing," he said, his voice catching a bit. "Hell of a goddam thing. I've known Vitus Papageorge for, oh, twenty years or more. Did a lot of business with him. Played a lot of golf with him. Went out to dinner with his wife and him. Intense little guy, but he was a good friend. It's a hell of a thing."

We stood there in silence for a moment. There was nothing much else to say. Finally, he shook his head and sighed aloud. We shook hands. He walked off slowly towards the parking lot.

Hell of a damn thing.

FIFTEEN

Upstairs, Jack and his pals were still engrossed in their poker game. I went down to the telephone closet and called my home machine. There was a message from Tony Zec at the B.C. Open, saying he had just sent over the day's stories to my email address, and one from Mary Jane Cappaletti.

"Hi, Hacker," her cheerful voice said on the tape. "I know you're worried sick, so I thought I'd let you know that Ducky is doing just fine. He's used the kitty box three times now, so he's back in my good graces. We took him on a walk to the park this morning. Everyone said he looked great in the earmuffs. Call us when you get home, or give us a call if you get bored with all the drinking and golf and such! Ha ha ha. Victoria says hi! Later."

I smiled.   Mister Shit was getting more attention in two days than I had given him in the last six months. Then I dialed the *Journal's* city room and asked to speak to Branson Tucker, one of our regular columnists and our longtime Mob reporter.   Tucker's knowledge of the various New England and East Coast *familias* was legendary, and he had sat through all of the trials, reported on all the gangland shootings, and knew where most of the bodies were buried.   He probably knew enough secrets to get himself buried, or dumped in the harbor wearing his cement galoshes, but the Mob seemed to tolerate Branson Tucker, figuring if they needed a mouthpiece for their side of the story, he was the go-to guy.

"Tuck?" I said when he picked up, "Hacker. Got a second?"

"For you, Mister Hacker, I can spare all of five minutes," Tucker said in his broad Yankee Brahmin accent. "Then I have to finish tomorrow's work of genius."

"Right," I said. "I won't hold you up. I've come across a name up here in Lowell that's been nagging at me. Whaddya know about Herbert Incavaglia?"

"Herbie the Vig?" Tucker sounded delighted.   "I haven't heard his name in a couple of years.   The man is a financial genius. Started as a street collector for Carmine Spoleto years ago – hence his name – then worked his way up the ladder. He knew fifty ways to hide, launder, reinvest and otherwise increase ill-gotten gains, and that was before breakfast! I swear, if he had gone to Wall Street, he would have been a zillionaire. Maybe he is anyway, who knows?"

"Yeah, well, this zillionaire has been working as the general manager for a country club up here in Lowell," I told him.

"Really?" Tucker was flabbergasted. "Herbie the Vig waiting tables? I find that hard to believe. Wait a moment…"

I could hear his fingers drumming on his desk as he thought.

"Yes, I do recall someone telling me a year or so ago that Herbie had moved up to Lowell. Said he was now working for Rene the Lip."

"And that would be?" I prompted. Keeping up with the Mob monikers was a full-time job, and mine was keeping track of 18-year-olds from Texas who could hit a golf ball 350 yards.

"Rene Lemere, dear boy," Tucker said. "He runs Lowell and Lawrence. And with all the Cambodian and Vietnamese gangs moving in, he's had his hands full keeping order. But if he's got Herbie Incavaglia working for him, he must be moving funds around somewhere. That's Herbie's specialty...taking dirty money and turning it into pristine, spendable hard cash."

"At a country club?" I asked. "How do you do that?"

"Well, I don't know," Tucker said. "All I can tell you is that Herbie has an angle going somewhere, somehow. He's a genius, I told you."

I thanked him for his time and rang off. I sat there for a while, thinking. Little pieces of the puzzle seemed to be falling into place, but not quite connecting. Vitus Papageorge, a known mover and shaker with a somewhat murky past, had wormed his way into the Shuttlecock Club where he hired, as general manager, one of the Boston Mob's most talented money men. That was interesting, all by itself. Now, poor old Vitus had ended up dead, in the definitive, not-coming-down-for-breakfast kind of dead. That made it even more interesting. Plus, I had seen Vitus' lovely wife playing tongue tag with somebody, not her husband, but presumably a member of the club. That was interesting in its own way, Andrea Murphy's objections notwithstanding, but I wasn't sure if the two events were twined.

And I still didn't know what Herbie the Vig's gambit was. According to Tucker, the man could practically spin gold out of straw. But how, short of blackmailing the ten richest members of the Shuttlecock Club, was Incavaglia skimming money?

I went back upstairs in search of my erstwhile partner, thinking two heads might be better than one. But I forgot that Jack had been boozing and card playing for the last couple hours. His head wasn't in the same space as mine.

"Hack-Man!" Jack greeted me, a fat cigar clenched in his teeth. "Ronnie and his partner Joey here are bored and they've challenged us to a little match. Whaddya say? Up for a little golf? Get outside into the fresh air and chase away the cobwebs?" He struck a match and started puffing away at his cigar.

"Cobwebs are one thing," I said dryly, "But what about the alcoholic fumes you're about to set afire?"

The card players laughed, and Jackie waved away the clouds of smoke he had emitted. "C'mon," he said cheerfully. "Let's get it on. McDaggert said we can go tee off on 10 so we don't get the cops all discombobulated. I'm feeling steady as a rock...look at this..."

He tried to put his cigar down in the big ashtray to one side and then hold his hands out to show us all how steady he was, but his hand knocked his glass of bourbon flying across the floor. The room convulsed in laughter, and I had to join in. Jack looked crestfallen at his fallen soldier leaking alcohol on the floor, then added his own deep guffaws to the laughter ringing in the room.

"Jeez," I said, "I hope to God we're not playing for money."

We arranged with Ronnie and his partner to meet them on the 10th tee in ten minutes and went back to Jack's locker to change shoes. He was still laughing as we sat down on the bench.

"Think they bought that?" he chuckled as he pulled on his spikes.

I looked at him closely for a moment. He seemed perfectly sober.

"I think you've been hanging around the late Vitus for too long," I said. "You've picked up some of his bad habits. Shame on you!"

"Yeah," he said. "Shame on me. Let's go kick some golfing butt."

In the cart riding out to the distant 10th tee, I filled Jackie in on what I had learned about the identity of the club's general manager. He was astounded.

"Herbert is a mob guy?" he said, incredulous. "He's so quiet, so mister behind-the-scenes, so don't-rock-the-boat."

"He's not a leg-breaker," I said. "He takes dirty money and makes it clean. Like an accountant, only he tries to break the law instead of follow it."

"Yeah," Jack said, smirking, "Just like the accountants do."

"What do you know about this Rene Lemere guy?" I asked.

"I see him around town some," Jack said. "He runs a legit business, grading and foundations for construction. But everyone knows he's the go-to guy for Spoleto and the Boston interests. He's tied in tight with the unions, obviously. Lotta the local politicians go to him. It's not like he's hiding from the law, or anything. People expect him to keep the city peaceful, and he mostly does."

"Tucker said the Asian gangs were trying to move in," I said.

"Yeah, it's a big problem in Lowell and downriver in Lawrence, too. A lot of Cambodian and Vietnamese families have moved in over the last 20 years, and now they have a generation of young men who don't know anything but the gang life. And they can be brutal. And dirty. Lemere cut his teeth bringing in illegal booze and tax-free cigarettes down from Canada, and running the usual numbers and loan-shark rackets in town. But that's small potatoes, and not a very violent business usually. These triad gangs are importing heroin from Thailand by the boatload. That's an altogether different industry. "

"And one that can get you killed pretty quick if you get on the wrong side," I observed.

"Well, as I understand it, Rene has carved out a territory for the Asians and leaves them alone. They're supposed to do the same for him," Jack said. "Except for an occasional shooting here and there – usually in the summer when tempers get hot – they manage to get along fairly well."

"Lotta demand for heroin here in the placid Merrimack valley?" I wondered.

"Lotta demand for heroin everywhere, pards," Jack said.

We arrived at the tee, where Ronnie and Joey were waiting. Ronnie, the Shuttlecock member, was about fifty and had a beer gut on him the size of a prize-winning watermelon. I always wonder where guys like that buy their clothes. His partner, Joey, was short and barrel-chested, with short, stocky legs. Watching him loosen up, I noticed his baseball-bat grip and flat swing with little body rotation – it was all hands and arms. We arranged our wager, shook hands and let 'em rip. It felt good to get outside, in the warm fall sunshine, and forget about everything but golf.

Jack and I dispatched our opponents with surgical precision. Something got into my partner – I think it's called sobriety – and he played amazingly steady and good golf. Which was lucky, since my driver began to go disturbingly awry. My gentle draw deserted me and my shots began drifting ever further to the right. It seemed I spent the entire afternoon playing either from the woods or the rough.

Jack saved us, time and again. I could tell it was going to be one of those days for him, one of those glorious, can't-do-anything-wrong kind of days, on the eleventh, our second hole. Jack had a 35-footer that he needed to get down in two to halve the hole.

Jack Connolly is an adherent of the Fuzzy Zoeller school of putting. He strolls around the green nonchalantly for a minute, eyeing the putt out of the corner of his eye (Fuzzy usually whistles tunelessly to himself while he does this part). Then, without further ado, he steps up to the ball and hits the putt. No plumb bobbing, no crouching, no endless practice swings, no asking anyone for a second read. Just look, step up, and boom.

Anyway, on the eleventh Jack did his minimalist routine with his long, across-the-green putt, and the instant he hit the ball he said "Boink."

"What do you mean, 'boink?'" I asked as the ball rolled across the smooth green grass.

"I mean 'boink,'" he said. "It's in."

I was about to say "you sure?" when the ball rolled straight into the dead solid perfect heart of the cup and disappeared from view with a definitive rattle.

"Told you," Jack said and he turned and strolled casually off towards our cart. I smiled and retrieved the ball for my partner. Our opponents, now down a hole, looked crestfallen as I replaced the flagstick.

"What are you guys, bunch' a comedians?" one of them asked.

I just smiled and shrugged. But that's when I knew that this was Jackie's day. And it was. He made another monster birdie putt to win the 13th, and on the par-three

14th, he had a ticklish, downhill, curving 12-footer. This time, I was watching from the side when he hit the putt, and this time, I was the one who said "boink" as soon as he hit it. It was obvious that the damn thing was going in, and it did. Dead center.

We were five-up after the first nine, and while we cooled down some on the second nine, the result was the same. I was still spraying my driver all over the map, but I made some good escapes and some better up-and-downs from the fringe, and contributed a bit to the team effort. Jack continued to play solid golf, contending on every hole, and with his handicap shots, we did well. He only made one "boinker" in the afternoon, but we closed them out easily.

A half hour later, we were back in the grille, nursing beers. Inside, it was strangely quiet for a weekend afternoon, as most of the contestants in the tournament had gone home. There were perhaps a dozen others who had decided to play, and a few stragglers from the morning's excitement were still there, looking pretty much the worse for wear. The Lowell cops and their fancy crime scene machine had departed, leaving behind only the yellow crime-scene tape draped across the front of the cart barn. I wondered how Ted McDaggert was going to get his carts charged up for the morning, when the tournament would resume in a one-day free-for-all.

But I forgot all that as my friends and I relaxed and replayed the highs and lows of the day's round. Jack took a lot of well-deserved ribbing for his Brer Drunk act, and a lot of well-deserved praise for his magnificent putting. After a long day on the golf course, there is almost nothing so delicious as a cold beer. I have never understood those who come off the 18th and immediately jump into a Scotch on the rocks. They have obviously forgotten the cold, frothy and slightly bitter taste that speaks to a man's soul. That first sip always takes me back to my first beer, stolen from a cooler at a family picnic when no one was looking, hidden under my flapping tee-shirt, cold against my belly flesh. I had run into the woods, hoping no one had seen me, and finally, safe in isolation, taken the prize out, twisted off the cap and tipped the bottle up.

For some reason, a cold beer after a long, hot day of golf always brings me back to that first stolen, teenage pleasure. I wish I could remember my first love with the same detail.

Outside, the twilight began to deepen. I noticed a steady stream of cars begin to pass down the long drive that bisected the first fairway. I yawned. My stomach growled. I remembered that I had forgotten to eat anything all day.

"What manner of debauchery have you got planned for the evening, Jack-off?" I asked, draining the last of my third, or maybe fourth, long-neck. "And I hope it involves food."

"You guys going to the luau?" Ronnie asked.

"Luau?" I echoed, looking at my partner, who was sitting back, sunburned face beaming happily.

"Well," he said, "Some of the guys had been talking about making a run down to Foxwoods," he said, mentioning the nearest Native American gambling reservation down in Connecticut. "But that probably got called off when Vitus got himself killed. I suppose the club decided to go ahead with the luau since they probably had already bought all the food and everyone made reservations. It might be kinda fun to see how everyone's taking the news."

"They gonna have a spit-roasted pig and everything at this luau?" I asked.

"Oh, hell, yes," Ronnie said. "They do it up...roast pig, poo-poo platters, tiki torches, mai-tais...everything!"

He made it sound like it was the dining extravaganza of the year.

"Well then," I said, pushing back, "You can go have fun eavesdropping. I'm gonna go eat half that pig."

The tiki lamps that flickered along the walkways in front of the clubhouse set a festive tone for the evening's event, but once the sun went down, the September night turned frosty, and most of the guests attending the Shuttlecock Invitational's annual luau party headed inside for the warmth of the ballroom. The roasting pig rotated morosely on a spit set up on the broad lawn in front of the main entrance, but the buffet tables holding the rest of the feast had been moved inside, set up in what was normally the main dining room.

Still, the ballroom had been festooned with enough palm fronds to make one believe that Jesus could come riding in on his donkey any time, to the hosannas of the crowd. Tables had been set up with fringed straw hats as the centerpieces, and the wait staff wore flowered Hawaiian shirts and red bandanas, cinched at the neck. They managed not to look too displeased at being made spectacles.

Somehow, the party organizers had found, in this decidedly non-Caribbean region of New England, an actual steel-pan band that had set up in one corner, and the glistening black faces of the players were expressionless as they clanged out their rendition of "Yellow Bird." Nobody was dancing. But I could tell that a conga line snaking around the tables was going to be part of the evening's entertainment.

Jack headed for the bar, of course, while I split off and went for the buffet line. I was famished, and I loaded my plate high with juicy chunks of pork that had been sawed off the unfortunate beast outside and brought inside to be kept warm on a Sterno-heated tray. I ladled on the tangy barbecue sauce, added some spicy rice-and-beans, fried plan-tains, corn fritters and a mound of cole slaw. I passed on the ubiquitous New England clam chowder, which I don't think they have in the islands, mon.

When I finally staggered back into luau central, I nod-ded at Jack, who was surrounded by a gaggle of buddies at the bar, and found myself a mostly empty table at the cor-ner of the room farthest away from the steel pan band. It's not that I don't like music that comes from rejiggered fifty-five-gallon drums whacked with sticks, but after a few min-utes of Bob Marley's greatest hits, my head begins to throb.

There were two couples sitting at the table, and they seemed to be enjoying themselves and the music. I nodded and smiled at them politely and we all silently agreed to ignore each other. Which suited me just fine, as I tucked into my heaping plate of food.

I was about halfway through the process of shoveling it in when my cell beeped at me from my blazer pocket. Without breaking stride with my fork, I pulled it out, flipped it open and barked into the receiver.

"Emphth-o?"

"Hacker? Is that you? Are your batteries low?" The voice was female.

I swallowed, stopped eating and tried again.

"No," I said, "I'm here. Who's this?"

"Angela Murphy," she said. She paused for a second, listening. "Where the hell are you, Jamaica?"

"It's a luau," I told her. "You're interrupting my wor-ship at the altar of roast suckling pig."

"Yuck," she said. "Have you ever considered going ve-gan?"

"Considered," I said, picking at some escapee rice grains that had fallen onto the tablecloth and popping them back in my mouth, "And rejected the idea."

"Do you know what animal protein does to your intestines?" she asked.

"No," I said, "And I really don't want to know. But is it OK if I go get more pig now?"

I could hear her shudder over the phone.

"Listen," she said, "I'm down at the Lowell Public Works department."

"Angie," I said, "It's Saturday night. The Lowell PWD can't possibly be open."

"Not normally, no," she agreed. "But I got my pal Ginny here to come open up the office for me. She's the assistant to the director. I've pulled the records on the Shuttlecock sewer job. Guess what?"

"It was a stinking mess?"

"I'm sure it was," she said, not laughing. "But it was financed by Merrimack Bank & Trust."

"Isn't that…"

"The bank owned by the late Vitus Papageorge," she finished for me. "The club had to get a bonded underwriter since it was a project that tied into a city-owned sewer line, and the financing had to be guaranteed. I guess that's so in case they got halfway through and the construction company took a powder, the money would be there to finish the job and keep the country club's poop from falling in the river. At least, that's what Ginny told me."

"What else does Ginny say?" I wondered.

"Well," Angie said, "It all looks pretty cut-and-dried. The job was done pretty much by the book. All the required permits are here. City inspection reports. They had to tear out the old brick culverts and install cast concrete conduits, plus build a new pumping station to move the crap under the creek and tie in with the main line that follows the river downstream underneath Highway 113 there. Big job. Two-point-six million."

I had a corn fritter speared and ready to disappear. I stopped, momentarily sparing its life.

"What a minute," I said. "What was that figure?"

Angie ruffled some papers. "Yeah, here it is," she said. "Financial bond posted by Merrimack B&T was $2.6 million. That included the 10 percent contingency funding."

My fritter hung in the air while I thought about that.

"So the bank forwards the money to the city, and the city pays the construction company when the job is completed according to code, right?" I asked. "And the bank collects from the country club."

"You got it," Angie said. "It all looks pretty cut and dried. Ginny remembers the project. Said she didn't see any funny business."

"What was the construction company on the job?" I asked, finally popping the golden fritter into my mouth, holding the phone away so Angie wouldn't hear my enthusiastic mastication.

"Hold on…" She riffled through some papers. "Here it is. Adams Construction in Dracut." I could hear a female voice in the background. Angela said "Really?" to her friend Ginny and then spoke to me again. "Guess what, Hacker?" she piped, excited. "Ginny says Adams Construction is part-owned by Rene Lemere. And guess who he is?"

"The local mobster," I said, chewing softly. "That's not the half of it," I continued over Angie's disappointed silence. "The club manager here is supposedly a close friend, if not affiliate, of the very same Mr. Lemere."

"Do tell," Angie said, whistling softly.

"And I remember some of the members here at the club told me that the cost of the sewer job was $4 million, not $2.6. Each member here at Shuttlecock had to pony up several thousand bucks each to cover the bill."

I could hear her pen scratching as Angela scribbled some notes.

"Well," she said. "I guess we have established a motive for someone to knock off Vitus Papageorge. One of the members must have discovered that Vitus siphoned off a cool million and a half for himself and decided to do something about it."

"Well, that's one possible interpretation," I agreed, chasing some cole slaw around my plate with my fork. "But it also means that any of the 500 or so members here is a suspect. And frankly, I'm not convinced that was the reason why Vitus was killed."

"How come?" Angela wanted to know.

"Well, if I was a member and I learned that there had been some financial shenanigans with the bookkeeping at the club, even if it made me really mad, I don't think I'd go looking for someone to kill. You know?"

"Yeah," Angela said. "You have a point."

"But what if I were a local mob boss and somehow or other a good chunk of that $1.4 million skim was supposed to come to me, and for whatever reason, it didn't?"

"You might send a leg breaker out to have a little chat with Mr. Papageorge," Angie finished.

"Exactly," I said. "And knowing what a world-class prick Vitus could be, it's not hard to imagine a scenario where a little leg-breaking job could turn into something more drastic. If he could piss me off just playing golf, imagine what he would do to some bent-nose guy named Guido."

"Well," Angela said, "Even though you are abusing the stereotype of Italian-Americans, I think I get your drift."

"Te amo," I muttered sweetly.

"Bite me," she muttered back. "Listen, I have to take Ginny here out for dinner. It's too late to file anything for tomorrow's paper anyway, so let's sleep on this and plan our next move. Call me tomorrow?"

"We're supposed to resume our golf tournament," I told her, "But I'll be in touch at some point. If I dig up any other clues, I'll let you know."

"Ain't you the crimestopper," she said, unnecessarily snide, I thought, and, chuckling softly to herself, she rang off.

I polished off the rest of my pig and went back to the buffet line for more. On the way back to the table, I caught Jack's eye and motioned that I wanted to speak to him. After a minute or two, he broke away from the bar, amid huge gales of laughter, and plunked down in the seat beside me.

"How's the grub?" he asked, reaching over and spearing a succulent chunk of roasted pig from my plate. I would have stabbed his hand with my fork except for all the years of training put in by my sainted mother.

"Outstanding," I said. "What I've just learned is even better." In between bites, I filled Jack in on the information from Angie. I could tell he was interested because he didn't attempt any further sneak attacks on my dinner.

"So that's what that little son-of-a-bitch was up to," he said. "Nice little scam. Gets his underworld contacts to submit a nice fat overbid on the cost of the new sewer project, the job is paid for by all the rich folks here at the club and he pockets a couple million."

"Yeah," I said. "And chances are he was supposed to spread the wealth around more than he did. Can't you just see Vitus arguing with some goomba that he deserved more of the take? No wonder he got strung up."

"It fits," Jackie nodded. "Or maybe they were afraid that the cover was going to get blown and decided to eliminate the witnesses."

I pushed some fried plantain around my plate.

"I wonder what role the club manager had in all this?" I mused aloud.

"Herb?" Jackie said, perking up. "Why don't we go ask him?"

"Right now?" I said.

"No time like the present," my insane partner chortled. "C'mon, Hack."

He grabbed his tumbler of bourbon, jumped up and headed out of the ballroom. I pushed my plate away, looked longingly at the key lime pie on the dessert table nearby, sighed and followed.

SIXTEEN

Down the hallway past the main dining room, a small staircase led to the second floor of the Shuttle-cock Club. Jack had told me that in the past, the club maintained a half dozen guest rooms for the use of out-of-town members or those in town who had perhaps over-celebrated and needed a bed in which to sleep it off. With all kinds of new state laws dealing with overnight accommodations, the club had pretty much abandoned this perk of membership in the 1960s. Now, the only rooms used on the second floor were for the offices of the club's manager and his assistant.

It was cold upstairs, and the air was dank and dusty. A long corridor extended off to the right, disappearing into the darkness. Harsh light spilled from a room at the top of the stairs, creating a square of brightness that illuminated the hallway's threadbare carpeting.

Jack and I walked through the empty outer office and into the manager's den beyond. Herbert Incavaglia was sitting at his crowded desk, peering through wire-rimmed bifocals at a ledger book open before him. He looked to be in his late 50s, with greying hair clinging hopefully to the sides and back of his head, having long since abandoned his shining pate. He was dressed in a dark suit, white dress shirt and conservative tie. His office was small and tidy. One wall was covered by a bank of file cabinets, another by a large cork bulletin board. His dark-stained desktop was mostly empty, except for the In/Out box on one corner and the ledger book on his blotter. An ell-extension at one end held his computer terminal and telephone. The room smelled faintly of burned coffee.

Incavaglia stood up when we walked in, closing the ledger.

"Mr. Connolly," he said, holding out his hand for Jackie to shake. "So good to see you again. Can I be of some assistance?"

Jack threw himself down in one of the two chairs that sat in front of Incavalgia's desk and put his drink down on the man's desktop. "This is my guest, Hacker," he said nodding at me. "We want to talk about Vitus Papageorge's murder this morning."

Herb Incavaglia grasped my hand. His was large and warm and hard at the edges. He looked at me for a moment, his eyes dark and narrow. I felt as though I was being sized up.

"Ah, Mister Hacker," he said. "You are a writer for one of the Boston newspapers, correct?" He raised his eyebrows and I nodded. "I had heard you were going to honor the

Shuttlecock Club with your presence this weekend. How unfortunate that these tragic events have spoiled what had been one of our most popular events. I do hope that you will be able to return next year and enjoy our Invitational tournament again."

While he was making his address, he opened a side drawer of his desk, took out a cardboard coaster and placed it neatly under Jack's glass. I sat down in the other guest chair, and Herb sat down behind his desk. He leaned back in his chair, laced his fingers together and rested them on his lap.

"How can I be of assistance?" he asked again. "And may I ask if this interview is to be considered on the record?"

"Why would you ask that?" I wondered.

Incavaglia smiled at me as if I were a child. "Please, Mr. Hacker," he said icily, "Don't be silly. Mr. Connolly here is the publisher and owner of the local newspaper and you are a journalist with a large metropolitan daily. It would be foolhardy of me not to inquire as to the ground rules for our conversation. If this is an official visit, then the club's only comment is that we are deeply shocked and saddened by the events of this morning at the Shuttlecock Club, we are cooperating fully with the police authorities, which are investigating Mr. Papageorge's death, and we will have no further comment at this time. How else can I be of assistance?"

Jack and I looked at each other. Herb had slammed a roadblock down in front of us before we got going. Jack picked up his tumbler of bourbon and threw me a wink over the rim.

"How long have you been here at Shuttlecock?" I asked Herb.

"I'm in my fifth year of service to the members," he answered.

"Bit of a change from your last job, isn't it?"

"Not at all," he said easily. "I was the comptroller for a chain of restaurants on the North Shore and I managed a gentleman's club in Boston for several years."

"Who's the easier boss to work for," I asked, "Vitus Papageorge or Carmine Spoleto? Or do you have to answer to Rene Lemere?"

Herbert Incavaglia stared at me silently. I smiled back at him. Jack smiled at him. The silence hung in the air.

"I - I don't believe I know either of the gentlemen whom you mentioned," he said.

"Can we see the records on the sewer construction project?" Jack said. "We have information that there may have been some cost overruns on that job."

Incavaglia stared across his desk at us for another long moment. I felt sized up again, and it made the hairs on the back of my neck stand up a little.

"Actually, that project was completed on time and on budget," Herbert said. "But all records and reports must be released by the chairman of the Building and Grounds Committee, Mr. Cameron Campbell. You will have to see him. I'm afraid I don't have the data in this office."

"And if I go see Jocko Campbell," Jack said, "He'll tell me that all the paperwork has been put into storage and it'll take him six months or a year for him to remember to dig it out. In the meantime, you all will hope I forget about it while you move the money you skimmed down to the Cayman Islands or Antigua."

Incavaglia rocketed forward in his chair. "I am not certain," he said, "But I believe I heard some statements that could easily be construed as libelous should they ever see print, Mr. Connolly."

I heard a sudden exhalation behind me — it sounded like a muttered "men!" — and turning, I saw Leta Papageorge walk into the office. She was dressed in jeans and a long, wooly green sweater that draped down to her thighs, her glistening blond hair pulled back in a tight ponytail, and she held in front of her a small, silver gun that glistened nastily in the harsh overhead light. She had it pointing right at Herbert Incavaglia.

"Sorry to interrupt your little sword fight, fellas," Leta said, her cheeks flushed. "But I got just one question for ole Herb here, and I don't have time for all the bullshit." She took another step closer to the desk and held the gun steady at Herb's head.

"Who whacked him, Herb?" she asked softly. "And why?"

Herbert Incavaglia turned white, and shrunk back in his chair as far as the laws of physics allowed. "Mrs. Papageorge," he said in a suddenly high-pitched, strained voice. "I assure you ..."

"Can it Herb," she snapped. "Who? And why?"

He held his arms out wide, supplicating.

"I—I don't know," he said. "Really, I don't. But it wasn't one of ours."

"That's crap, Herb," Leta began. But in arguing with him, the arm holding the gun dropped a bit, no longer aimed between the man's narrow little eyes.

I made my move and made it fast. I jumped out of my chair, gave Leta a hockey-style hip check to knock her off balance, and at the same instant, I grabbed her wrist and pushed it and the gun upwards toward the ceiling. With a sharp twist, I managed to yank the gun away, as Leta gave a tiny yelp, equal parts pain and surprise. She recovered her balance and sprang at me. I held her off with one arm and held the gun away with the other.

"Damn you!" she cried, trying to grab and hit at the same time, until she finally realized the futility and began to weep, grabbing my lapels and burying her face in my chest. I held the gun at arm's length. Jack had stayed in his chair, but gave me a nod of appreciation and reached over to take another sip – a longer and deeper draught – from his cocktail.

Herb Incavaglia's face went from pale to deep red in an instant. He started to stand up, but I swung my arm around and pointed the gun at him again.

"I don't think you've answered the lady's question yet, Herb," I said. "Who whacked Vitus and why?"

He was flabbergasted. "Wh-why, you can't do that," he stuttered. "This woman threatened my life. You witnessed it! I can have her arrested for assault and you for aiding and abetting!"

"Go ahead," I said, holding the gun steady. "Call the cops. We'll start by telling them that you said the killer, quote 'wasn't one of ours,' end quote. Which will lead them to ask what you meant, which will rip the cover off your little can o' worms here. So be my guest...pick up the phone and call. I think the number is 9-1-1."

Herb didn't move. His eyes peered at me, this time with undisguised hatred.

"This is highly unethical," he said.

"Hey, Herb. Here's a little news flash for you: Journalists aren't ethical. So answer the lady's question or I might give her the gun back."

Leta Papageorge had stopped crying all over my sport coat and was staring at Herb. He, in turn looked beseechingly at Jack, seeking some help from the only club member in the room. Jackie smiled and shrugged.

"Better start talking, Herb," he said. "My friend here is notorious for being unconventional. I can't predict what he's gonna do."

"I can't tell you anything," Incavaglia finally said. "My, ummm, business associates are as perplexed as you are. Mr. Papageorge's business relationships were in good order. We are also interested in finding out who perpetrated this crime. Everything I just said was off the record and I will deny any or all of it if it sees print."

Leta Papageorge snorted softly. While she had stopped crying, she continued to hold my coat's lapels tightly. My non-gun-holding hand had come up and wrapped itself protectively around her waist, and her body warmth floated upwards, mingling with her subtle perfume, a not unpleasant experience.

"Always covering your ass, huh Herb?" she said. She pulled away from me. "C'mon fellas. Let's get outta here."

"Wait a minute," Incavaglia protested. "You mean you're going to let this woman barge in here, threaten my life and just…leave?"

Jack and I looked at each other.

"Yes," we said in unison. Leta and Jack walked out, and I, still holding the little silver pistol, followed, backing out of the office.

Going down the stairs, I heard Jackie giggle.

"Journalists aren't ethical?" he said. "I gotta remember that one."

SEVENTEEN

W e stumbled down the stairs, past the dining room and made it as far as the foyer when Jackie suddenly pulled up, said "hang on a sec," and made a sharp right towards the ballroom. I had Leta's little pistol hidden in the palm of my hand, and I surreptitiously handed it to her. Guns make me very nervous.

"Is it loaded?" I asked.

She smiled at me as she tucked it away in her waistband, hidden beneath her oversized wooly sweater.

"Yeah," she said. "But it probably woulda just winged him. My shooting instructor said that beyond a range of about ten feet, the bullet tends to bounce off things. But if I had stuck the barrel in his ear ..."

She smiled at me again. It was not a pleasant smile.

"Maybe you should take tae-kwon-do," I suggested. "Learn how to kill someone with just two fingers, or a credit card or something."

She kept smiling her evil little smile. But her eyes were a little different.

"Oh, shit," I said, smacking my head. "You have, haven't you? Taken martial arts?"

She nodded, still smiling. "My instructor said I was one of the most dangerous women he knew," she said.

"You got a thing for instructors, don't you?" I said.

She let it hang.

Jackie came running back, carrying a new, full bottle of Jack Daniels.

"A little fortification for the road," he said.

"Where are we going?" I asked.

Jack nodded at Leta. "I think we should take the lady home. It's obviously been a rather long day for her," he said.

"I can drive myself," she said hotly. "I made it down here didn't I?"

"Don't get her mad," I told Jack. "She's rearmed and dangerous."

"Yeah, well, go ahead and shoot me if you want," Jack said laconically. "But we're taking you home. We can help get your car back tomorrow if you want. But I think it would be safer if you went with us. Besides, we can talk a little on the way."

Leta Papageorge thought that over. Then she nodded her agreement.

"Can I have some of that?" she asked, nodding at Jack's bottle of Jack Black.

"That's why I got it," he said, and led the way outside.

The late Vitus Papageorge lived in a new gated subdivision, one of a thousand like it, that had been built in the hilly country of southern New Hampshire, designed to appeal to a generation of young commuters who didn't mind making the traffic-clogged 90 minute drive down to Massachusetts and Boston in return for lots of cold fresh air, a homogenous community of other white, upper-middle class businessmen, and New Hampshire's beneficial state tax system, which is to say no taxes at all. On anything. Which compares very favorably with the Commonwealth of Massachusetts, which has a tax on everything. Of course, Massachusetts does offer some state services to its citizens, while New Hampshire's attitude is "live free and die."

Jack drove out of the club, turned left on the river road and headed north. He took the bottle of Jack from between his legs, took a pull and passed it over to me. I looked at it sadly, and passed it on to Leta, riding shotgun in the back seat of Jack's sedan. I heard her gentle gurgle.

"Aren't there open container laws in New Hampshire, too?" I wondered, sounding like a little old lady to myself.

"Only if we get caught, Hacker," Jack grinned. "And I'm absolutely the best drunk driver in New England. Never been caught yet."

"Always a first time," I said, mostly to myself.

Jack was taking the scenic route, even though the night was black and moonless. The car rumbled over the frost-roughened country roads. I rolled down my window and took a draught of the cold, fresh air. We drove through the occasional pool of light from the odd streetlamp, and the sounds of the tires were reflected back up into my window from the ancient stone walls that lined the road. We passed the occasional house, each one of which had one window reflecting the blue glow of a television inside. I thought about the first settlers who had used the strength of their own backs and the help of a team of oxen to move these boulders out of their fields, acre after slow acre, in order to grow enough food to survive another harsh New England winter. It seemed a hopeless cycle of struggle against an unyielding land.

We passed an open meadow over which a blanket of mist hung like wispy fluff. Crickets sang morosely, knowing their days were numbered. After the first hard frost would come the cricket holocaust. The road dipped suddenly, and I felt the temperature of the air drop as well. I rolled my window back up and shivered.

Leta passed the bourbon back up to me. "Looks like you could use a shot, Hacker," she said.

I turned and shot her a quick smile.

"I'm just trying to make heads or tails of this thing," I said. "We keep taking two steps forward and running into brick walls. I thought this nice little scam Vitus had cooked up over the sewer project provided the perfect motive for someone to kill him, but Herb said not."

"If you can believe Herb," Jack reminded me.

"Oh, I believe him," Leta said.

I turned again. "How did you know about it?" I asked.

She smiled her evil little smile again, her teeth flashing white in the darkness of the back seat.

"Oh, Hacker," she sighed. "You are such a nice man. Naïve, but nice. Do you have a computer?" she asked.

"Sure."

"Do you back it up every week like they recommend?"

"Well, no," I admitted. "But I know I should."

"Well," she said. "I was the back-up for Vitus. Everything he did, I knew about, and filed it away. Not documents or anything like that – I told him years ago that if he ever got caught, I would deny knowing anything and everything, take all his money and go live in the south of France. And I made sure that I wasn't personally connected to any of his deals. But at the same time, I made sure I knew everything about all of his deals. After all, it was my future at risk, too."

She reached over the seat and grabbed the bottle out of my hands.

"He knew that I would turn on him at the first inkling that something was going bad," she said, after tipping the bottle back again. "Eventually, he came to rely on me as a sounding board. He was a smart little operator, but I made him smarter. And safer."

"So you knew about the scam?" I asked.

"You mean the sewer deal? Oh, hell yes," she said. "And next was going to be the new bridge over the river, and after that, a new irrigation system, and then probably a major reconstruction of all the greens. Vitus and Herb had a whole series of improvements planned for the next five years."

"And they were going to skim off the top?"

"Yeah," she said, smiling again. "I don't think any of the other projects would have brought in as much as the first hit. But a couple hundred thousand every year or so — all hidden from taxes — doesn't hurt at all. And I heard Vitus say that Herb had been thinking about torching the clubhouse. The rebuild would have been expensive, but insurance would have paid and paid and paid."

Jack whistled softly. "How would Vitus have convinced the members to keep paying for all this?" he asked. "We lost a bunch of old members over the sewer project."

"And Vitus signed up twice as many new members at the increased membership fees to replace them," Leta answered. "There just aren't enough country clubs in the state to keep up with the demand. He was going to launch a new membership drive, mostly in Boston, which would have raised something like five million. That would have gone into the long-term capital fund to pay for the improvements.

The club would get the new stuff, it's just that Vitus and his friends would keep about one dollar out of every four for themselves. Clean, shiny, legal dollars that couldn't be traced."

"Thanks to Herb Incavaglia," I said.

"Man's a genius," Leta nodded. "Personally I always thought he was a weasel, but he knew how to move dollars around so fast that nobody could discover where they had gone."

"Was Vitus this dirty in his other businesses?" Jack wanted to know.

"My husband loved only one thing," she said, with a trace of wistfulness. "And that was getting away with as much as he could. Up here in New Hampshire, where the political parties come every four years for the presidential primary, he made a killing. See this? ..." She held out her arm to show us the glistening diamonds on her inch-thick tennis bracelet. "Came from the Clinton campaign in 1992. Vitus' bank served as their campaign finance headquarters. He charged them low rates for the banking, and a nice hefty fee for 'consulting.' We consulted before he bought it for me."

"And your marriage?" I asked. "Did he get away with as much as he could there, too?"

She laughed. "Oh, Hacker," she said. "I knew it. I had you pegged as a romantic. Look, people get married and stay married for all kinds of reasons. Some people want to settle in with a house, bunch of kids, relatives coming every holiday. I knew from the outset that Vitus wasn't interested in all that. He wanted to make money, to make people do what he wanted, and to get away with stuff. It made him feel...I don't know... alive."

"And you?"

190 DEATH AT THE MEMBER-GUEST

She took another pull on the bottle. "I guess I got away with stuff, too," she said. "I had a pretty nice life. Did what I wanted. Lived on the edge. I guess it made me feel alive, too." Her voice caught, at the end.

"You loved him, didn't you?" I asked.

She didn't answer. The car rolled through the dark countryside. I turned and looked into the back seat. Leta Papageorge was crying, silently, tears coursing down her cheeks.

EIGHTEEN

We dropped Leta Papageorge off in her driveway, like high schoolers after a dance. Vitus's imposing French chateau sat way back from the road. We passed the elaborate brick-and-wrought-iron entrance, crossed a wooden bridge over a marshy area, and wound up a hill covered with oaks and maples. A fancy outdoor lighting system had been installed, the uplights creating a dramatic leafy vista across the broad lawn. Jack stopped the car in front of Vitus' five-car garage, where several other cars had parked. Bright floodlights from the house cast a harsh pool of light onto the driveway.

"You want us to come in?" Jack asked.

Leta took a last hit from the bottle. "Nah," she said. "It's pretty grim in there. Have you ever been to a Greek wake? The men are all sitting in the living room, smoking cigars, and the women are all out in the kitchen, making stuff. They're all his people, so I'm pretty much persona non grata."

"You have no relatives?" I asked.

"Only child," Leta said. "Parents died years ago."

"I'm sorry," I said.

"Don't be," she answered. "I learned how to take care of myself a long time ago. If I don't get asphyxiated by the cigars or clog up all my arteries with the baklava, I'll survive these next few days and then figure out what to do next."

A man, dressed in somber black, had come out of the house and was standing on the front walk, peering at our car. Leta got out of the backseat and waved at him. The man turned and walked back inside.

"See?" she said, as Jack rolled down his window. "I have this strange desire to go in there, turn on the CD player with some Rolling Stones greatest hits and dance around. But they would all just keel over dead if I did."

Jack and I laughed at the image of the blond Leta boogeying around a half dozen black-suited Greeks, mouths agape, cigars sending swirls of blue smoke into the air.

Leta smiled at us and turned to go inside. After a few steps, she stopped, turned and came back to the car.

"You guys realize that Herb is gonna call somebody, right?" she said. "He's just a finance guy, not a muscle guy, but he knows the people who hire the muscle guys. You might want to think about that before you do something stupid."

"Yeah, I figured," Jackie said.

"I didn't," I said. "Can I borrow your little six-shooter?"

Leta laughed, but not in a mean way. "Naw," she said. "You might get hurt worse."

"Worse than what?" I wanted to know.

She smiled enigmatically at me and walked away.

When she was inside, Jack turned around in the driveway that was big enough for an 18-wheeler, and drove away. We rode in silence through the black night for a while, thinking about what Leta had said.

"So," I said. "Do we have a plan?"

"A plan?" Jack echoed.

"Yeah. You know…what we're gonna do next. What we're gonna do if Herb's leg-breakers come calling. What we're gonna do if they actually break something. When we're gonna call Detective Tierney and ask for police protection and the witness protection program? That kind of plan."

Jack laughed. I guess it was my gallows humor. "Don't get hysterical on me, Hack," he said. "We've just yanked on a piece of string. Whatever happens next depends on who, or what, is tied to the other end."

"And you don't care if the other end is attached to Guido with a baseball bat and an unhappy disposition?"

"Che sera sera," Jack said.

"Swell," I said.

He laughed. "Actually, Hack, this is one of those rare times when our profession serves us well."

"The other is the buffet lunch at the U.S. Open, right?" I said.

"Perhaps," Jack laughed. "But the way I figure, no one is going to bust our legs or throw us into the river. I am, after all, the all-knowing, all-seeing, and all-powerful publisher of the Lowell *Citizen*. And you, after all, write about golf for a major Boston paper." He paused.

"On second thought," he said, "Your ass may be grass."

I laughed. "I get your point, you shithead," I said. "The mob isn't going to waste us because that would rain down upon them lots of unwanted attention."

"A veritable cloudburst," Jack nodded.

"So what are they going to do?"

"Probably try to scare us a little," Jack said. "I know Rene Lemere, and he's not a big-time criminal. He isn't going to rock his boat by throwing us over the side. But he may want to talk tough to us and let us know he's very displeased."

"And what do we do?" I wondered.

"Play dumb and find out what he knows," Jack answered.

"And when does all this take place, O great knower of everything?"

Jack smiled at me. "Probably when we least expect it," he said.

We rode in silence into the city, the dark river silent beside us. We rumbled over the metal grating of one of the bridges, cut down a few empty city streets and finally pulled into Jack's semi-hidden riverside estate. The house was quiet inside. I waited in the living room while Jack went and checked his messages. He was soon back. "Nothing," he said. We agreed to rise early and head for the club for the final day's tournament rounds.

"Sleep tight," he said.

"Yeah, right," I answered.

And it was a long night of tossing and turning. Every breath of wind, every creaking of a tree or rustling of a leaf, every barking dog or rumble of tires on the road outside caused me to bolt upright in bed. About 3:30, I gave up and turned on the light to read. Sometime shortly thereafter, I fell asleep, the lights still on, the book on my chest. It must have worked, for the boogeyman didn't come.

NINETEEN

J ack woke me at seven. I felt around the bedsheets care fully, checking for horse's heads. Nothing. I breathed a sigh of relief.

"I called the pro shop," he said. "We're not scheduled to tee off until 10:30."

"How is this gonna work?" I asked, yawning. "We gotta play five nine-hole matches in one day?"

"Naw," Jack said. "Teddy said everybody will just play two matches today, and any flights that are tied will have a sudden death playoff. Or flip a coin."

"So if we still have three hours, I can go back to sleep," I said hopefully.

"You could," he said. "But I think we should go have a big breakfast. Get carbo-loaded for the day. I know a diner not far from here that makes the best Bloody Marys. They don't have a liquor license, of course, but that's why they're so good."

"You should have been a moonshiner," I said. "You have the right attitude for it."

"I knew a lot of those guys back at Wake Forest," Jack laughed. "Salt of the earth fellows. Really fine people."

I groaned, but I hoisted myself out of bed and into the shower. Half an hour later, Jack and I were tooling north away from the river. I scanned the front page of the Lowell *Sunday Citizen*, filled with the lurid story of the country club president murdered in the cart barn. Police were said to be following several "promising leads" in the case. There was a sidebar under a nice black-and-white photo of Vitus, dressed in his banker's pinstriped suit, which painted a portrait of a powerful local pooh-bah, cut down tragically in his prime. Nothing about Papageorge's former trouble with the federal banking authorities, nor, of course, anything about his scam with the sewer lines. Just a long list of his business accomplishments, his club memberships, his donations to the Boys Club, along with some nice quotes from the governor and junior senator from New Hampshire.

"Nice reporting job," I said, as Jackie drove down a bumpy country road. "Makes Vitus sound like the second coming of Andrew Carnegie."

"Yeah, well, you don't want to publish the guy's warts in his obit," Jack said. "Save that for the blockbuster scoop to follow in a couple days."

"We're gonna rip the cover off?" I asked, smiling.

"Indubitably," he grinned back.

We finally pulled into the parking lot in front of a small, cinder-block shack tucked underneath two large maple trees on a mostly deserted state highway. Which state and which highway, I had no idea: Jackie had taken a shortcut through some neighborhoods, behind a strip center and around a sparkling lake. A small sign in a darkened front window announced that we had arrived at Bob's Eats. There were four other cars parked outside and a dusty yellow retriever lying across the threshold. He wagged his tail feebly a couple times as we stepped over him to go inside.

Bob was inside, manning the grill behind a long plywood counter. There were two plastic-covered tables crammed beneath a small, dirty window down at the far end, but the five other customers were draped on stools at the counter. Bob was a large man, with an even larger beer belly that protruded dangerously towards the hot grill. He wore a tiny little paper hat that was scrunched down into his greasy silver wisps of hair, had a cigar stuck behind one ear, unlit as far as I could tell, wielded a shiny stainless spatula in each hand and wore a white tee shirt, blue jeans and a mottled apron cinched tightly beneath his breasts. I believe the fashionistas call it the Empire line. He turned to give us a cursory glance, nodded at Jackie and turned back to his grill with a flourish of spatulas. He had an order of scrambled, two fried eggs, three blueberry pancakes, a rasher of bacon, a line of sausage links and half a grill of homefries going all at once.

I pulled up a stool to watch Bob's ballet. Jackie walked down to the end of the counter and poured two mugs of hot coffee. Bob deftly plated some eggs, scooped out a healthy order of potatoes, flipped the bacon up and on, and dusted the lot with a cloud of salt and red pepper. Turning, he put the plate on the shiny countertop, pointed at a fellow three stools down and slid the breakfast down. The fellow caught the plate, picked up his fork and looked happy.

Bob nodded in approval. He turned to look at Jackie. "The usual?" he grunted. "And who's your pal?"

"The usual," Jackie nodded. "And a couple Sunday specials, too. Hacker? Bob. Makes the best goddam breakfast in America. Tell him what you want."

I was ready. In fact, I was beginning to drool. "I'll have the pancakes, bacon and homefries," I said. Bob nodded his approval again. I'll bet he didn't nod if someone came in and asked for wheat toast without the crusts. Or an egg white omelet, no cheese, peppers on the side. Not at Bob's.

I saw a copy of my newspaper on the table under the window and went to get it. Back at the counter, while Bob went into his dervish dance at the grill, I sipped the hot, rich coffee and scanned Angela Murphy's take on Vitus' murder. The *Journal* had made the story the page 3 lead, and Angie had ended up with only about fifteen graphs. Someone had found a file photo of Vitus and Leta, dressed to the nines, at some Boston charitable ball. He looked grumpy, she looked divine. Angie mentioned Vitus' brush with the federal banking regulators, his close political friends, and his reputation for hard-nosed business practices. Good girl! I thought. I also silently thanked her for keeping my name out of the story. The piece ended with the usual police statements of promising leads, autopsy report to follow by Monday, nothing further to say at this time. In other words, Lt. Tierney had no earthly idea who had strangled Vitus Papageorge.

Bob served up someone else's order and slipped out into the back room. He came back a minute later with two tall paper cups filled with a mysterious red liquid, in which was jammed a talk celery stalk. He put them down in front of us.

Jack exhaled a long sigh of anticipation and relief. "Bob, my man," he said, "If you weren't so goddam ugly I think I'd kiss you on the lips."

Bob raised one eyebrow. "Mazeltov," he grunted.

My cellphone buzzed at me from my pocket. I flipped it open.

"Yo, Hacker," I said.

"Yo yourself!" said a nice female voice. "Hacker! I'm just sitting here reading the morning paper and read about this guy getting murdered right where you are! My God! Were you there? Are you OK?"

I smiled. "Hi Mary Jane," I said. "I'm fine. Yes, I was there. I'll tell you all about it when I get home tonight."

"Are you still playing golf?" she trilled, still excited. "I mean, this guy was killed! Dead! Ewwww, how icky it must be!"

"It's OK, " I said. "They took him away and everything. No muss, no fuss. They're gonna try and have everyone play today and then kinda flip a coin to decide who wins."

"My God," she said. "Listen, would you like to come over for dinner with Victoria and me? When will you be getting back to the city? I can bake a chicken or something. You can tell me all about it."

I laughed. "Great," I said. "Love to. I should be back around seven. Is that too late for Vic?"

"Nah," Mary Jane said. "I'll feed her early and get her into bed. OK, we'll look for you around sevenish. Listen, Hacker? Be careful, will you?"

"It's OK, really," said. "I'm more in danger of getting bonked with a golf ball or tripping over a bunker rake. I'll call you later. Is there anything I can bring?"

"Just your own sweet self," she said. "Bye."

I flipped my phone shut, still smiling. Jackie was looking at me with a smirk. "Hacker's got a girl friend," he sing-songed in his best sixth grade voice.

I laughed. "Just my downstairs neighbor," I said. "Nice lady, but not my girlfriend."

Jack was nodding sagely. "Son," he said, "If you could see the look on your face right now ..."

I was saved from having to defend my bachelorhood by the arrival of two sliding plates. Jackie's platter of eggs, bacon and sausage, toast and homefries went zipping past. I held out my hand to stop my own heaping plate of breakfast. Neither one of us spoke for the next fifteen minutes.

"Whew," Jackie said, pushing his empty plate away. "You ready to go golf your lungs out?"

Bob did a pirouette at the grill, grabbed both our plates, and swiftly deposited them with a clatter in the empty bin on his side of the counter. He was back flipping hot cakes and spatulating potatoes in a wink. The man was an ergonomic genius.

"I'm ready to go sleep for about four hours, roll over and sleep for three more," I said.

"Excellent," Jack said, pounding me on the back. "I read somewhere that you play your best golf when you're relaxed."

"How about catatonic?" I said.

Jack laughed and polished off the last of his Bloody Mary, smacking his lips. "Let's go get 'em!" he said, throwing down some bills on the counter. I groaned and followed him out to the car.

As we headed to the Shuttlecock Club, following another maze of bumpy macadam roads through the countryside, my phone buzzed at me again. I sighed and answered.

"Hacker," a voice rasped out at me unpleasantly. "Where the hell are you?" It was Frankie Donatello, my boss. I gulped.

"Ummm, where do you think I am?" I hedged.

"Well, I've got a stack of stories on my desk here that are datelined Endicott, New York," he said. "But they don't have your style."

"I have a style?" I said. "Aww, Frankie, that's the sweetest thing you've ever said to me."

"Shuddup," he growled. "What gives?"

"Frankie," I said, "Remember that j-school kid you saddled with me? I thought I'd let him see what a PGA tournament is all about. Gave him a chance to do some reporting. That's probably why some of the pieces read a bit different."

"You took the kid with you to New York?" Frankie said, sounding incredulous. "You ain't turned gay on me, have ya?"

"Frank, that's politically incorrect," I said, managing to pirouette around his question. "I have merely overseen the kid's work." Which was, of course, true.

"Yeah," Frank grumped. "And while the kid worked, you've probably been goofing off, playing golf or drinking yourself into oblivion. Nice scam, Hacker ..." He was starting to get worked up and ready to launch into one of his standard employers speech about responsibility and dedication to the company.

"Frank," I said sharply, "You're the one who made me do this. Don't start complaining to me about spending time with the kid. I didn't want to do it in the first place."

He was silent, fuming. "Fine," he said finally. "I want you back in this office tomorrow morning at 8 a.m. I've got a backlog of stories to do for the special high school gridiron special next Saturday. So cancel your dinner plans and be prepared to actually do some work for a change."

He slammed down his phone before I could compose a suitably smartass answer. But I was still grinning as I flipped my phone shut.

"Dodged a bullet there," I told Jackie, laughing. "Good thing the boss is a dumb as a brick."

Jack nodded. "My theory is that every newspaper has one or two solid people who make the thing happen," he said. "And it's never the guy at the top ."

"That mean you're expendable?" I chided.

"Oh hell yes," he said, laughing. "Anybody can smooze with advertisers and sell space. That just takes an iron stomach, creative lying, the ability to be constantly insulted without taking it personally and some degree of persistence. Not exactly brain surgery. Good writing and good editing…those are hard to find. Hard to do."

"Nah," I said. "It's really not that tough. Just gotta ask a lot of questions and then put the important stuff you find out at the top. Piece of cake."

"So," Jack said, glancing over at me. "Have we found any important stuff in the case of the Dead President? Or haven't we asked the right questions yet?"

"Well," I said, "What do we know?"

"Vitus is one dead s.o.b.," Jackie said.

"Correct."

"Someone killed his ass."

"Correct again. You're on a roll, pards."

"Wasn't you or me."

"Well, I know for certain it wasn't me," I said. "But I'll take your word for it that you didn't do it."

"We have determined that Vitus was involved in some financial shenanigans involving skimming some cash out of the Shuttlecock Club, aided and abetted by the general manager, who just happens to be connected to the Mob."

"I would say that those are all facts," I nodded.

"Can we therefore deduce that Vitus was done in by someone from the Mob who perhaps was unhappy with something Vitus did, or didn't do in that said scam?"

"We can suspect that," I said, "But I don't think we can say with certainty that's what went down. We do not have confirmation, just a lot of hearsay."

"Some of that hearsay came from the guy's wife, for Chrissakes," Jackie protested.

"Who might have been trying to cover her own ass, or throw us a false scent," I said. "I think there's a lot we don't know about Leta. Remember, I saw her smooching with someone in the dark. We don't know who."

"So you think the murderer could have been someone else at the club?"

"Could have," I said. "Maybe someone got wind of the skim job Vitus pulled and wanted revenge. Maybe someone just didn't like the bastard. Maybe someone was nursing a long grudge."

"That's a lot of maybes," Jack said, frowning. "I thought we were ready to arrest someone."

"Here's another maybe: maybe it was someone totally unrelated to the Shuttlecock Club. An old business partner or someone Vitus had screwed over in some deal. After all, even though it was early in the morning, there were cars driving in and out of the club that morning. Someone could have strung Vitus up and vamoosed before I found the body."

"Vamoosed," Jack echoed. "Great verb."

"From the Latin, vamoosa," I said, straight-faced. "Meaning to scram or otherwise make like a tree and leaf."

I think Jack wanted to pull over and beat me severely about the head and shoulders, but we had arrived at the club, so he pulled into the driveway.

TWENTY

The clubhouse was buzzing with activity. Play had begun early, but many of the golfers scheduled for later tee times had already arrived, and were sitting around discussing the previous day's events. A flustered waitress was trying to deliver plates of bacon and eggs to the crowded tables, while two bartenders were passing out Bloody Marys, screwdrivers and beer as fast as they could.

We found out that our tee time would probably be later than scheduled, as the course had backed up. The last day of play in a tournament is always slower since everyone takes their time over every shot and especially over putts, which could be the difference between victory and defeat. And with the tournament telescoped from three days into two, strokes were even more valuable. We had about 90 minutes to kill.

Jack and I went upstairs, and he unpacked our Brothers outfits for the day: jet black from head to toe, with black straw cowboy hats and even black golf gloves.

"Where did you find these?" I asked in wonder, fingering the brand new glove.

"Special ordered 'em from Titleist," he said. "Got a buddy down there. I wanted the full Gary Player look for today. Black power, babee."

"Right on," I said, giving him the upraised fist salute. "Hope the clothes help you keep the ball in the fairway."

"It's all attitude, Hack," he said. "Besides, I plan on riding your broad back all day anyway! I'm going to shit, shower and start drinking. How about you?"

"I'll just go hit some balls," I said. "Might work better than the black duds."

"Doubt it," he said, disappearing into the lavatory. "But help yourself."

I decided to stop off and see how Teddy MacDaggert was holding up. One of his shop assistants was holding down the fort in the crowded pro shop, but nodded his head towards Ted's private back office when I asked where the pro was. I ducked behind the sales counter and walked down a creaky hallway to find him.

McDaggert was on the telephone when I walked into his tiny warren, so I hovered in the doorway. His office came straight from central casting: country-club golf professional. His desk was covered in papers, brochures for golf equipment, catalogs from John Deere, and stacks of scorecards bound with rubber bands. The walls were completely covered by calendars from golf companies, postcards from traveling members, memoranda from the Shuttlecock business office, and a few framed photographs of Ted posing with various golfing celebrities. Leaning against the wall beside Ted's desk were three sets of irons, bound with twine and work-ordered for new grips. Three new putters, still in their polystyrene wrapping, lay across the beat-up old director's chair in front of his desk. It was all chaos, barely controlled.

As I stood there, I noticed Ted's face reddening slightly, and he turned away as if to make it harder for me to hear what he had to say, even though I was standing perhaps three feet from him in the doorway. I would have retreated, since he obviously wanted privacy, but he held up his hand for me to stay, and wound up his call.

"Well, OK," he said. "Just wanted to make sure you were OK and everything. If there's anything I can do …" His voice trailed off and he listened. "Well, I understand, but this is not a time to try and go it alone," he said. "Please, call me." He nodded. "Right. OK. Bye then."

He hung up and managed a half grin at me. "C'mon in, Hacker," he said, waving in the general direction of his guest chair. "That was Leta Papageorge. God, what a horrible thing to happen." He ran his hands through his fritzy hair and stared off into the distance, which ended abruptly at the wall 10 feet in front of his face.

"Nice of you to offer a shoulder to cry on," I said. He snapped back from wherever he had gone momentarily, looked at me, colored again, and blew out his breath.

"Hell, Hacker," he said. "Have you ever fallen hard for a woman? Even though you're not supposed to?" His look was a combination of hangdog, self-pity and pride to admit to a fellow member of the male tribe that he had, in some way, made a conquest.

Aha, I thought. The mystery kisser.

"Get out of here!" I gushed, trying to keep him talking. "You and Leta….?"

He nodded, smiling a little. "Yeah, she came in at the start of the summer and signed up for golf lessons," he said. "Vitus said he wanted her to be able to play in the mixed events with him and win. Typical Vitus—never mind having fun or wanting to play for herself. It was all about him, and he ordered her to learn the game and fast. She came in two or three mornings a week. I tried to make it fun, especially since it wasn't her idea in the first place. I think she liked that—not being serious. Everything about Vitus was always so goddam serious."

I kept silent, letting him vent.

"About a month ago, she gave me a little kiss at the end of the lesson. Just a little thank-you peck. But it was on the lips." Ted sighed, deeply from his soul. "I couldn't sleep the next couple of nights, thinking about that kiss, trying to decide what it meant. Hell, Hacker, I played on the Tour for a year, been around women who flirt. I'm not some 15 year-old kid who's never been kissed, y'know?"

"You ever been married, Ted?" I asked.

He nodded. "Yeah. Divorced about ten years ago. She didn't like New England much. Or the hours I have to spend here. Or me, if you get right down to it. She lives down in Virginia with the kids. Only get to see them every other Christmas, mostly."

He sighed. "Anyway, the next time she came in, I kept it light. She wanted to know how to move her hips in the swing. I showed her. Had to stand close, touch her body. Her perfume was nice. She was nice. One thing led to another, and she was kissing me again. Nothing light this time."

"Wow," I said. "You lucky duck. But didn't she have something of a reputation around here?"

"Yeah," Ted said. "I'd heard all the gossip. But when she's kissing you, you feel like the only male animal left in the world, y'know?"

I didn't know, but I nodded sagely. "So how far has it gone?" I asked as gently as I could.

He smiled at me, ruefully this time. "Not as far as I want, that's for damn sure," he said. "I've begged her to meet me somewhere away from the club, dinner, or lunch, or... But she says she couldn't ever get away. Said Vitus kept her on a short leash. It's been driving me crazy, I don't mind telling you."

"And Vitus?" I asked. "You think he ever knew?"

Ted McDaggert shook his head. "Naw," he said. "'Cause if he did, my ass would be outta here in a second. I've known Vitus Papageorge for years. He backed me on Tour. Hell, I'm still paying him off. I call it the never-ending debt." He sighed. "He was one ornery, cold-hearted son-of-a-bitch, and even though I've worked for him for a dozen years, he would have cut my heart out and eaten it in front of me."

"So what happens now?" I asked.

"Damn if I know," Teddy said, staring off into space again. "Doesn't want me to come over. She says once all this dies down a little, we'll talk. That doesn't sound like she's planning to spend the rest of her life with me, does it?" He looked at me, eyes haunted and hurting.

"From what little I know of her," I said slowly, "She seems like someone who takes care of herself first. Maybe it's a good time to take a step back and regroup."

He nodded, but he was off in that distant place again. Where unconquerable women submit, one's fantasies become real, and everyone lives happily ever after. Which is why they call it Never-Never Land.

TWENTY-ONE

I found my partner upstairs in the deserted lounge. With no one to play cards with, he was scanning the Sunday newspaper. He did have a half-empty Bloody Mary at his side, however, decorated forlornly with a stalk of wilted celery. He peered at me over the top of the paper when I walked in.

"How ya hitting them, Hack?" he asked. "Long and straight, I hope."

"Have you ever thought about warming up a little before a match?" I asked.

He put his newspaper down. "Pards," he said, "I figure I have about six, maybe ten, good shots in me per round. The last damn thing I'm gonna do is waste any of them up there on that hill, on a yellow ball with stripes. I know how to hit a golf ball…it's just up the golfing gods as to when and where the good ones come. And this, my friend…" he raised his tall Bloody Mary, " … is the sacrament I use to let the gods know I know what the game is. So, again I ask…how ya hitting them?"

"Never got there," I said. "I was doing a little reconnoitering and happened across some juicy stuff."

"Do tell," Jack said, putting his paper down.

I told him what I had learned. McDaggert probably didn't even realize, in his lovelorn state of mind, that he had catapulted himself into Prime Suspect No. 1. His torrid little affair with Leta Papageorge, which was not getting consummated all summer long, gave him an excellent motive for knocking off his boss, Vitus. Get the husband out of the way, and Leta could be his.

"But Teddy doesn't really seem like the violent type," Jack said, frowning.

"Most killers don't," I said. "Besides, he mentioned that he still owed Vitus money for backing him on Tour a decade or so ago, and he made it sound like the debt load wasn't getting any lighter. I think Vitus owned the guy. That adds another layer of motive into the equation. Maybe Vitus was calling in his note, putting the pressure on. Ted says he has two kids from a former marriage. That probably means child support, college educations and other costs. You and I both know golf professionals at country clubs do not make tons of money. It all starts to add up. Leta, money, Vitus' sparkling personality. Maybe he decides that life would be easier on a lot of levels if Papageorge shuffled off his mortal coil."

"You build a strong case, counselor," Jack said. "But it's all circumstantial. No smoking gun."

"He strangled the guy, for Chrissakes," I pointed out.

"Oh, yeah. Point taken."

"One more thing that's been eating at me," I said. "You told Tierney that Ted picked up the phone and called the cops when the cart kid came running in from the barn. But I remember that he came out to the barn, saw the body, and then went running off."

"Right," Jack nodded.

"So which was it? I think the natural reaction if a kid comes running in and says there's a body in the cart barn is to hightail it out there and see for yourself. Maybe the kid is mistaken. Maybe someone is pulling a bad joke. But you want to make sure. But if you *know* there's a body in the cart barn, because you were the one who did the deed there, then you play along, gasp in surprise and shock, call the cops and then go out to see for yourself."

"Elementary, my dear Hacker," Jack said drolly. "But unfortunately, still circumstantial. Maybe Teddy knew the cart kid was straight up, and if the kid said there's a body in the barn, then he knew he should call."

"Maybe only counts in horseshoes," I said.

Jack looked at me. I looked at him. Then we both started to laugh.

"Holy crap," I chuckled. "Agatha Christie would be pissing herself listening to us."

Jack was wheezing with laughter. "Inspector Clouseau!" he gasped.

We eventually calmed down.

"Still," Jack said. "You have uncovered what appears to be an interesting and perhaps important piece of the puzzle. I think we should go play some golf and think about it later."

"Capital idea, Holmes," I said in my best clipped British accent. "And if the Hound of the Golden Slipper happens to bite your ass on the back nine, don't say you were not forewarned."

"Indubitably, my good man."

We left the clubhouse arm in arm, which, along with our all-black getup, was duly noted by our fellow competitors with assorted hoots, hollers and homophobic comments.

On the first tee, we met our opponents. Bill, the member, was a mustachioed dentist and his guest was a young guy named Stanley, who wore a multihued baseball cap and wraparound dark glasses secured to his person by a bright pink strap that hung part way down his back. I decided to call him The Dude. We all shook hands, chatted, compared scorecards to get the stroke situation cleared, and teed off.

Jack and I must have been thinking about Ted McDaggert, his love life and finances, because we quickly lost the first two holes. Jackie quacked his drive off the first tee, the ball diving hard left through the screen of oaks and plunking into the dark river beyond. I buried my tee ball in the high-lipped bunker Mr. Ross had thoughtfully placed in the landing area of the right rough, just across the driveway. Three chops later, we conceded.

On the second, Jack hacked his way through the thickest rough on the golf course, while I nailed my drive forty yards off-line to the right and deep into the shady woods. I managed to get my second shot back onto the golf course, but then The Dude nailed a five-iron approach to near kick-in range. I got my ball on the green, but Stanley calmly sank his birdie putt to win the hole. He let out an excited, whooping yell, exchanged high-fives with his partner, and strode off towards the third green with the same swagger Jack Nicklaus used to have at Augusta.

My partner and I rendezvoused at the golf cart.

"I hate it when they yell like that," Jack said, cleaning the stains off his well-hacked ball.

"I'm getting kinda pissed myself," I said.

"What say we begin the general butt-kicking?" he suggested.

"I'd say it's about time," I answered.

"We bad," he said.

"We mad," I said.

"The Brothers!"

Our Palmer-like charge took a while to get rolling. We managed to stop the bleeding by halving the third. On the par-three fourth, across the river, Jack laid a little nine-iron within two feet of the cup and dropped the putt to win the hole. Neither of us whooped or yelled. On the par-five fifth, I made a nice birdie after nailing a three-wood approach to the edge of the green. But Bill, with a stroke in hand, managed a par five to tie. Still down one with four to play.

I made another birdie on the sixth, but the Dude tied me with his four-net-three. On the long seventh, I tried to cut the corner with my tee shot, but was stuck behind the trees and had to pitch sideways. I eventually carded a par five, but everyone else had strokes. Luckily, my partner also made a five to halve the hole with The Dude. One down, two to go.

The eighth is a long and tough par four, dogleg left and the green perched way above the fairway up a long hill. I tried to draw a three-wood around the corner, but got under it just a hair and the ball didn't carry all the way down to the flat area. My partner blocked one right and short, ending up in the rough. The tooth jockey hit a rope down the left side, dangerously close to the out-of-bounds stakes along the road, and his partner sliced a banana ball off to the right where we heard it knocking around in the pines.

"This bodes well," Jack said as we rode after our shots.

"Forsooth," quoth I. "Fortune is merry and in this mood will give us anything."

"Huh?"

"I don't guess Shakespeare translates well in golf," I said.

"Will you please shut up and play golf?" my partner griped. I guess the pressure was getting to him.

As it turned out, fortune wasn't as merry as we hoped. Both our opponents were able to chop their balls back onto the fairway, in good position on the flat part of the fairway, perhaps 100 yards below the hilltop green. Jackie whacked his ball out of the rough, and it scooted up the hill and dribbled into a bunker left of the green.

I had the dreaded hanging lie. My ball had somehow managed to stop on a steep downhill section. The ball lay below my feet and on an uncomfortable angle. I knew the shot was likely to shoot off to the right, but I had to guard against overcompensating to the left, because of the road, trees and out-of-bounds waiting on that side. And with bunkers on both sides, the entrance to the green, some 175 yards away at the top of the hill, looked as narrow as a rich man's gateway into heaven.

On the downhill angle, it was difficult to make a balanced swing, much less get the clubface moving on anything resembling a square path. I made as easy a swing as I could, trying not to rush and just make good contact, and the ball took off with a reassuring sound. But the hill-imparted sidespin soon took over, and the ball began drifting slowly and inexorably to the right.

"Hold on, honey!" I yelled at it. "Get on the ground!"

Fortune laughed. The ball plunked into the bunker on the right.

With both of us in trouble, our opponents had new life. I watched as they talked over their next shots: easy uphill pitches to a large open green. Bill went first and hit his a little thin: it flew up the hill and landed in the middle of the green, running to the back edge. He would have a long, bending and very fast downhill putt. Stan the man hit next, and, guarding against doing the same thing, chunked his just a tad. His ball thunked down on the front edge of the green, hopped forward once and then rolled backwards, stopping in the frog hair on the collar. He had about 30 feet to the hole, but his was an uphill putt, unlike his partner's.

We rode up to the green and parked on the left, next to the bunker where Jackie's ball lay. He had a good lie, but the green sloped steeply away from him.

"Just pooch her out and let it run down to the hole," I said.

"Right," he nodded, his face taut with determination, and he climbed down into the bunker.

His pooch turned out to be a Rottweiler. Jackie got all ball and no sand, and the ball rocketed high over the green, through a stand of small bushes, past an ancient stone wall, and disappeared into the darkness of the forest primeval. He held his pose, club over the left shoulder, and watched his disaster. Then, still in the classic finish position, he began to curse in soft, quiet strings of obscenities. Things related to both men's and women's bodily parts and excretion functions, both alone and in combinations, both possible and beyond the imagination of the most feverish pornographer. Somewhere, a monsignor shuddered and crossed himself. Somewhere a puppy died. In a perverse yet creative way, it was quite an amazing elocution.

He finally slowed down and stopped, but not before the three of us, standing there on the edge of the green, were teary with laughter. He dropped his pose, looked up at us and flashed the famous Connolly grin.

"That's my horse," I said wearily. "Clutch player of the year."

I walked around to the far bunker to find my ball. Lady Fortune was having a high ole time with us, the bitch. My shot had landed on a slight upsweep in the bunker and plugged. It was a classic ham-and-egg lie, the ball nestled deeply into a perfect halo of sand created by the incoming missile of the ball. Instead of being able to toss the ball out lightly on a perfect, soft cloud of sand, I would have to dig it out. That meant any control of what happened to the ball once it got on the green was lost: it could run for days, or stop short. I figured it would run. And not only was my lie impossible, but I had to get the ball in the air quickly to get it over the high lip in front of me. With both my opponents looking at a possible two-putt for five-net-four, I really needed to get up and down to halve the hole. Or else our goose was cooked.

I took a deep breath and a moment to compose myself. Despite all the possible disasters this shot presented, I knew this was not a particularly difficult shot to pull off. Most amateurs get tense and excited in the sand, tighten up and flail away wildly. Getting out of the sand is really pretty easy, as long as you slow it down and make a smooth, relaxed swing.

I pictured the shot I wanted to make, picked out a target on the green where I wanted the ball to land, dug my feet in, made my arms relax, and put an easy swing on it. The result was not too bad, considering. Ball and sand flew up in the air. The ball popped up high in the air, came down pretty close to my target spot and ran towards the hole. As I had feared, there was no backspin, so the ball kept rolling, just missing the cup and continuing on for about twelve feet. I was left with a slightly uphill putt with some sideways break. Tough, but not impossible.

Now it was their turn. The dentist, putting down the hill from the back of the green, made a gentle stroke, but once the ball got rolling down that hill, it refused to stop. It zoomed past the cup and kept going and going, finally dribbling to rest nearly fifteen feet past the hole.

"Shit," he said helplessly. "I just breathed on that one."

"I don't think you could get it any closer from up there," I told him, consolingly.

He marked his ball and went over to help The Dude read his uphill attempt. Thirty feet. Break to the right. Again, Stanley seemed to have been influenced by his partner's strong putt. His putt died quickly going up the hill and stopped six feet short. Knee-knocker time.

Bill was away, and took some time looking at his putt, but his fifteen-footer never was on line and skittered past. Six-net-five. We were still alive. I was next. I studied my putt. The amount of break was determined by the speed: if I hit it firmly, it was just an outside left edge read. But if I tried to die the ball into the hole, I'd have to borrow about eighteen inches. I figured what the hell, no sense pussyfooting around with it. I decided to take the break out and just hammer the thing home. That's what Tiger would do, I told myself.

I learned a long time ago that successful putting is all about trusting your reads and just letting go. Internal urgings to do this or don't do that will kill you every time. The secret is to pick the line, make sure the putter head goes back and forth along that line and hit the putt with the inner certitude that it's going to go in the hole. It doesn't always go in, of course, but it does more often than not when you can trust and let go.

So I finally stepped up to the ball, aimed along the left edge and let her rip. At first, I thought I had powered it way too hard: the ball zipped along the grass up the slight incline, and didn't begin to curl a little right until it was maybe two feet from the hole. I began to see it in almost slow motion at that point, even though in real time, the ball was humming along. But I saw it bend slightly to the right, in line with the left edge I had been aiming for. Ball and hole came together in those last few nanoseconds, and just before it slipped past, the ball moved oh-so-slightly to the right again, enough to catch just a piece of the hole and drop in with a definitive rattle.

"Jeezus," the Dude said with awe in his voice. "What a great goddam putt. You rotten rat bastard."

I smiled and thanked him, and pulled my ball out of the hole. I looked over at my partner, who nodded at me with approval. No histrionics. Not for The Brothers. The Golf Assassins.

Stanley still had his knee-knocking six-footer left to tie me, but I suddenly knew he was toast. I would have bet my mortgage – if I had one – that he couldn't put his ball in on top of mine. The pressure, the psychology of the moment, the sudden need to deliver ... altogether too much for his brain to handle. Besides, an old golf pro I knew said you can never putt well wearing dark glasses. The old pro was right, and so was I. Stanley's attempt was wide right by three inches.

We were all square heading to the last.

The par-three ninth is a great hole for deciding a close match. It was playing right at 190 yards today, with a slight breeze against. From the elevated tee, the green looked miles away and impossible to hit, perched atop the far hill and surrounded by sand, trees and that imposing false front that dropped down into the purgatory below.

We had the honor. Jack took out his five-wood and pushed it into one of the bunkers to the right of the green. He slammed his club down hard in frustration.

"That's OK, pard," I reassured him. "You got that shot."

He laughed.

I took my three-iron and cut it in from left to right. The pin was back left but my goal was to get it somewhere –anywhere—on the green. Mission accomplished, my ball landed in the middle and stuck, about forty feet to the hole. I figured a three would be tough to beat.

Our opponents weren't giving up. Both of them hit good shots. The dentist knocked a three-wood all the way to the back of the green, and his partner fetched up hole high, but on the left edge. Neither could be called a legitimate birdie attempt, but either one should be able to get down in two for par. And there was always the chance of a lucky putt falling in from long distance. Fortune can be both merry and spiteful when she wants.

On the green, the three of us marked and waited for Jackie to come out of the bunker. He entered looking glum, remembering his disastrous swing on the last hole. He stood in the bunker for a moment, swishing his sand wedge back and forth and looking at his shot.

"How close do you want it, pards?" he called to me.

"Anyplace in bounds would be nice," I replied.

Give him credit, he had his skull swing grooved. Once again, his fierce downward blow caught all ball and with a terrifying click the ball shot out of the bunker and rocketed across the green at about knee height. I felt myself flinch when I heard the thin connection and registered the blur of the white missile. My brain had but a split second to realize that his ball was heading, once again at warp speed, for the deepest of the woods.

But somehow, some way, on its path to oblivion, Jack's ball ran smack into the center of the yellow flagstick sticking out of the hole. There are probably about 76 things that could have happened once the relentless speed of the ball came into contact with the immovable force of the metal stick. The ball could have ricocheted off in almost any direction. Instead, the ball hit the flagstick with a resounding clang absolutely dead center, about halfway up, and dropped like the dead straight down and into the hole. Slam dunk. The white Shuttlecock Club flag atop its pole fluttered a few times as the pin swung back and forth as if waving in surrender. And then all was still.

Fortune, wherever the hell she lives, must have been watching all this and peeing herself with laughter. The rest of us were struck dumb in amazement. It was such an improbable result from such a bad shot that there was nothing one could say. It was pure, dumb, animal, golf luck. I shook my head, more to clear away that vision that was echoing through my mind, and to convince myself I wasn't dreaming. I looked over at my partner. He was standing in the bunker, in that classic finish pose again, and this time, he was grinning from ear to ear.

"I meant to do that," he said innocently.

That was it. Game, set and match. The Dude and the dentist were ashen faced, as I would have been in their shoes. They had been hoping to drop one of their long putts, and now one of them had to make it to tie.

"Gentlemen," I said. "After a shot like that, there is only one honorable thing to do. We concede both of your putts—good, good." I waved at them to pick them up. "I cannot in good conscience allow our team to win this excellent match with a shot of such pure, unadulterated bullshit as that last one was. Pick 'em up boys. Match ends all square and let's go have a drink."

I shook hands with both of them, who by this time were grinning. Then I walked over to the hole, pulled out Jackie's ball and hurled it deep into the woods where it belonged. Jackie, after raking the bunker, came onto the green and congratulated our opponents on a fun match. We headed off to our cart.

"Easy game, golf," he said, putting his sand wedge away.

I just shook my head.

We drove the half-mile or so through the woods, across the main road and over the entrance bridge to the Shuttlecock Club's island, and finally pulled up beside the clubhouse where all hell had broken loose. There were two Lowell police cars parked haphazardly at the rear entrance to the golf house, and a TV truck from Boston, it's corkscrew antenna poking through the oak branches looking for a clear sightline to the heavens.

One of the cart kids was standing there. "What the hell's going on?" Jackie asked the kid.

"McDaggert's been arrested," the kid said. "Cops got him handcuffed in his office."

"Crap," Jackie said with a straight face. "We're supposed to tee off in ten minutes."

The kid looked at Jackie as if he were retarded, until I burst out laughing. Then he grinned, although he kept glancing at Jack to see if he was serious or not.

"I – I think the rest of the tournament's been cancelled," he finally said.

"Crap," said Jack, heaving himself wearily out of the cart. "Let's go see what kind of cock-up the Lowell PD has committed this time."

Abandoning our cart, we walked around to the front of the golf house. Jack pushed his way into the crowded grill. But I saw Angela Murphy talking on her cell phone across the parking lot, and veered off towards her. She snapped her phone shut just as I got to her.

"Wassup?" I said, nodding a greeting.

"They got reasonable cause on McDaggert," she told me. "Found out that he was in hawk to Papageorge. More than $25,000. And Vitus was about to foreclose the guy's house. That gave him motive, and he was definitely here early that morning. One of the cart kids saw him running out of the cart barn about 30 minutes before you found the guy hanging back there. Tierney thinks its pretty cut and dried."

"What do you think?" I asked her.

Angela shrugged and looked away. "Dunno," she said. "Sounds plausible to me. Guys have been killed for less." She shook her head at some silent thought and then glanced back at me. "What do you think?" she asked. "You knew him."

"I find it hard to believe," I said. "Ted McDaggert doesn't strike me as a violent man. And he's been in debt to Vitus for years: Papageorge financed his years trying to be a touring professional. I can't believe that Vitus would call in his note. He'd get more benefit for himself by keeping Teddy in debt: free golf lessons on demand, a cut of the pro shop profits, able to cheat on his handicap." I shook my head. "Nah, I can't see Teddy as the perp."

"Well," Angela said. "Guess we'll find out at the trial, huh?"

A cop came out of the rear door to the clubhouse and gave Angela a little signal. We hustled over. So did the cameraman from the TV truck. Another cop came out and opened the back door of the squad car. Then two more beefy cops, each holding the arm of Ted McDaggert, his hands handcuffed behind his back. His face was red and sweaty, his eyes unfocused. The cops stopped briefly in a pool of sunshine.

"Ted, Ted," yelled the TV guy, his camera rolling tape. "Did you do it Ted?"

McDaggert just stared at the guy for a moment, then turned his head away. Angela had whipped out her handheld tape recorder.

"Any comment, Mr. McDaggert?" she asked, her tone gentle but firm.

He looked at her and saw me standing next to her. He nodded at me in greeting. "I didn't do it, Hacker," he said to me. "It wasn't me."

The cops decided that was enough interviewing, and hustled Ted into the back of the squad car, shut the door and drove him away. A small crowd of members and their guests had wandered outside from the grill room, and they watched as the police car made its way down the main entrance drive, across the first fairway and over the bridge. No one said anything.

I motioned to Angela and we went inside, making our way through the pro shop and back towards McDaggert's tiny warren of an office. Lt. Tierney was sitting at Ted's desk, and Jack was sitting across the desk, making some notes on the back of a pink While You Were Out pad.

"Ah," Tierney said as we walked in. "The rest of the media horde has arrived. C'mon in. Might as well only say this once."

Tierney explained that Ted McDaggert was being held on suspicion of first-degree murder. He said the police's preliminary investigation of the crime had established a motive – Ted's ongoing debt to Papageorge – and that witnesses had placed Ted at the scene during the time the crime was supposed to have occurred.

"'Suspicion of homicide' is different from actually charging him with the crime, isn't it?" Angela asked. "Doesn't that usually mean you think he's the guy, but you're not quite sure?"

Tierney gave her a hard look across the desk.

"We believe we have the perpetrator," he said. "The investigation will continue as we still have a few details to clean up."

"Such as?" I chimed in. No sense letting Angela have all the cop-baiting fun.

"No comment," he said, frowning. "I'm not going to tell the goddam media all the details of our investigation."

Jack looked over at me. "That means they had to make an arrest to keep the good citizens of Lowell happy," he said. "But Teddy was just the easiest move. If they had him dead to rights, they'd be giving us the DNA scans, and a filmed re-enactment of the crime."

"Probably the mayor told the cops to haul someone's ass in today," I mused aloud. "Make it look like they're making some progress for the next news cycle."

Lt. Tierney stood up, his face red. "Are you two jokers finished?" he bellowed. "We made a goddam arrest. Now go and put that in your freakin' newspapers."

He noticed Angela was scribbling notes furiously in her notebook.

"And that was off the freakin' record, Murphy," he said, his face getting redder.

Angela nodded, but kept writing.

Tierney started to push past me in the doorway, but stopped and looked at me with a smirk.

"Say," he said. "I hear that Rene Lemere wants to have a chat with you."

"Yeah," I said. "I heard that too. Have you happened to learn exactly when and where?"

He smiled evilly. "Rene and the Lord work in mysterious ways," he said. "When he's ready, you'll know."

"I don't suppose the Lowell PD wants to furnish us with some protection?" I asked hopefully.

Tierney snorted. "What for?" he laughed. "I haven't heard anything about the threat of bodily harm. Just that he wants a little chat. Nothing illegal about that, compadre. If you piss him off, I can't be responsible for what happens."

With a final smirk, he walked out.

Jack and I looked at each other for a moment. Angela broke the silence.

"Why does the local Mob guy want to see you, Hacker?" she asked.

I shrugged. "Get a few tips for his golf game?" I suggested. Jackie laughed. Angie did not.

"Seriously, Hacker," she said, gnawing on the end of her pencil. "What have you done?"

"Well," I said, " I think Jack and I kinda pissed off the club manager."

Angie raised her eyebrows.

Jack chimed in helpfully. "It was probably threatening him with that gun that did it," he said.

Angie drew in a sharp breath.

"But I saved him from being shot by Papageorge's widow," I said plaintively. "Some people are just impossible to please."

Angie had buried her face in her hands and was shaking her head back and forth. "Holy Mother of Jesus," she said. "You guys are a couple of pips, y'know?"

"So what do we do now?" I asked.

Angela looked at her watch. "You could probably make it to the Canadian border in four hours, be in Montreal by 10. Maybe there's a late flight to Switzerland. I understand they're neutral. You might be safe there."

I laughed sarcastically. "We ain't running from no small-town hood," I said.

Angie looked at me. "Hacker," she said. "He may be a small-town hood, but he's got guns and people who work for him who will use them to shoot you and then go home for dinner with their wives. And he's also connected to a big-time hood, which is to say Carmine Spoleto. Do *not* fuck around."

"Angela's right," Jackie said suddenly, standing up. "But so is Hacker. We can't screw around any longer and we ain't running."

"Are you thinking what I'm thinking?" I asked Jack.

"I doubt it," he grinned at me. "But you tell her."

"What?" Angela asked, exasperated.

"Instead of waiting for Lemere to find us, we go find him," I said. "Ask him what he wants."

"Beard the bear in his den," Jackie said, nodding.

"Just go knock on his door and say 'Hey, Rene, we were in the neighborhood, thought we should chat?'" Angie said incredulously.

"Exactly," we said in unison.

"Clear the air," I said. "Action's better than inaction. Besides, I gotta get back to town. Frankie's got a load of crap for me to do tomorrow."

Angie blew out her breath in frustration, and probably would have smacked her forehead but she was holding a pencil and might have poked her eye out. But she was getting ready for a big long lecture. I could feel it coming.

"That's probably the dumbest plan I ever heard," she started.

Jackie cut her off at the pass. "Maybe so," he said, but it's the only one we got."

"Right," I agreed.

"So," he said. "It's decided. Let's go have a drink."

"Like the last cigarette before the execution?" I laughed.

"No," he said, "Like the first drink in about an hour."

TWENTY-TWO

Angela was not to be stopped from delivering her sermon. We were being irresponsible, it was dangerous walking into a situation for which we were not prepared, we were going to get hurt, would likely end up going on a deep-sea fishing trip in which we would function as the bait, this was not to be taken lightly, whatever were we thinking, were we crazy, was our life insurance paid up, how would she explain my certain demise to my employer at the Boston *Journal*, not to mention our families ... and so forth.

We eventually told her we'd call as soon as we could to assure her of our continued safety and escaped to the men's locker room upstairs. Jackie ordered a tall vodka on the rocks. I asked for a club soda. Jack looked at me accusingly so I had Roland put a slice of lime in it as well.

"So," I said when our drinks arrived. "Do we have anything that resembles a plan of action?"

"Hacker," Jackie said as he took a long pull of his 16 oz. glass of vodka. "We are so far from having a plan it isn't funny. All we know is what we know. So we go see what Rene wants from us, we ask him to answer our questions and then maybe we all go out for a beer and a shot."

"Or skip the beer part and just get shot," I said.

"Whatever," Jackie said, waving his hand in dismissal. "Nothing ventured, nothing gained, I always say."

"Never heard you say that before, pards," I told him.

"Whatever," he said again, and drained his drink. But my accounting, that was 8 oz. per swallow. I cannonballed my club soda, choked a little, and slammed the glass down.

"Just do it," I said.

Outside, dusk was beginning to creep out from beneath the hedges and trees, softening the edges of everything and turning the world gray. But even from 50 feet away, as we walked towards Jack's car, we could see the blond woman leaning against the rear bumper. She wore black Capri pants, a red pattern sweater and had a suitcase-sized woven bag hanging over her shoulder.

"Hiya, fellas," said Leta Papageorge as we approached. "Goin' my way?"

"Dunno," Jack said, not breaking stride. "Which way are you going?"

"Well," she said, "I was hoping you'd take me down to police headquarters so I can bail poor Teddy out. I don't think he was the one who killed Vitus."

Jack and I looked at each other silently.

"I brought lots of cash," she said, "See?" She opened her bag. There were blocks of wrapped bills inside. Lots of them.

"Might take more than cash to get him out," I said. "Might have to give them the killer. Until then, they think Ted's the one and I don't think he's gonna get bail."

"Oh," she said, and her face fell for a moment. Then she brightened. "Then I guess I'll go wherever you guys are going."

"Don't you have a funeral to plan or something?" Jackie asked, unkindly.

"Up yours, Connolly," she said. "Vitus' family is handling all of that, and frankly, we're both glad that I have nothing to do with it. It's scheduled for Wednesday and I'm still trying to decide if I'm going."

"I know the name of a good grief counselor if you want," Jack said. "Help you to buck up and all that."

He unlocked the car and Leta popped the back door and jumped in. Jack and I looked at each other and shrugged and got in.

"Are you armed and dangerous?" I asked as Jack wheeled us out of the parking lot and down the long, curving entrance road.

"Of course," Leta said cheerfully from the back seat. "You think I'd go out with all this cash and no means of protection?"

"Well," I said, "You got us, now, and where we're going, I'm afraid having a gun might not prove to be the best idea."

"Where are we going?" she asked, excitedly.

"To see Rene Lemere," Jack said.

Leta Papageorge blew out her breath. "Holy crap," she said.

I turned around in my seat and looked at her. "You know him?" I asked.

"Ahhh...know *of* him," she answered, her eyes not meeting mine, but looking out the window at the passing scenery. "If it's all the same to you, I think I'll keep my pistol."

I shrugged. "Your funeral," I said. Jackie laughed.

Jackie was driving down the river towards Lowell. We passed an ice cream store, the old waterworks, and a new pavilion alongside the water whose sign read: "Lowell Sailing Center."

"Hey," Leta said. "Did you guys know that Vitus had a son?"

"Really?" I said.

"Yeah. Surprise to me, too. My beloved husband never mentioned him to me. Turns out he was married twice before, the first time for about six minutes apparently. One of Vitus' aunts took great pleasure in telling me. Apparently she told the son, too, 'cause he's flying in for the festivities."

"Where's he live?" Jack asked.

"Jesus," Leta said. "Someplace in Hicksville. Ottumwa, Iowa or some damn place. Auntie Kay said that Vitus never liked the kid and he tried to get as far away from his father as possible. Which I guess is Ottumwa."

"But he's coming back for the funeral," I said.

"He's coming back to make a claim for the inheritance," Leta said sharply. "I'll probably have to buy him off. Little shit. I don't like him either and I've never met him."

"Would you like some cheese with that whine?" I said sarcastically.

There was a rustle from the back seat and something round and hard was thrust into the back of my neck at the base of my brain.

"Hacker," she said coldly, "Are you sure you want to be insulting someone who's carrying a loaded firearm?"

I felt the blood drain from my face. Then, out of the corner of my eye, I saw Jack try to stifle a grin. He failed. I whirled around. Leta was holding the thick end of a fountain pen. She and Jack burst out in peals of laughter.

"Bite me," I said, which was the best I come up with to regain some dignity.

We rumbled across one of the suspension bridges that span the mighty Merrimac near downtown Lowell, and worked our way through the center of town. The town hall, a huge monolithic turreted structure constructed out of gray granite blocks, rolled by on the left. A long four-story red brick building stretched off to the right for several blocks: one of the miles of mills that made up this rusty old town.

"You know where we're going?" I asked Jack.

He nodded. "I think Rene keeps something of an office in one of these old buildings on the canal," he said. "I'm looking for a sign."

"Lemere Legbreakers?" I asked. "You call, we haul, that's all? The best pain money can buy? Don't leave your loansharking to an amateur...call the best!"

"Hacker?" Jackie said gently. "Are you wigging out on me?"

"Sounds like it," said the voice in the back seat.

"There it is!" Jack said. "Teamsters Foundations. Doesn't that sound like a nice little law-abiding business?"

He pulled into a small, cobblestoned parking area. The building was brick, three stories high, and filled with large windows, most of them on the upper floors boarded up. Next to the parking area was a loading dock, the bay shuttered tight, and a gray door above which hung a lone metal light. It was dark and getting chilly. A lone streetlight a few yards away threw dark shadows across the sidewalk. There were no lights on inside the building that we could see, and no other cars in sight, except for a beat-up pick-up truck parked down near the corner. The only sounds were a dull rumbling of cars from a main street a few blocks away and the mournful cries of the crickets in the weeds. They knew their goose was cooked.

We got out of the car and looked at the dark facade. I was encouraged by the lack of lights. Leta was not. "Shit," she said, "No one's here." Good, I thought, maybe we can get out of here with our brains intact.

"You never know," Jackie said. He walked up to the door beside the loading dock and pushed the bell. We heard a ringing echoing inside. He waited a few moments and pounded on the door. Nothing.

"Oh well," he said. "Let's try Plan B."

I was about to ask him what the next brilliant strategy was when the door creaked open, spilling bright light into the parking lot. A guy with a large head of brilliantined hair stuck his head out the door.

"Th' fuck you want?" he grunted.

"We're looking for Rene Lemere," Jack said. His voice, I noticed, had just the smallest quiver in it.

"You got an appointment?" the guy asked, his frown causing his entire massive face to droop.

I laughed out loud. I didn't mean to, of course. But the question struck me as absurd. That one would need an appointment to see a hood. In a dump like this. At seven o'clock on a Sunday night. Leta, standing next to me, gave me an elbow shot to the ribs, but it was too late.

"Th' fuck's so funny?" the guy grunted, not looking happy in the least.

"My friend is a little on edge," Jack smoothly interjected. "We're trying to find Rene and have a little sit-down with him. My friend here is Hacker, and we understand Rene's been looking for a meeting. Thought we'd save him some time and effort and drop in."

The guy looked Jack and up and down, and then focused his dark and beady eyes at me and gave me the up and down thing too. Then he turned to Leta, who said "Keep your eyes to yourself, bozo."

That was enough. The guy threw the door open and motioned us inside.

"Ah," Jack said, sounding proud of himself. "So he's here?"

"Naw," the guy said. "But you three pieces o' shit ain't goin' nowhere until he says so."

"Well," Jack said, "Thanks anyway, but we'll wait until …"

"You'll wait until nuttin'" the guy said. He pulled back his jacket to show us his pistol tucked in his waistband. "Get your sorry asses in here. Now."

Our asses, sorry and not, went inside.

TWENTY-THREE

The inside of Rene Lemire's crime syndicate headquarters looked more like Joe's Insurance office. The slick-haired guy pointed us down a narrow corridor and into a tiny airless room at the back with one half-boarded-up window. Outside, there was a small dark canal and, across a weed-choked vacant lot, another long brick warehouse, all as dark as the thoughts of the condemned. The room was covered in cheap dark paneling of the kind that every off-price home improvement store carries and illuminated by three banks of harsh fluorescent lights overhead. The walls were empty save two items: a gilt-framed 10 x 12 color photograph of an elderly woman with a huge bouffant white hair-do and thick rhinestone glasses, hanging behind the desk; and, tacked above a colorless three-drawer file cabinet, a color calendar showing Miss September pulling downwards on her tight white tee-shirt so as to highlight her twin cantaloupes. Her lidded eyes were half closed and she was chewing on her lower lip as if she was ravenously hungry for something. My guess was that it wasn't a Caesar salad with the anchovies on the side she was hungry for.

Slick motioned at the three of us to park it on a thread-bare sofa covered in a red-plaid tweed. We sank down simultaneously, which caused a stringy shriek from the ancient couch. We stared across three feet of space at a gray metal desk, the top covered in fake wood veneer. There was a black telephone, a large calendar-type desk pad and a stapler arranged on the desk. There was not a lot of warmth in Rene's office, but I relaxed, figuring the worse Rene Lemere could do to us was try to staple us to death.

I nodded at the photo of the old woman on the wall. "Nice photo," I said to Slick. "Is that …?"

"Rene's mother," Slick said. "And don't get funny. He's very protective of his mother."

"Which one is Mom?" Jackie asked, looking innocent. Slick pulled back his hand as if to give Jack a whack upside the head, but didn't. He walked around the desk and heaved himself down into the desk chair, which also squeaked in protest. Slick's head was enormous and glistened in the fluorescent light of the office. He had no neck to speak of, a thick, round chest, and a bit of a gut. But he looked like he could move fast if he had to. He had a red, bulbous nose which looked like it might have been broken a few times, and his upper lip was thick and sweaty. He looked across the desk at us with small, dark, unblinking eyes, almost as if he didn't even see us sitting there.

"What's the plan, Stan?" Jackie asked. "I got things to do."

Slick shrugged, an almost imperceptible movement of his shoulders.

"Rene's on the way in," he said. "When he gets here, we'll all find out."

He sat back and fixed us again with those small, dark, unseeing eyes. I tried to watch to see if ever blinked.

My cell phone rang. I pulled it out of my pocket, flipped open the top and answered.

"Mister Hacker?" came a scratchy high-pitched voice. "Tony Zec here. I'm on the New York Turnpike, heading back to Boston. We're all done here. Sam Tennyson won in a playoff. Shot a terrific last-round 63. It was amazing ..."

"Zec," I cut him off sharply. "Shut up. Did you send me the stuff?"

"Yessir," he quavered over the line.

"Good," I said. "Good job. Drive safely. Why don't you come in to see me tomorrow afternoon?"

I saw Slick's left eyebrow go up about two centimeters.

"Check that," I said into the phone. "Can you come in Tuesday?"

"Yessir...as long as it's in the morning. I have a class at two. It's my Law and Journalism seminar, and ..."

"Zec!" I barked again. "Tuesday morning. Ten."

"Okay," he said. "See ya."

We hung up. Slick didn't move a hair. Jackie and Leta were looking at me.

"It was my college intern," I said. "He was covering the tournament for me up in New York."

"You have a college intern?" Leta asked with some amazement in her voice. "You?"

"Wasn't my idea," I said. "It's a long story."

"Well, I certainly don't have anything better to do at the moment," she said, sounding a bit peevish. She folded her arms and waited.

I was going to say something smartass to her when my phone rang again. I jumped at the sound. Angrily, I flipped the top open.

"Goddam it Zec, I'm busy here," I snapped into the phone.

There was a pause. "What's a Zec?" came a cheerful feminine voice. "And why are you busy when you're supposed to be at my house eating baked chicken and ziti?"

I felt myself go red. "Oh, hi Mary Jane," I said sheepishly. "Sorry. Thought you were someone else."

"You thought right," she said. "I am someone else. Where the hell are you?" In the background, I could hear little Victoria say "Mommy, you said hell."

"Damn," I said. "I'm sorry."

"You guys celebrating a win?" Mary Jane laughed softly into the phone. "Maybe you'd better sleep it off instead of driving home."

I had a sudden brainstorm.

"Listen," I said. "I've been called into a sudden meeting up here in Lowell with Lemere. Do me a favor and call your father-in-law and apologize for me. Tell him if I could get out of this I would, but I can't. He'll understand."

There was dead silence on the other end. I kept talking.

"Yes, I know, but he'll understand," I said. "He's been in this situation many times. Just tell him there's no way I can get out of this right now."

"Hacker," Mary Jane said in a soft whisper. "Do you know who my father-in-law is, I mean, was? Why are you talking about him? What the hell is going on?"

I heard Victoria say 'Mommeee..." Mary Jane said nothing. "Thanks Mary Jane," I said. "And again, I'm very sorry. Yes, give your father-in-law my regards. Of course. Yes. Right. Bye."

I hung up and silently prayed that Mary Jane would understand. Or, even better, not understand anything and call her former father-in-law and ask him what the hell was going on. Victoria would be mortified, but you can't win them all.

Everyone was looking at me. I took a moment to put my phone away, hoping that the few extra seconds would help me calm myself down.

"My downstairs neighbor," I said to the room at large. "She had invited me to dinner tonight with her family. Her father-in-law is an avid golfer, and he wanted to hear some of my stories about the tour. We'll just have to reschedule I guess."

"I guess," said Slick.

We sat there in silence again. Leta shifted her heavy shoulder bag around on her lap. All those wrapped bills must have been heavy. Not to mention her little silver gun. I started having a fantasy that involved the three of us shooting our way out of Rene Lemere's tawdry little office, but quickly shook my head to clear it away. Anything like that would no doubt result in someone dying, and I suspected it wouldn't be Slick.

A bell rang insistently from down the hall. Slick stood up and headed out of the room to answer it. He stopped and held his hand out to me. "Phone," he said. I reluctantly reached into my pocket and handed him the cell. Slick pocketed it and went to answer the door.

"Finally," Jackie said. "Some action. I was about to start singing 'Some Enchanted Evening.' This sitting around drives me crazy."

"What are your feelings about gunplay?" I asked incredulously. "That seems to be our only option here."

He was about to answer when Herb Incavaglia came bursting into the office. He stared at the three of us sitting on Rene's couch. "Oh, for fuck's sake," he muttered and turned on his heel. He slammed the door to the office shut with his heel and began yelling at Slick. We couldn't hear exactly what he said, but it didn't sound like he was happy to see us gathered there. Slick's deep bass voice answered Herb in staccato, angry bursts.

"I guess we have established a relationship between Herb and Rene," Jackie said.

"I coulda told you that," Leta laughed. "In fact, I think I did."

"So what are we doing here again?" I asked no one in particular. "Besides risking life and limb?"

"I don't know what you're doing here," Leta said sharply, "But I'm trying to find out who killed my husband."

"And Hacker, you're here because you heard Rene the Lip wanted to see you, so you thought you'd drop by before you headed back to Boston," Jackie reminded me helpfully. "And me? I'm just the designated driver."

That struck all three of us as rather funny, and we were giggling on the couch when Herb Incavaglia came striding back into the office, looking red and sweaty, followed by Slick, his face impassive as always.

"What the hell is so funny," Herb almost shouted. "Do you know how much trouble you're in?"

We stop giggling and all three of us looked up at Herb standing there, hands on hips, hair somewhat wild, eyes large and round. Then, without planning, all three of us uncrossed our legs and crossed them again. It was like a Rockettes number. That also struck all three of us as instantly funny and we began to howl with laughter.

Herb had reached the end of his rope.

"Bust 'em up, Bennie," he said to Slick. "Start with that guy," he motioned at me. Slick Bennie bounced on the balls of his feet, light as a cat.

"Whoa," I said, holding one hand up and wiping the tears out of my eyes with the other. "No need for violence here. We're all just a little on edge and we're waiting to talk to Rene. He probably wouldn't be too happy if he got here and found us all mashed up."

Bennie looked at Herb, who nodded. "Yeah," he said. "Well, just shut the fuck up then." He stalked out of the room. Bennie went over and sat down behind the desk again and stared at us. Jackie sighed, Leta giggled, and I stared back. He blinked. Which I guess proved that, at the very least, Bennie wasn't a lizard.

I don't know how long we sat there. Jackie eventually began humming what sounded like something by Lerner and Loewe. That made Leta giggle. I gave her an elbow shot, which landed mostly on the side of her breast. "Ooo, Mister Hacker," she cooed, "Aren't we getting a little fresh?" I snorted an aborted laugh. Bennie blinked again, reached under his jacket and pulled out his gun, flipped the safety off and ratcheted a bullet into the chamber.

"Next one who makes a sound gets one in the knee-cap," he said. He put the gun down on the calendar mat and stared at us with those tiny, dark eyes. I think we all believed him, because for the next half-hour or so, we sat motionless, and silent, waiting for Rene the Lip.

TWENTY-FOUR

The appearance of Lowell's foremost gangster was a bit of a letdown, after all the anticipation and buildup. Jackie was snoring softly at the far end of the sofa, and Leta had pulled out an emery board and was busy shaping and smoothing. That left Bennie and me to stare at each other.

Finally, I heard the door out to the loading dock swing open, and footsteps as someone walked down the hall. I could also hear a soft, tuneless whistle.

Rene "the Lip" Lemere came into his office carrying a Coke from Burger King and his cell phone, both of which he put down carefully on his desk. "Get out of my chair," he said to Bennie, who shot up as if he had been goosed. Then Rene turned to look at the three of us.

He was an avuncular sort, with white, thinning hair, large sagging ears and bushy eyebrows that pooched out of his careworn forehead. Rene was wearing a blue plaid sport shirt and baggy khaki trousers. Two pens were clipped to his breast pocket, and a brown belt failed to corral his spreading midsection. He looked more like someone who had just finished mowing the lawn than the head of a crime empire. He peered at us through black eyes. He had a severe overbite condition, which made his top lip protrude outwards, giving his countenance a permanent frown. Hence, I figured, his colorful Mob moniker.

"So," he said, his voice sharp and hard-edged, unlike his appearance. "What do we have here?"

I stood up. "Name's Hacker," I said, sticking out my hand. "Heard you wanted to talk. This is John Connolly, owner of the Lowell Citizen," I motioned towards Jack, who had, thankfully, woken up. "And this lady is Leta Papageorge, whose husband was murdered yesterday out at the Shuttlecock Club. We all would like to know what you know about that."

Rene listened to me, his eyes locked on mine, arms folded, nodding slightly as I introduced everyone. Bennie stood motionless leaning against the wall. I had no idea where Herb had gone.

"Right," Rene said. "Let's talk about that." He walked around his desk and sat down in the chair. He reached over for his Coke and sipped some through the straw poking out of the plastic to-go cup. He picked up his black desk telephone and punched a button. "Herb," he said into the receiver, "Get in here."

"First of all," he said after hanging up, "Let me express my sincere condolences to you, Mrs. Papageorge. Vitus was a friend of mine, and his death is a tragedy. I will miss him." He nodded at Leta.

Herb Incavaglia came into the office, his face flushed. He went and stood next to Bennie.

Leta looked back at Rene. "Thanks, Rene," she said in a strong, firm voice. "But I wanna know which one of your slimeballs killed him."

Herb came off the wall, twisting his hands. "Dammit," he said. "You can't talk like that in here!"

Lemere held up his hand. "I'm sure Mrs. Papageorge is just overcome with grief," he said calmly. "No offense taken."

"Oh, can the polite bullshit, Rene," Leta snapped. "You know who snuffed Vitus and I'm not leaving here until you tell me."

Lemere's face reddened and his eyes narrowed dangerously. Bennie came to attention against the wall.

"In fact, lady, I do not know who killed the son-of-a-bitch," Lemere growled. "I just know that it has royally screwed up a pretty good piece of my business. That's why Herb is here."

The bell from the loading dock rang again, startling us all.

"And that'll be Fred," Rene said, glancing at his watch. He motioned with his head and Bennie went out to open the door.

Herb began having another hissy fit. "Rene," he said, "For Christ sakes. These guys are from the newspapers. Did you go off the record?"

Rene and I both burst out laughing. We exchanged a look and shook our heads.

"Off the record?" Rene said, chuckling to himself. "I think these gentlemen know that if anything they see or hear gets printed, they themselves will be taken off the record. Isn't that right, Mr. Hacker?"

"That's kinda what I assumed," I said, smiling at him. "Still," I added, "The story of Vitus Papageorge's murder leads to his, shall we say, unconventional financing techniques for various construction projects at the Shuttlecock Club, which in turn leads, from what we understand, to you. So keeping this story under wraps may prove difficult."

"Then you are dead men," Rene said.

There's not much one can say in rejoinder to that definitive sentence. It hung chillingly in the air for a moment.

Bennie came back into the office, followed by Fred Adamek. He was wearing blue jeans and an old sweatshirt, beat-up sneakers and a Red Sox baseball cap. He stopped short when he saw the three of us sitting on Rene's sofa.

"W-what is this?" he stammered, looking from us to Rene.

"Shut up, Fred and go stand over there," Rene said, motioning to the wall next to Herb. Bennie had brought a metal folding chair in from the hall and he set it up next to the door and sat down in it. His face was still impassive.

"How's Rita?" Rene asked Fred.

He took off his baseball cap and wiped his forehead. "She's OK today," he said. "The air is drier and she can breathe a little better. Still a struggle, but today was one of the good days."

"That's good," Rene said, nodding. He looked at us. "Rita has the emphysema," he said "Last coupla years, she's been on the oxygen. Summer is a bitch, right Fred?"

Fred nodded, looking nervously at Jack, Leta and me.

"So," Rene said, after taking another sip of his Coke. "Looks like our little program at Shuttlecock is over. Vitus dead and all, seems like we can't go on. That doesn't make me happy."

"Then why did you kill Vitus?" Leta demanded. "With him gone, your nice little Shuttlecock Club skimming operation is caput."

"Wait a minute," Herb Incavaglia said from his spot along the wall. "Why do we have to stop? I'm still in place. We can keep it going. Find a new president, cut him into the deal. It can still work, Rene, I know it can…"

"Shut up, Herb," Rene said sharply. "I said it's over. One, it doesn't work without Vitus' bank. Two, too many people know about it. That makes it dangerous, especially for me. It's over."

"I still don't get it," I said. "If losing Vitus meant losing the money from the Shuttlecock scam, why'd you kill him?

"I'm telling you, I didn't kill him!" Rene said, his voice raised in frustration. "He was a freakin' golden goose. He and Herb came up with all the projects that the club needed, his bank helped guarantee the financing, and Freddie here handled the construction part. It was perfect. I wish I knew who killed the guy. I'd take care of him myself."

Fred had pulled out a handkerchief and wiped his forehead. He seemed to be sweating a lot.

"What are you gonna do with them?" he asked Rene, motioned at us.

Rene blew out a breath. "Tell you the truth, I don't know," he said.

"You gotta get rid of them," Freddie said. "Can't let 'em walk out of here. They're goddam newspaper guys. Shit will really hit the fan, then. We'll all go to jail, for Christ sakes. I can't leave Rita alone." His voice sounded pinched.

Rene looked at Fred, nodding to himself.

"It was you," I said. I was looking at Freddie. "You killed him. I should have realized it before. Adams Construction…Fred Adamek. You were part of the program."

"What are you talking about?" Freddie protested, his face red and sweaty.

"It all fits," I said. "Jack," I turned to my partner at the other end of the couch. "Remember that little argument about the bridge on the fourth hole?"

Jack nodded. "Yeah," he said, "Fred and Vitus seemed to be disagreeing about something."

"I'll bet that Vitus was going to hire another construction company to do the job," I said. "He was like that. Liked to keep people on their toes, or just be mean for no good reason."

"But Freddie here was pissed," Jackie chimed in. "Real pissed."

"Probably needed the money," I continued. "I'll bet having a sick wife at home on oxygen, nurses, doctors...costs a lot of bread. Freddie probably couldn't afford not to get the bridge job."

"So when he found out Vitus was going to hire someone else, he freaked," Leta said.

"He was there that morning," I said. "Came in early to hit balls, he said. Probably followed Vitus out to the cart barn, arguing his case. Vitus probably said something smartass, Vitus being Vitus."

"And Freddie gave him one in the kisser," Jackie said.

"He's left-handed, remember? Vitus was punched in the right eye before he was strung up," I said. "Had to be a lefty."

"Would take a strong guy to lift him onto the cart," Jackie observed. "Like someone in construction."

"SHUT UP!" Fred Adamek shouted. "Just ... shut...the...hell...up." His voice trailed off to a near whisper. He slumped back against the wall, and covered his eyes with his handkerchief.

The room was silent. Herb's face had gone white and he stood as if frozen. Bennie sat in his chair, impassive as a rock. Rene had his arms crossed and his oversized lip was pursed in thought as he rocked slightly in his office chair.

"I was going to make a hundred grand," Fred said softly, pulling his hanky away. "Vitus wanted me to take less. Cheap bastard. He's got plenty of money. But me? I owe Rita's doctor fifty thou, and it's gonna take another year for her to …" His voice caught. "When he told me he was giving the job to Dracut Contracting, he was laughing. He knew what that job meant to me. He was laughing."

Freddie looked at Leta. "I'm sorry, missus," he said softly. "But he was one supersized son-of-a-bitch, and I'm glad he's dead. I'd kill him again if I could."

"Bennie," Rene said, his voice cutting and hard. He motioned with his head. Bennie stood up, put the chair aside and stood back to let Freddie walk out in front of him.

"Rene," Fred said, holding his hands out. "We go back a long way. And what's Rita gonna do without me? C'mon, you gotta give me a break here."

Rene stared at Freddie for a moment. Cold, unblinking. Then he gave him a slight, sideways motion of the head.

Freddie sighed in resignation. He stumbled towards the door, his head hanging.

He was quick for an old guy.

As he passed Bennie, he suddenly swung his thick, powerful forearm into Bennie's neck, slamming his head back against the wall. It sounded like someone had dropped a melon on the sidewalk. Bennie sagged and started to go down. With his other hand, Fred reached under Bennie's jacket and came out with his gun. The whole thing took maybe two seconds.

Fred wheeled and pointed the gun at Rene.

"You don't want to do that, friend," Rene said, smiling. "Kill me, and there's no place you can go. Except hell."

"I'm already there," Fred said in a soft, resigned voice. "And you put me there."

There was a soft pfft sound. Freddie started, a surprised look crossed his face, then he slowly crumpled to the floor. Bennie's gun fell out of his hand and skittered next to the desk.

Leta gasped as a tall figure in a black trenchcoat came through the doorway, following a long gunmetal silencer attached to his gun.

Rene, still sitting in his desk chair, looked at Freddie lying on his floor and then looked up at the tall man standing there. He had the collar of his trench coat turned up and wore a wide-brimmed hat like something Sam Spade might have, so we couldn't see his face very well. I saw some olive-toned skin, and, below the hem of the coat, well-creased woolen slacks and finely polished black shoes.

"Rufus," Rene said. "Your timing is impeccable."

"Carmine sent me," Rufus said in a hoarse whispery voice. "Wanted to make sure nothing happened to someone named Hacker."

Rene turned and looked at me, eyebrows raised in surprise.

"How'd you know that wasn't me?" I asked, pointing to the dead Fred on the floor.

"Been here a while," the guy said.

"Well, thanks, Rufus," Rene said. "But I can take care of these people. I'm afraid they know a little too much. I'm sure Carmine will understand."

Rufus shook his head. "Nope," he said. "Carmine said Hacker and his friends are leaving. He wants you to come see him tomorrow morning. Eight a.m. sharp." He looked at Herb Incavaglia who's face had gone even whiter. I wondered where his blood was pooling. "You, too," he said. Herb made a little moaning sound. Rene sat back in his chair and said nothing.

"Right then," Jackie said, getting to his feet. "I think our work here is done. Nice knowing ya, Rene." He stepped over a groaning Bennie as he walked out.

Leta and I followed Jackie down the hall and into the darkness of the parking lot outside. The temperature had dropped, and the chill cut straight to my bones. At least, I think it was the chill making me shiver. Rufus the enforcer followed us outside. He lit a cigarette. Leta went up to him.

"Thank you," she said.

He smiled enigmatically but said nothing. Jack had his car running, and Leta went over and climbed in the back seat.

Rufus pulled out a cell phone, flipped it open and punched in a number. He waited, said "Yo," listened and handed it to me.

"Hello?" I said.

"Mister Hacker," said a soft, Italian-accented voice. "Carmine Spoleto here. Is everything all right?"

"Yes, thank you," I said.

"My former daughter-in-law tells me that you never said anything to her about you and me."

"That's right," I said. "Never thought it necessary to bring up."

"Quite right," he said. "But I'm an old man, and I know things. I believe that you might have a problem with Mary Jane now."

"I'll talk to her," I said.

"Do that," he said. "I'm fond of that girl. And my granddaughter, too."

"Me, too," I said.

"Bene," he said. "Buona notte."

TWENTY-FIVE

J ack peeled out of the parking lot and headed for the bright lights of downtown Lowell.

"Well," I said, "That was a fun weekend. Thanks, pard."

"Not at all," he said. "Maybe we can do it again next year."

Leta was sniffling from the backseat. "One minute he was standing there, and the next, he was on the floor," she said, voice wavering. "Poor Freddie. He came to our house for dinner just last week."

"He was also the one who killed your husband," I reminded her.

"Yeah, I know," she said. "And I hope he rots in hell for that, the rotten bastard. But it's still all so sad. And what is his poor wife going to do now?"

I glanced at Jackie, who shook his head. He knew better than to try to introduce logic into the midst of a woman's emotional state.

"We'll go over to my house," Jackie said. "Get a drink, regroup, decide what to do next."

"Damn," I said. "Bennie still has my cell phone."

"Here," he said, opening the compartment that separated the car seats. "Use mine."

I called Angela and told her we were still alive.

"What happened?" she demanded.

"Ummm, I'll get back to you on that," I said.

"Hacker!" she screeched. "I gotta file a story in one hour. You cannot hold back on me now! What the hell happened?"

"A bit of heck broke loose," I confessed. "But we all still have all ten fingers and toes. We're heading over to Jackie's place." I gave her the number. "Call me there in about 30 minutes."

I hung up. I wasn't ready to talk to Mary Jane yet. But she might be worried. I sighed and decided to wait a bit.

"Pards," I said to Jackie, "We've got to decide how to handle this. We both have a story to get out, but we don't want to get a visit from Bennie."

"Or Rufus," Jackie nodded.

"Exactly. "

"But you've got to get Ted out of jail," Leta piped in from the backseat. "I told you he didn't do it. We should go tell the cops everything and get him out tonight."

I shook my head. "Not a great idea," I said. "That would make us eyewitnesses to a Mob murder, and there's three things that don't last long: dogs that chase cars, pros putting for pars and eyewitnesses to Mob hits."

Jackie laughed.

Leta said "huh?"

"Slightly abridged Lee Trevino quote," I said. "But it's better for all of us to try and keep tonight's fun and games to ourselves. "

"So we all heard and saw Fred Adamek confess to killing Vitus and you guys can't run that in the newspaper?" Leta said. "I can't believe this!"

"I didn't say that," I said. "We just have to figure out a way to run the story without involving any of us. After all, I was supposed to be in Endicott, New York this weekend covering a stupid golf tournament."

"Which is worse?" Jackie mused aloud. "Having the Mob trying to kill you or having your boss mad at you?"

"Depends," I said. "If he's got coffee and doughnuts, Frankie's usually in a passable mood."

We pulled into Jackie's riverside home. The phone was ringing as Jackie let us in. He answered and held the receiver out to me.

"Okay, whaddya got?" Angela demanded.

"Here's the deal," I said. "We found out who the murderer was. It ties back into the financial scam at the Shuttlecock Club. But you can't run the second part yet."

"How come?" Angela demanded, fire in her voice.

"Because if you do, me and Jackie and Mrs. Papageorge here might have to enter the witness protection program," I said. "If we make it that far."

"So?" she said.

"I can feel the love," I said, "But that's the deal. Part one today, part two later."

"How much later?" she asked.

I thought of Rene Lemere's upcoming meeting with Carmine Spoleto.

"Maybe as early as tomorrow," I said. "In fact, I can give you some pretty good leads tomorrow that might get you the rest of the story."

I heard here drumming her pencil as she thought about it.

"OK," she said finally. "Tell me."

So I did.

TWENTY-SIX

I spent the night at Jackie's Sunday and slept like the dead. The house was empty when I awoke early Monday morning. It had turned cold and was threatening to rain. Jack and Leta were gone. A copy of my newspaper and an advance print-out of Jack's were on the kitchen counter. The Boston *Journal* led with an exclusive, front-page story that reported "sources close to the investigation" had evidence that pointed the finger at one Frederick G. Adamek of Dracut, president of Adams Construction Co., as the possible killer of his sometime golf and business partner Vitus Papageorge. The motive? Anger over the loss of the upcoming bridge contract and his need for money to help his desperately ill wife. It noted his proximity on the morning of the crime.

The Lowell police were quoted as saying the investigation was ongoing and that they would have no comment. However, the police spokesman said nothing to defend its arrest of Ted McDaggert, and Angela quoted police sources as saying Teddy might be released. Attempts to contact Mr. Adamek were unsuccessful, the story continued. A housekeeper and nurse at the Adamek residence said Mr. Adamek had not returned home that night and his whereabouts were unknown.

Jackie left me a printout of the story that would appear in that afternoon's Lowell *Citizen*. The headline read: "Golf Pro Released: Admits He Saw Body." According to the account, McDaggert admitted he had wandered into the cart barn after Vitus has been strung up, saw his body dangling from the electrical cord, but did nothing about it. "He was already dead," Ted said in the story. "I should have called for help, but I didn't. I don't know why." The police said he could be charged with obstruction in a police matter, but had dropped all pending murder charges.

The Lowell paper also said a search was continuing for Fred Adamek, but quoted sources saying that his sudden disappearance might be Mob related. It mentioned a close working relationship between Freddie's Adams Construction and Rene Lemere. Phone calls to both Adams and Teamsters Foundations had gone unanswered, the paper said.

I showered, packed up and drove back into Boston. Thanks to the usual traffic mess, I didn't get into the office until around 10. Frank Donatello greeted me with a dirty look and a thick stack of copy to edit, mail to sort through and assignments to get done. "Vacation's over, bub," he grumped at me.

On top of the stack were all the stories that Tony Zec had sent to me over the weekend. The first one was headlined "Tennyson Wins With Sparkling Final Round." It started off "On a gorgeous Sunday afternoon, Sam Tennyson, the 94th ranked player in the world, put together a round for the ages, firing a stunning 64 at the En-Joie Country Club to overtake a dumbstruck Brad Faxon and claim his first PGA Tour title in more than six years." It went on in that vein for another three pages.

I dug out a copy of Monday's sports section and read the AP wire story that had run, buried deeply in the gutter on page D-13, under the heading "GOLF." It was one graph long. "Sam Tennyson's final round 64 was good for a two-stroke win in the BC Open yesterday in Endicott, NY. Tennyson won $545,000."

I smiled. My intern had a lot to learn. But at least he had enthusiasm going for him. That might, or might not, help him carve out a career in the newspaper business. Where enthusiasm is usually the first thing to go.

I pushed the rest of the papers around my desk all morning. It was hard to concentrate on the statistics from last Saturday's football game between Acton-Boxborough and Westford High. I was thinking somewhat deeper thoughts about life and death, anger and revenge, and the limits of human forebearance. I was thinking about Rita Adamek, struggling for oxygen with every breath, and now with no one to hold her hand.

The telephone kept interrupting my reveries. The first call was from Branson Tucker, the paper's Mob correspondent.

"Hacker, my lad," Tucker's deep voice drawled through my phone. "I had the most amazing thing happen to me this morning."

"Well, I said, "I hear Viagra works pretty good. The missus must be pleased."

"Very funny, dear boy," he said dryly. "No, I am talking about a telephone conversation I just had with one Herbert 'the Vig' Incavaglia. He tells me that he has surrendered to the feds and wants to talk a little."

"Is that right?" I said.

"Indeed," he said. "And I find it quite amazing that it was just a day or two ago that you asked me about him. And that you were in Lowell. Where, according to our fine newspaper, some interesting events have been going on over the weekend."

"Could be coincidence," I suggested.

"Dear boy," Branson clucked at me. "There is no such thing as coincidence in the world in which these people live. I wonder if you could perhaps tell me a little more about what you know?"

"I have a better idea," I said. "Get Angela Murphy to help you interview the guy. She was on the scene all weekend up there. Tell her I said it's time for Part Two. If Herb is singing, he will fill in all the blanks you need."

He was silent for a moment. "Sounds quite intriguing," he said. "Why don't you want to get involved in the story?"

"I'm just a golf writer, Branson," I said. "My world is all about fun and games. Not life and death."

"Quite so," he said. "I'll call Angela."

I pushed the papers on another lap around the desk before the phone rang again.

"Hacker!" said a woman's voice, "Leta Papageorge. How are you feeling this morning?"

"Emotionally bruised," I said. "You?"

"Oh, not too bad, actually," she said. "Vitus' son got here late last night. We had a long talk over breakfast. He's actually not a bad young man. Don't tell anyone, but I kind of like him!"

"Your secret's safe with me," I said, laughing. "So what's next for you?"

"Well, " she said, "I'm actually thinking of taking over management of the bank."

"Really?" I said, amazement creeping into my voice.

"I know, I know," she said. "Doesn't sound like me. But you know, I already know a lot about the business, just from looking over Vitus' shoulder all these years. And I think I can keep things going, and maybe even do it a little better. You know, if you're not trying to screw someone all the time, you can sometimes help people in this business."

I pounded the telephone on the desk. "Hello?" I said. "Will the aliens who have captured Leta Papageorge please let her go at once."

She laughed. "And Alexander – that's Vitus' son? – he and I have been talking all morning. He might be interested in coming back east and working with me."

"Really?" This time, I didn't even try to keep the amazement out of my voice.

"Yeah," she said. "He's smart and a nice kid. Got a wife and a baby. He wouldn't mind coming back East."

"That would make you a grandmother, kind of." I pointed out. "Instant family."

There was silence on the other end. Followed by a sniffling sound.

"I think that's nice, Leta," I said. "Good for you."

She hung up without saying anything else.

Tired of staring at my desk, I played some solitaire on my computer until my stomach told me it was time for lunch. I was making neat stacks with the papers before leaving when the phone rang again.

"Hack-hack-hack-man!" chirrped my erstwhile partner. "Can you get away for a while?" he asked. "I'm going over to London for a week. We can play Sunningdale, Wentworth,

Stoke Poges, all those stuffed shirt clubs. Start a food fight, goose the secretary, get a little blood flowing. Those Brits need us, Hack!"

"Can't," I said sadly. "Gotta write a piece about an All-American field hockey player at Stone Hill College and then there's a fierce gridiron tilt this weekend between Hingham and Mashpee. Both teams are 0 and 3."

"Jeezus," Jackie groaned. "What a waste of talent."

"That's what I say," I said. "But I guess one's gotta earn his keep somehow."

"Well," he said, "If you change your mind, I'm leaving Thursday. Give me a call."

"Yeah," I said. "Vaya con Dios, and all that."

"Cheerio," he said.

There was a pause.

"Hack?" he said.

"Yeah."

"You done good."

"Yeah," I said. "You, too."

I didn't go out for lunch. Instead, I drove over to the North End, found a parking spot about two blocks from home and walked down the narrow, cobbled street. I stopped at Enrico's bodega and bought a bouquet. Fall mums, some angel's breath, couple of asters. Then I walked across the street and went up to the second floor and knocked.

Mary Jane opened the door. I held out the flowers. She stared at me, then took them and held them. Mister Shit came out of the living room and rubbed up against Mary Jane's leg, arching his back in happiness. He stared at me with contempt, stretched and walked away contentedly. Turncoat.

Mary Jane leaned forward, head against my chest, and my arms came up around her. We stood like that for a long time.

Then she backed up a half-step and punched me, hard, in the shoulder. She looked up at me with wet eyes.

"You bastard," she said. "I was worried sick."

"I know," I said. "I'm sorry."

"You never told me you knew," she said, and hit me again, a little softer this time.

"Wasn't sure how to bring it up," I said. "And you never talked about it. Never seemed important, before."

"Before?" she asked.

I reached over and wiped a tear from her cheek with my thumb.

"Are you OK?" she asked softly, eyes shining now through her tears.

"Think so," I said, "Thanks to you."

"Well, I think you'd better come in so we can make sure," she said.

She grabbed my jacket and yanked me inside. I closed the door with my foot.

THE END